The War of the Crowns

BY CHRISTIAN JACQ
FROM CLIPPER LARGE PRINT

The War of the Crowns

The Queen of Freedom Trilogy

Christian Jacq

Translated by Sue Dyson

W F HOWES LTD

This large print edition published in 2006 by
W F Howes Ltd
Unit 4, Rearsby Business Park, Gaddesby Lane,
Rearsby, Leicester LE7 4YH

1 3 5 7 9 10 8 6 4 2

First published in France by XO Editions under the
title *La Guerre des Couronnes*, 2002
First published in the United Kingdom in 2003
by Simon & Schuster UK Ltd

A CIP catalogue record for this book is available
from the British Library

ISBN 978 1 84632 833 6

Typeset by Palimpsest Book Production Limited,
Grangemouth, Stirlingshire
Printed and bound in Great Britain
by Antony Rowe Ltd, Chippenham, Wilts.

I dedicate this book to all those men and women who have devoted their lives to freedom, by fighting against occupation, totalitarian regimes and inquisitions of every kind.

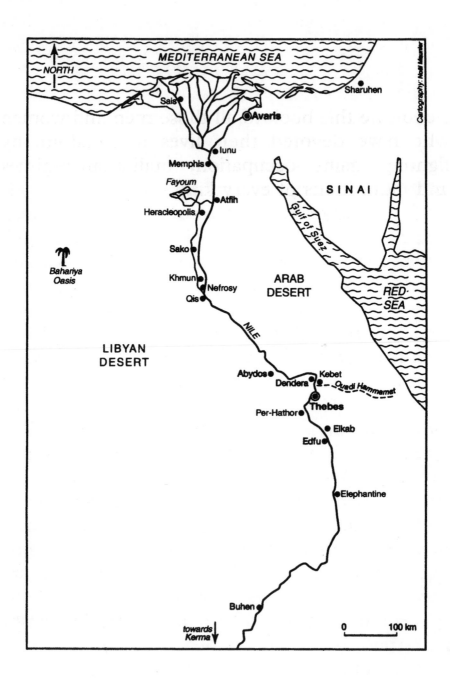

CHAPTER 1

The general of the charioteers sat at the left hand of Apophis, Emperor of the Hyksos. It was a much-sought-after honour to sit beside the most powerful ruler in the world and watch the ordeal of the bull, yet he was extremely worried. The inhabitants of Avaris, the imperial capital in the Egyptian Delta, spoke of this ordeal with fear, even though they did not know exactly what it was.

The two men were sitting on a platform, over-looking an arena and a circular structure called the 'labyrinth'. It was said that no one emerged from the labyrinth alive.

The general looked down at it. At first glance, there seemed nothing dangerous about the place. It was made up of a twisting, turning path marked out by partition walls, which were covered here and there with greenery. It looked impossible to go wrong: there was only that one winding path, and it led towards the way out.

'You seem rather tense,' commented Apophis in his hoarse, blood-chilling voice.

'Yes, I am. Majesty. Your invitation to the palace,

here to the labyrinth . . . I don't know how to thank you,' stammered the general, not daring to look at the emperor.

Apophis was a tall, very ugly man, with a prominent nose, flaccid cheeks, a bulging stomach and thick legs. He allowed himself only two small vanities: an amethyst scarab mounted on a gold ring, which he wore on the little finger of his left hand, and an amulet in the form of an ankh,⋆ which he wore round his neck and which endowed him with the right of life and death over his subjects.

As 'Beloved of the God Set', Apophis had proclaimed himself Pharaoh of Upper and Lower Egypt and had tried to write his coronation names on the sacred tree in the city of Iunu, as the rites required. But the leaves had proved unwilling, refusing to accept him. So Apophis had murdered the High Priest, ordered the closure of the temple, and announced that the ritual had been carried out correctly.

For some time now, the emperor had been dissatisfied.

Much was going well. In the islands off the coast of Mycenae, Jannas, the impressive and ruthless commander of the Hyksos war-fleet, was hunting down pirates who had dared to attack the empire's trading-fleet. Several small Asian princedoms had displayed a wish for independence, but elite troops

⋆The looped cross that is the hieroglyphic sign meaning 'life'.

were putting an end to such wishes by massacring the rebels, burning their towns and villages and bringing back droves of slaves to Egypt.

These episodes had served Apophis's grand design: to increase still further the size of his empire, which was already the largest ever known: Nubia, Canaan, Syria, Lebanon, Anatolia, Cyprus, the Mycenaean islands, Minoa and the Asian steppes had all bowed their heads before him, and feared his military might. But this was only a stage in the process, and the Hyksos invaders, who included soldiers of many diverse races, must continue their conquest of the world.

The centre of that world was Egypt, the Egypt of the pharaohs. The Hyksos had invaded and overrun the country with surprising ease, putting an end to long centuries of civilization based on the rule of the goddess Ma'at: justice, righteousness and unity. The Egyptians had proved feeble soldiers, and their resistance to the invaders' brute force and new weapons had been pitiful. Now he, Apophis, was Pharaoh.

He had set up his capital at the small town of Avaris, which was dedicated to the cult of Set, the god of storms and violence who had rendered him invincible. The town was now the principal city in Middle Egypt. Over it loomed an impregnable citadel, from whose walls the emperor liked to gaze down upon the port, which was always filled with hundreds of warships and trading-vessels. Inland from the port, the town itself had, in accordance with Apophis's wishes, assumed the appearance of one gigantic barracks, a paradise for his soldiers, who were waited upon by Egyptians forced into slavery.

The pharaoh should have been wholly content. But, incredibly, in the south of this defeated, destroyed Egypt, a rebellion was taking shape. At the insignificant and moribund town of Thebes, an equally insignificant prince named Seqen and his wife, Ahhotep, had dared to take up arms against the emperor.

Apophis scowled at the general. 'What, precisely, is happening?' he demanded.

'The situation is under control, Majesty.'

'Where is the battlefront now?'

'At the town of Qis, Majesty.'

'Qis? That's seven days' march north of Thebes, isn't it?'

'Approximately, Majesty.'

'That means Seqen's ridiculous army has conquered a huge amount of territory – far too much.'

'Oh no, Majesty!' said the general hastily. 'The rebels sailed down the Nile surprisingly quickly, and they tried to break through our lines with a lightning strike, but they have not established their rule over the provinces they passed through. In reality, their actions were more spectacular than dangerous.'

'All the same, we have suffered several setbacks.'

'The rebels took a few detachments by surprise, but I took rapid action and halted their advance.'

'At the cost of heavy losses, it would seem.'

'Their weapons may be archaic, but these Egyptians fight like wild animals. Fortunately, our chariots and horses give us enormous superiority. And also, Majesty, do not forget that we killed Seqen.'

Apophis kept his expression unreadable as he thought, 'Only because we have a spy at the heart of the enemy's organization.' Aloud, he asked, 'Where is Seqen's body?'

'The Egyptians managed to recover it, Majesty.'

'A pity. I'd have liked to hang it from the tallest tower in Avaris. What about Queen Ahhotep? Is she still at liberty?'

'Unfortunately, yes. But she's only a woman, after all. Now that her husband's dead, all she can do is surrender. The tatters of the Egyptian army will soon disperse, and we shall destroy them.'

'Ah!' exclaimed the emperor, turning to look down into the circular arena. 'The entertainment is beginning.'

An enormous bull with blazing eyes and pounding hooves came thundering into the arena, into which a naked, defenceless man was immediately flung.

The general went pale. The unfortunate victim was his own second-in-command, who had fought courageously at Qis.

'The game is as simple as it is amusing,' said Apophis. 'The bull charges at its adversary, whose only means of survival is to seize its horns and

5

execute a perilous leap over its back. A Minoan painter, Minos, is decorating my palace, and he says it is a very fashionable sport in his country. A clever man, Minos. Thanks to him, my paintings are more beautiful than the ones at Knossos, don't you think?'

'Oh yes, Majesty.'

'Look at that bull. He's a real giant, and he has a thoroughly vicious temper.'

He was right. The bull instantly charged its victim, who made the mistake of turning and trying to run away. The monstrous horns sank into his back. Snorting, the bull tossed the dying man through the air, trampled on him and gored him again.

Apophis grimaced in disgust. 'That worthless creature was as disappointing in the arena as he was in battle. Running away – that's all he was good for. But the responsibility for our defeats rests with his superior, does it not?'

The general began to sweat profusely. 'Nobody could have done better, Majesty, I assure you, I—'

'You are a fool, General. First, because you failed to foresee that attack; second, because your soldiers were defeated several times on Egyptian soil, and did not conduct themselves like true Hyksos; lastly, because you think that the enemy has been beaten. Stand up.'

Dumb with horror, the general obeyed.

The emperor unsheathed the golden-hilted dagger he always wore. 'Go down into the labyrinth, or I shall slit your throat. This is your only chance of winning my pardon.'

Apophis's murderous gaze banished all hesitation from the general's mind, and he leapt down into the labyrinth, landing on his hands and knees on the twisting path.

When he reached the first partition, he saw a blood-stain on the ground. After a moment's thought, he decided to leap over it, as though over an invisible obstacle. It was just as well he did, for two blades shot out, one from either side, brushing the soles of his feet.

The emperor was highly entertained. Since he had improved the layout of the labyrinth, few candidates had succeeded in getting past this first stage.

The general did the same thing as he emerged from the second bend, and that was his mistake. As he landed, the ground disappeared beneath his feet and he was flung into a pool where a hungry crocodile was waiting. The man's cries troubled neither the crocodile nor the emperor. A servant hurried to bring Apophis a bronze finger-bowl, and while the crocodile devoured its prey he washed his hands of the matter.

CHAPTER 2

Ahhotep, Queen of Egypt, was in her husband's tomb, meditating beside his body. Since the flagship had brought back the body back from the front, she had not left it for a moment.

Seqen's body was disfigured by several mortal wounds. On Ahhotep's orders, they had not been disguised during mummification: she did not want the signs of Seqen's courage to be wiped away. He had fought fiercely against the Hyksos hordes until he was eventually overwhelmed, and his bravery had given new heart to his soldiers, who had been terrified by the horse-drawn war-chariots, a new and formidable weapon.

Seqen had fallen passionately in love with Ahhotep, who admired him for his purity and nobility, his thirst for freedom and his readiness to sacrifice his life to restore Egypt's former greatness. Hand in hand, Seqen and Ahhotep had faced many ordeals before they were able to attack the enemy positions north of Thebes and thus begin to break out of the Hyksos encirclement.

Ahhotep had had the idea of creating a secret

desert camp where the soldiers of the army of liberation could be trained for war. She had entrusted this project to Seqen, and as Queen of Egypt had recognized him as Pharaoh. The office was an onerous one but, though born of a humble family, he had proved himself fully worthy of it, right up to his last breath.

The empire of darkness might have turned the royal couple's life into a wasteland of tears and blood, but there had also been a few shared moments of intense happiness. In Ahhotep's heart, Seqen would always represent youth, strength and love.

Footsteps sounded in the passageway outside, and the queen's mother, Teti the Small, came into the tomb. Although the old lady looked incredibly fragile, she was always impeccably dressed and made-up, and fought stubbornly against the dull exhaustion that forced her to sleep in the afternoons and retire early to bed. Devastated herself by Seqen's death, she was afraid Ahhotep might no longer have the energy she needed if she was to emerge from her suffering.

'You must eat,' she advised her daughter.

'Seqen's very handsome, isn't he? We must forget these ugly wounds, and think only of our king's proud, resolute face.'

'Ahhotep, you are now the sole ruler of the country. Everyone is awaiting your decisions.'

'I shall stay at my husband's side.'

9

'You have kept vigil according to our rites, and the period of mummification is over.'

'No, Mother, I—'

'Yes, Ahhotep. And I must say the words you are afraid to hear: the time has come to carry out the funeral ceremonies and seal the tomb.'

'I won't do it.'

Frail though she was compared to her magnificent daughter, Teti was unyielding. 'By behaving like a mere grieving widow, you're betraying Pharaoh and making his sacrifice pointless. He must now journey to the stars and we must continue the struggle. The soldiers call you "the Queen of Freedom", don't they? Then act like one. Go to Karnak, where the priests will transform you into the incarnation of Victorious Thebes.'

The authoritative tone and words pierced Ahhotep's heart like a dagger-blade. But she knew Teti was right.

Closely guarded, and accompanied by her two sons, Kames and Ahmose, Ahhotep set out for the Temple of Amon at Karnak, where the priests chanted incantations day and night for the immortality of the royal soul.

Since the beginning of the Hyksos occupation, no work had been done to enlarge or adorn Karnak. Protected by an encircling wall, the temple was composed of two main shrines, one with square pillars and the other with pillars carved in the form of Osiris, proclaiming the resurrection of the god murdered by his brother Set. There was a prediction that the door of the shrine containing the statue of Amon, 'the Hidden One', would open of its own accord if the Egyptians succeeded in defeating the Hyksos.

When the royal party arrived, the High Priest came to greet them. Fourteen-year-old Kames stood up very straight, but Ahmose, who was only four, clutched his mother's hand tightly.

The High Priest bowed low before the queen, who was wearing her mother's gold crown. 'Majesty, are you ready to embody the conquering fire of Thebes?'

'I am ready. Kames, take good care of your brother.'

Ahmose began to cry. 'I want to stay with you – and I want my daddy.'

Ahhotep kissed the little boy tenderly. 'Your father is in the heavens with the other pharaohs, and we must honour him by finishing his work. To do so, I need the support of everyone, especially our two sons. Do you understand that?'

Gulping back his tears, Ahmose went to his brother, who took him reassuringly by the shoulders.

The High Priest led Ahhotep to the shrine of the goddess Mut, whose name meant both 'Mother' and 'Death'. It was she who had given the young queen the strength to carry on a near-impossible fight, and it was she who would transform the modest city of Thebes into the heart of the war to liberate Egypt.

The High Priest attached a gold uraeus to Ahhotep's crown, then handed her a bow and four arrows. 'Majesty, do you swear to fight the darkness?'

'I swear.'

'Then may your arrows reach the four corners of the earth.'

Ahhotep shot an arrow to the east, then one to the north, the south and lastly the west. Her noble bearing impressed all the priests.

'Since the heavens look favourably upon you, Majesty, here are the life you must preserve and the magic you must use.'

The High Priest took an ankh and a sceptre, whose head was shaped like the beast of Set, and held them up before the queen's eyes.

Strong vibrations passed through Ahhotep's whole body. Henceforth, she would be the incarnation of an entire people's hopes.

After the soldiers from the training-camp had paid final homage to the dead pharaoh, the funeral procession set off for the cemetery. Four oxen drew the sarcophagus,* which lay on a wooden sledge. At regular intervals, priests poured milk on to the ground in front of the sledge, to make the runners glide more smoothly.

*It is preserved in Cairo Museum (CG 61001).

In this time of war, traditional craftsmanship had been reduced to its most crude and basic form, so Seqen's funerary furniture was very modest, utterly unworthy of a royal tomb: a scribe's palette, a bow, sandals, a ceremonial kilt and a crown. Thebes no longer had a single great stone-cutter or sculptor: every one had long since been executed by the Hyksos.

Ahhotep was accompanied in the procession by her sons and her mother, by Qaris, head steward of the palace, and by Heray, who, though his official title was Overseer of Granaries, was also responsible for Thebes's safety and for catching collaborators with the enemy. There was one notable absence from the ceremonies: Emheb, governor of the town of Edfu, had had to go to Qis to maintain the morale of the troops at the front.

Outside the entrance to the little tomb, which was derisory compared to the pyramids of the Golden Age, Qaris and Heray stood the sarcophagus upright. Before it was entrusted to the Goddess of the West, who would absorb Seqen into her breast where he would be reborn, his mouth, eyes and ears must be reopened.

The funerary priest handed the queen a wooden adze. As soon as she touched it, it broke.

'We haven't another one,' he lamented. 'That was the last one dedicated when Pharaoh ruled Egypt.'

'The sarcophagus cannot remain lifeless!' protested Ahhotep.

'Then, Majesty, we must use the adze called "Way-Opener".'

'But it is in Asyut,' said Qaris in alarm, 'and Asyut is far from safe.'

'Nevertheless, we must go there at once,' said the queen.

'Majesty, I beg you not to,' said Qaris. 'You have no right to run such a risk.'

'My foremost duty is to ensure that Pharaoh has a peaceful journey to the paradise lands of the afterlife. If I were to fail in that duty, we would be doomed to failure.'

CHAPTER 3

The ancient town of Asyut – known as 'Way-Opener' because of its association with 'the Opener of the Ways', the jackal-god Wepwawet – lay six days to the north of Thebes. Asyut was in enemy-held territory, and was virtually in its death-throes, but a few brave people still fought on. Two battle-hardened officers in Ahhotep's army, the Afghan and Moustache, had contacts among them.

Moustache was an Egyptian from the Delta, who had joined the rebel movement almost in spite of himself, though it had since become his reason for living. The Afghan's livelihood had been destroyed by the invaders. His prime concern was to restore the trade in lapis-lazuli with an Egypt which once again respected the laws of commerce. Together, the two men had braved many dangers. They were wholehearted admirers of Queen Ahhotep, the most beautiful and intelligent woman they had ever met, and would fight with her to the end, whatever might happen.

Ahhotep consulted the two officers, and it was decided to send a message by carrier-pigeon, to find

15

out how things stood in Asyut. The message was entrusted to a bird called Rascal, the fastest and toughest of the flock. The mission was dangerous and, besides, if Rascal did not return Ahhotep would have lost one of her best soldiers. The white and brown pigeon seemed to listen attentively when Ahhotep warned it of the danger: its head was erect and its eyes sparkled as if confident of success.

Two days went by, while the queen searched the sky in vain. Then, at dusk on the second day, she made out her messenger in the distance. The bird was flying more slowly and awkwardly than usual, but it was definitely Rascal. When he alighted on Ahhotep's shoulder she saw why: his right flank was drenched in blood.

He proudly presented his right leg, to which a small, sealed papyrus was attached. The queen praised him and stroked him gently, then removed the message and entrusted the brave messenger to Teti the Small.

'He must have been wounded by an arrow,' she said. 'Take good care of him.'

'It's only a superficial wound,' said Teti, examining it closely. 'Rascal will be fit and well again in a few days.'

Much relieved, Ahhotep unrolled the papyrus and read the brief message. It said that Asyut had been almost completely destroyed, with the exception of the ancient tombs. It now housed only a small Hyksos garrison, which received supplies from the oases at Khargeh and Dakhla.

'We must leave at once,' decided Ahhotep. 'Have a boat prepared for the voyage. And we'll take my dog, Laughter, and my late husband's donkey, Way-Finder, because they both have a keen instinct for danger.'

Sailing at night was dangerous – there was a risk of running aground on a sandbank or disturbing a herd of hippopotamus, whose anger could be terrifyingly destructive. But in daylight the Nile was even less safe, because here and there the Hyksos were always on the prowl.

It was nearly dawn when the boat reached its destination. The moon, Ahhotep's ally, lit up the countryside and the town. Once a thriving, bustling port, Asyut was now virtually abandoned. Old boats and a leaking barge were rotting at their moorings. The town was sheltered by a cliff-face, in which tombs had been excavated. One of them, that of a High Priest of Wepwawet, contained the adze needed to give life back to Seqen's mummy.

Laughter and Way-Finder sniffed the air, and could detect no danger, so they led the little party off the boat. Besides the huge dog and the donkey, Ahhotep's guards were the Afghan, Moustache and ten young archers, all on the alert for the slightest sign of trouble.

The Afghan looked around warily. 'If I were the Hyksos commander,' he said, 'the burial-ground cliff is where I'd post my sentries. It's an ideal lookout point.'

'Then we'd better check,' said Moustache. 'If you're right, it'll mean one or two fewer Hyksos.'

The two men climbed the cliff with the speed and ease of seasoned fighters. Less than half an hour later, they returned.

'Four sentries, all fast asleep,' said Moustache. 'The way is clear.'

Ahhotep had undergone the same training as her soldiers, so she had no difficulty in scaling the cliff. Several tombs had been defiled, and unfortunately they included the High Priest of Wepwawet's, which the Hyksos were using to store weapons and food. With fury in her heart, the queen explored the ravaged tomb by the light of a torch.

Eventually she reached the small chamber near the back of the tomb where the ritualists generally placed the most precious objects. On the ground lay fragments of storage-chests and statues. She searched through the chaotic jumble and at last, underneath the wreck of a basket containing mummified food, she found the adze of sky-metal that was used in resurrection rituals.

The door of Seqen's tomb was closed once more, and Kames, aided by Qaris, placed the funerary seal upon it. Now that Ahhotep had opened the mummy's eyes, mouth and ears, Pharaoh's soul was no longer chained to the earth.

'Majesty,' ventured Qaris as they walked away, 'we must discuss the military situation.'

'Later.'

'You must stop the attack at once.'

'Governor Emheb will hold the front. All I want is to share my husband's death.'

'Majesty, I hardly dare believe—'

'I must enter the House of the Acacia, and no one shall stop me.'

There were only three of them left: three old priestesses who made up the reclusive community of the House of the Acacia. They would have starved to death if Queen Ahhotep had not granted them accommodation and provisions so that they might pass on their knowledge.

Ahhotep sat with them at the foot of an acacia-tree armed with fearsome thorns.

'Life and death are contained within it,' said the oldest priestess. 'Osiris gives it its green foliage, and inside the mound of Osiris the sarcophagus becomes a ship capable of sailing across the universe. If the acacia dies, life leaves the living, until the father is reborn in his sons. Isis creates a new pharaoh, healed of the wounds inflicted by Set, and the acacia is once again bedecked in leaves.'

The prophesy was clear: Kames was to become king.

But Ahhotep needed more. 'I wish my spirit to remain eternally linked with Seqen's, beyond death.'

'Since death is born,' replied the priestess, 'it

will itself die. But what existed before creation does not undergo death. In the celestial paradise, neither fear nor violence exists. The righteous and the ancestors commune with the gods.'

'How can I enter into contact with Seqen?'

'Send him a message from your heart.'

'But what if he doesn't reply?'

'May the god of destiny watch over the Queen of Egypt.'

Ahhotep's most valuable possession was a pillar-shaped wooden box, elaborately gilded and encrusted with semiprecious stones. It bore an inscription, '*The queen is beloved of Thoth, master of the divine words*', and in it she kept her writing-brushes and inks. She needed it now.

On a pristine sheet of papyrus, she wrote a love-letter to Seqen in beautiful hieroglyphs, begging him to drive away evil spirits and to help Egypt regain its freedom. She implored him to give her an answer, to prove that he had indeed been reborn.

Ahhotep attached the message to an acacia branch. Then she made a clay statuette of Osiris lying upon his deathbed and laid it at the foot of the tree. Finally, she sang and played the harp, so that the harmonious chords would ensure Seqen a serene journey to the afterlife.

But would she receive an answer from the husband she loved so much?

CHAPTER 4

Although Jannas was still fighting the pirates in the Mycenaean islands and trying to put down the Theban rebellion, the customary ceremony of paying tributes was taking place in Avaris. Apophis enjoyed this moment, when envoys from every province of the empire grovelled before him and gave him impressive amounts of money and valuables. Unlike former pharaohs, he kept the greater part for himself, instead of putting it back into the cycle of trade.

Khamudi, the emperor's ruthless right-hand man, always made ample use of it, with the blessing of his master, whose safety he ensured. He took for himself a proportion of all sizeable trading operations, and had gained control of papyrus cultivation in the Delta. He was a corpulent man, with jet-black hair plastered to his round head, slightly protuberant eyes, and plump hands and feet – he had grown fatter and fatter since his appointment as High Treasurer. His nickname among his slaves was 'His Royal Self-Importance'.

His interest outside his work was indulging in depraved sexual practices together with his voluptuous blonde wife, Yima, who came originally from Canaan. Here, too, Apophis, who liked to think of himself as austere and moralistic, turned a blind eye. He would keep it turned as long as Khamudi remained in his proper place – in other words, second in rank to himself.

As they did every year, the storehouses of Avaris were filling with gold, precious stones, bronze, copper, rare kinds of valuable timber, fabrics, jars of oil and wine, ointments and countless other riches which ensured the imperial capital's unequalled prosperity.

When the Minoan envoy approached the emperor, dressed in a tunic patterned with red diamonds, Khamudi touched the hilt of his dagger and gestured to his archers. At the slightest suspicious sign from the diplomat, they had orders to kill him. But the Minoan bowed as low as the others, before launching into a long speech in which he praised the greatness and power of the Hyksos emperor, whose faithful vassal he was. (During this boring eulogy, Apophis's sister, Windswept, a magnificent woman, took the opportunity to caress her lover Minos, the Minoan painter who was adorning the palace. The young man blushed but did not resist.) The envoys's servants laid swords, silver vases and intricate items of furniture at the emperor's feet. Minoa was proving equal to its reputation.

'Jannas is cleansing the Mycenaean islands,' declared the emperor in his harsh voice, which made the listening throng shiver, 'and the campaign is costing me dear. As Minoa is close to the battle zone, she shall pay me an additional tribute.'

The envoy bit his lip and bowed again.

Apophis was very pleased with the Minoan decoration of his fortified palace and the furniture he had gathered there. It included a royal bed stolen from Memphis, incense-burners and silver basins placed on alabaster tables in his bath-chamber, which had a red limestone floor, and in particular some splendid lamps comprising a limestone base and a sycamore-wood stem topped with a bronze dish. After washing, the emperor donned a fringed brown tunic and went to the apartments occupied by his wife, Tany. He had refused to grant her the title of Empress, so as not to concede even the smallest crumb of power.

'Aren't you ready yet?' he demanded.

Short, fat Tany was probably the ugliest woman in Avaris. She was forever trying new ointments and lotions in the hope of improving her looks, but the results were disastrous. She made up for it by taking daily revenge on the once-wealthy Egyptian women who had been forced into slavery and now served her, who had herself once been a servant. The emperor was indifferent to his wife's ugliness, but he thoroughly approved of her hatred of Egypt, which had inspired him to some excellent ideas.

Tany held out a necklace whose beads looked

like pearls but were made of a strange material. 'Look at this, Apophis. Isn't it strange?'

'What is it?'

'According to my new slave, who comes from Memphis, it's called glass. It's made by melting quartz with natron or ashes, and you can make it whatever colour you want.'

'Pearls made of glass? These are a bit opaque, but I'm sure we'll be able to improve the process. But come on. I'm in a hurry to see our two plans take shape – yours and mine.'

'I'm just finishing my make-up.'

Tany plastered her forehead and cheeks with a thick layer of kohl, and squeezed herself into a brown and white striped dress. Head held high, she followed her husband out of the palace, always one pace behind him.

Khamudi and the imperial guard were waiting for them. 'All is ready, Majesty.'

The procession made its way to the last Egyptian burial-ground in Avaris, where the ancestors who had lived there before the invasion were buried. Hundreds of Egyptian slaves had been herded together there, on the orders of the guards. All of them feared a mass execution.

'All traces of the vile past must disappear,' decreed Apophis. 'This old burial-ground takes up too much space, so we're going to build houses here for army officers.'

An old woman managed to push her way out of the crowd and knelt before him, imploringly. 'No, my lord, do not attack our ancestors. Let them sleep in peace, I beg of you.'

With one violent blow of his hand, Khamudi broke the insolent woman's neck. 'Get rid of that,' he ordered the guards, 'and kill anyone else who dares interrupt the emperor.' He turned back to the crowd. 'Henceforth, you will bury your dead in front of your houses or even inside them. They must not take up space in my city. There will be no more offerings or prayers for the dead. The dead no longer exist, there is no "Beautiful West", or "Eternal East", or "Light of Resurrection". Anyone caught performing the duties of a funerary priest will be executed immediately.'

Lady Tany was delighted: with his usual genius, Apophis had not only made use of her idea but had even improved upon it.

Nothing could have plunged the Egyptians more effectively into despair. To be deprived of all contact with their ancestors would at last make them recognize that a new world had been born.

To reach the small island on which the Temple of Set had been built, the imperial retinue took the royal barge. The brick-built shrine, now the main temple in Avaris, was also dedicated to the Syrian storm-god, Hadad. A rectangular altar stood in front of the entrance, surrounded by oak trees and by ditches filled with the bleached bones of sacrificed animals, mainly donkeys.

The priests bowed very low before the emperor, who had come to consecrate a shrine to his own glory. It was entirely decorated in gold leaf and bore witness to the empire's wealth and its master's divine status. The ceremony ought to have been the signal for rejoicing, but many people were casting anxious eyes at the sky. Threatening clouds were gathering right over Avaris.

Looking perfectly serene, Apophis entered his shrine and pronounced the craftsmen's work satisfactory. All the provinces of the empire would be informed that he was the son and equal of Set.

When he emerged from the temple, lightning was zigzagging across the clouds. Large raindrops began to fall on to the altar, where a Hyksos priest had just killed a fine white donkey, its hooves tightly bound together.

'Majesty, the anger of Set is warning us of a great danger! We must—'

The priest's words died in his throat as Apophis slit it with his dagger.

'Do you not understand, imbecile? The Lord of Storms hails me as master of the empire, and has rendered me invincible.'

CHAPTER 5

High Treasurer Khamudi had established a gigantic taxation centre at the heart of Avaris, guarded by the army. From this base, he kept tight control of the taxes received from the various provinces of the empire. As the years went by they kept on growing, demanding an equal growth in the number of officials.

Apophis wielded absolute power, and himself commanded the army, but he delegated management of the empire's wealth to his High Treasurer, who would pay with his life if he concealed anything from him. Khamudi was too enamoured of his position to play that game. So he told the emperor about everything he appropriated for himself in order to increase his personal fortune.

The Egyptians and vassals were bled white, but Khamudi kept dreaming up new taxes, or lowered one tax the better to raise another. Convinced there were no limits to the extent to which the empire's subjects could be exploited, he was determined to improve his results. As for the senior officials, who had themselves accumulated considerable wealth since the start of Apophis's reign, they had come to an arrangement with Khamudi.

The High Treasurer's secretary burst into his office, a look of terror on his face. 'My lord, it's the emperor – he's here!'

An unexpected visit from Apophis? Khamudi had a sudden need to scratch his left leg. Problems set off a skin-rash which even the strongest salves had difficulty in soothing. Thousands of figures ran through his head. What mistake had he made?

'Majesty, what a great honour to welcome you.'

His shoulders stooped, the emperor threw him a chilling sidelong glance. 'You have made yourself very comfortable here, haven't you? The luxury is rather ostentatious, with this modern furniture, this army of scribes, these vast archives and your bustling papyrus factory. Still, you have one invaluable quality: efficiency untainted by conscience. Thanks to you, the empire grows richer by the day.'

Khamudi felt somewhat relieved.

The emperor flung his heavy frame into an armchair decorated with wild bulls. 'The Egyptians are mere cattle,' he said in a tired voice, 'but most of our soldiers have gone soft and must be constantly harassed to prevent them resting on past glories. Our generals' incompetence is infuriating.'

'Do you wish them to be . . . cleansed?'

'Their replacements would be no better. We have lost ground in the South of Egypt, and that is something I will not tolerate.'

'And neither will I, Majesty. But this is only a

temporary situation. The rebels have been halted at Qis, and they won't get any further. As soon as Commander Jannas returns from the Mycenaean islands he will smash their front.'

'Yes, but that affair is much more serious than I thought,' grumbled Apophis. 'Jannas isn't dealing with simple pirates; he's facing a well-organized enemy war-fleet.'

'Our troops will be back from Asia – the rebels there have been virtually crushed.'

'No, they must stay there a while longer, to ensure that the flame has been properly extinguished.'

'In that case, Majesty, let us send our garrisons from the Delta.'

'Absolutely not, my friend. While we are waiting for Jannas, we shall make use of another weapon at our disposal: false information. You are to have two series of scarabs engraved. The first will be for our vassals, announcing that the Hyksos empire continues to grow. The other will be for the Egyptians who have taken up arms against us. I shall dictate the message to you; take great care in transcribing it into hieroglyphics.'

'Take cover!' roared Governor Emheb. 'They're using their catapults!'

The soldiers of the army of liberation threw themselves belly-down on the ground, or sheltered behind the reed huts that had been built on the front line. The volleys of missiles continued for

29

some minutes, but were not followed by an attack. When they were able to move again, the soldiers investigated, and were surprised to discover hundreds of limestone scarabs, all bearing the same inscription.

They brought them to Emheb.

As he deciphered the text, the governor realized the danger. 'Destroy every one of them,' he ordered.

Emheb copied the message on to a slip of papyrus, which he entrusted to Rascal so that the queen would be alerted quickly.

Ahhotep was hoping for a sign which would prove that Seqen's soul had been reborn, but nothing came, even though all the rites had been carried out correctly. She could think of no other way to make contact with her husband.

As the days wore on, the beautiful young woman seemed to begin fading away, and no one could comfort her. However, she was still very attentive to her sons, who had been very shocked by their father's death. Kames tried to forget his pain through weapons training with his instructors, while little Ahmose spent most of his time playing with his grandmother.

Thebes was sinking into sorrow. How long it seemed since the first days of the campaign to free Egypt!

Qaris, the head steward, steeled himself to approach the queen, who was sitting at the foot of the acacia-tree where she had placed her letter to Seqen.

'Majesty, may I speak with you?'

'From now on, silence is my country,' said Ahhotep sadly.

'It is serious, Majesty, very serious.'

'What could be more serious than the death of Pharaoh? Without him, we have lost our strength.'

'Apophis has had scarabs engraved, announcing your death. If this false information spreads everywhere, the rebels will soon lay down their arms and the emperor will have won without a fight.'

Ahhotep looked even sadder. 'Apophis is right. I am dead – to this world.'

The usually imperturbable Qaris lost his temper. 'That is not true, Majesty, and you have no right to say it! You are Regent Queen of the Two Lands, of Upper and Lower Egypt, and you have sworn to carry on the work of Pharaoh Seqen.'

The queen smiled faintly. 'An implacable enemy occupies the Two Lands. When he killed Seqen, he killed me, too.'

Suddenly Qaris gasped. 'Majesty, your letter . . . It's gone!'

Ahhotep stood up and looked at the branch to which she had attached the papyrus. Sure enough, the scroll was no longer there.

Qaris's face lit up. 'Pharaoh Seqen has received your message, Majesty. Isn't this the sign you have been waiting for?'

'Yes, but I need more than just that.'

She bent down to look at the clay statue of Osiris lying on his death-bed that she had laid at the foot of the tree. Ears of wheat had sprung forth from it. The sight of them took Ahhotep's breath away and she almost fainted.

Qaris smiled even more broadly. 'Pharaoh Seqen has been reborn, Majesty. He lives for ever among the gods, and he will guide you in all you do.'

In Thebes itself, the rumours were spreading like wildfire. Some said that Queen Ahhotep was dead, others that she had lost her mind and from now on would live as a recluse within the temple at Karnak. Governor Emheb prepared himself to surrender and beg the emperor for mercy.

And then the good news was announced by Heray, Overseer of Granaries. Ahhotep was alive and in good health, and she would address her troops the following day, at dawn.

Many soldiers were sceptical, but when the sun rose in the east the queen emerged from the palace, crowned with a slender gold diadem and dressed in a long white robe. Her beauty and nobility were greeted with respectful silence.

'Like this reborn sun, the soul of Pharaoh has been born again in the light. As regent queen, I shall continue the fight until Kames is able to command the army. I intend to remain absolutely faithful to the dead king. Therefore today, at Karnak, I have created the office of "Wife of God", which I shall be the first to hold. I shall never remarry, and my only companion shall remain my husband, who rests in the secret heart of Amon. When Egypt is once again free, if I am still in this world I shall withdraw into the temple.'

CHAPTER 6

Rascal and his small flock of carrier-pigeons had left Thebes in the early morning, bearing messages for the front. They announced that Queen Ahhotep was in perfect health and that the fight against the Hyksos was continuing. The order was given to destroy the scarabs spreading the Hyksos' lies.

From now on, the military camp to the north of the City of Amon was no longer to be a secret. It was to become the official headquarters of the army of freedom, with its palace, its forts, its school for scribes, its barracks, its weapons workshops and stores, and its dwellings. A special detachment of soldiers protected Thebes, where no one now had any thoughts of collaborating with the Hyksos. Seqen's sacrifice, his first victories and Queen Ahhotep's bearing had restored the entire population's taste for battle.

Using the silver mined from a rich seam she had discovered in the desert, and with her mother's help, Ahhotep had set about bringing back royal dignity to the House of the Queen. The old institution was still a long way from its past splendour, but the official buildings in Thebes and at the military base were no longer decrepit and neglected. Under Qaris's direction, skilled artists were working there again, scribes and craftsmen competing to see who could work most zealously.

The queen, her mother and Heray were standing before Qaris's model of Egypt, which represented the whole country from the mouth of the Delta in the north to Elephantine in the south. When Ahhotep had seen it for the first time, only one place had been free of the occupying forces: Thebes. Today, although the situation was still far from good, it had improved a great deal.

'Thebes, Elkab and Edfu,' said Qaris, pointing to them on the model, 'are the three towns we can rely on. Further south, Elephantine is under the control of the Nubians, allies of the Hyksos, and we must not forget the great Hyksos fortress of Per-Hathor, between Thebes and Edfu. To the north, very close to Thebes, Kebet is still not completely free. Titi, its governor, assures us that his network of rebels will be sufficient, but we'll probably have to send him reinforcements. Much further north, Khmun is still the main Hyksos barrier. And then, of course, there's the Delta, which is entirely under the emperor's control.'

'What is the latest news from the front?' asked Ahhotep.

'Thanks to our carrier-pigeons, we are in constant contact with Emheb, who has set up his front-line camp outside Qis. The Hyksos in the town can do little more than fire sporadic volleys of arrows, because the way our troops are deployed and occupy the terrain prevents them from launching a mass attack using chariots.'

'But why doesn't Apophis attack us?' asked the queen in astonishment.

'If we wish to be optimistic,' said Heray, 'we must suppose that he has enough other problems to postpone until later dealing with the small one we present.'

'Each day,' added Qaris, 'Emheb strengthens our hold on the front.'

'What about supplies?'

'They are secure, Majesty, because the peasants in the area have rallied to our cause. The networks of rebels set up by the Afghan and Moustache have proved extremely effective.'

The queen thought for a moment. 'Our weak point is still weapons, isn't it?'

Qaris sighed. 'I'm afraid so. We have neither chariots nor those strange animals called horses, which pull them at an incredible speed.'

'That doesn't mean we must be satisfied with our ancient weapons,' replied Ahhotep. 'Summon all the craftsmen.'

In her left hand, the Regent Queen of the Two Lands held a wooden sceptre bearing the head of Set. In her right, she held the sacred Sword of Amon, a curved bronze blade covered with silver and inlaid with an alloy of gold and silver. Beside her, his face proud and solemn, stood her elder son. During his childhood he had been called Kames, but he now used his true name, Kamose.

'With this sceptre,' Ahhotep declared to the many assembled craftsmen, 'I shall measure Egypt when she is free. But, before we can carry out that peaceful task, we must use the sword the god of Thebes has given us. With it, I consecrate my elder son as war-commander, not for death but for life. May this ray of light illuminate his thoughts and give him his father's courage.'

Ahhotep touched Kamose's forehead with the point of the Sword of Amon. The light that flashed from the blade was so dazzling that those watching had to close their eyes.

The look in the boy's eyes suddenly changed, as though his consciousness had been opened to realities whose existence he had never suspected before. 'In the names of Pharaoh and of the Queen of Freedom,' he vowed, so solemnly that a shiver ran around the watching throng, 'I swear to fight to my last breath so that Egypt may become herself again and joy may once more fill the hearts of her people. Until I have accomplished my task, I shall not allow myself a single moment's rest.'

Kamose kissed the Sword of Amon and prostrated himself before the queen. Childhood had just died within him. Ahhotep raised him to his feet and he again took his place at her side.

Turning back to the craftsmen, the queen said, 'Everyone knows the enemy's weapons are much better than ours. It is up to you, the craftsmen of Thebes, to redress the balance. You are to make new spears, longer and with sharper bronze heads, and new wooden shields, also strengthened with bronze. In future, the footsoldiers' heads are to be protected by helmets and their chests by thick copper breastplates. Axes, clubs and daggers must be of better quality. And our best troops will be equipped with curved swords similar to the Sword of Amon. In hand-to-hand fighting, with these weapons and our will to win, we shall be better than the Hyksos. Now, craftsmen, to work!'

Her words were greeted with resounding cheers.

'What an amazing woman,' commented Moustache, who had hung on her every word.

'She has that power you call magic,' said the Afghan. 'And those eyes . . . With them she could conquer anyone.'

'I've already told you: whatever you do, don't fall in love.'

'Why not?'

'You had no chance before, Afghan, but you have even less now that Queen Ahhotep has become the Wife of God. From now on, no man can go near her.'

The Afghan frowned. 'She's far too beautiful to accept a fate like that.'

'She herself chose it. As you can see, she does not lack character or determination.'

'All the same . . . Remember when we first

became rebels? You thought defeating the Hyksos was impossible, too.'

'To be frank, I still do. Ahhotep makes our heads spin, and sometimes we almost forget the imbalance in our forces. But that doesn't matter. She gives meaning both to our lives and to our deaths.'

To strengthen the front, Ahhotep had decided to use the *heka*, the magic, light-born power whose guardian she had become when she travelled to Dendera with Seqen. The most intense *heka* was that of the sacred city of Iunu, which was in Hyksos hands, but the one she had would serve to keep the enemy pinned down, at least for a little while.

In the shrine of Mut, at Karnak, a priestess made wax figures representing Hyksos soldiers, tied up and unable to do any harm. On red bowls, Ahhotep wrote the name of Apophis and ancient incantations ordering the serpent of destruction to spit its venom and attack him. Then the figures were put into the bowls, which were held over a brazier.

'May breath enter these figures,' she chanted, 'and may it burn them. May the wax, born of the bee, symbol of the royalty of Lower Egypt and the Delta, become our ally.'

The flames crackled, the hideous faces of the Hyksos melted out of shape, and Ahhotep smashed the red bowls.

★　★　★

'May I speak with you privately, Majesty?' asked Qaris as the queen was leaving the temple.

'You look worried. Is there bad news from the front?'

'No, it's nothing like that. But I have done a great deal of thinking, and there are certain conclusions I cannot keep to myself. You alone must hear them.'

Qaris was a plump fellow, with round cheeks and a calm temperament, who usually managed to radiate good humour, even at the most difficult times. Ahhotep had never seen him so anxious.

'May we walk a little further away, Majesty? No one must hear what I am about to tell you.'

They went on to the landing-stage outside the temple, and walked along to the end.

'The enemy without is formidable,' declared Qaris, 'but the enemy within is no less so. Fortunately, Heray has rid us of collaborators, and the people are now devoted to you. Moreover, Thebes now realizes that there is no going back and that we must see the adventure through to its conclusion: destruction or freedom.'

'I know all this. Are you worried that support for collaboration will re-emerge?'

Qaris shook his head. 'No. Heray is too vigilant, and Thebes will not take a backward step, I am convinced of that. This is about something else, something equally serious.' The steward's mouth was dry. 'For many years, my main task has been to collect information and to extract what is important. Of course, I have closely studied the reports concerning the tragic death of Pharaoh Seqen.'

Ahhotep halted in her tracks. 'Have you found something amiss?'

'Majesty, I am convinced that your husband fell into a trap. The Hyksos were waiting for him at that place. They knew how to isolate him and were able to murder him because they had received information from someone very well informed.'

'You mean . . . Are you saying there is a traitor among us?'

'I have no absolute proof, but that is indeed what I believe.'

Ahhotep raised her eyes to the heavens. This was one treacherous blow she had not foreseen. 'Have you anything more solid than suspicion, Qaris?'

'No, Majesty, and I hope I am wrong.'

'If you are right, all my principal decisions must be kept secret.'

'As secret as possible, yes. And I would advise you not to trust anyone.'

'Not even you?'

'I have nothing to offer you but my word, Majesty.'

CHAPTER 7

The destruction of the last Egyptian burial-ground in Avaris provoked an unexpected revolt – by elderly widows and widowers. In desperation, they gathered together to march on the citadel and protest against the emperor's decision. The stunned guards watched open-mouthed as this tide of harmless folk poured in, many walking with difficulty. A few spears were enough to halt them.

'Go home at once,' an Anatolian officer ordered them.

'We want to keep our burial-ground,' protested an old man in his eighties, leaning on his stick. 'My wife, my parents, my grandparents and my great-grandparents are all buried there, and it's the same for most of us Egyptians. Our dead pose no threat to the security of the empire, as far as I know.'

'Orders are orders.'

With silent determination, the protestors sat down. Killing them all would be no problem, but the officer decided to consult his superior.

★   ★   ★

'Old men?' exclaimed Khamudi.

'They refuse to go home, my lord, and they want the emperor to see them.'

'Haven't these imbeciles realized yet that times have changed? Are they noisy?'

'No, not at all. How would you like me to execute them?'

'Execute them? I have a better idea. Go and fetch the lady Aberia. I am going to ask for the emperor's permission.'

Aberia was using her enormous hands to indulge in her favourite pastime: strangling people. For the moment, she had to content herself with a gazelle, whose finest cuts would be served at Apophis's table. But it was much less entertaining than wringing the neck of an enslaved Egyptian noblewoman. Thanks to the emperor's wife, Lady Aberia had no lack of prey, some terrified, others fighting back. Her thirst for vengeance was unquenchable, and Apophis approved of this policy of terror, which deterred the defeated from resisting him.

'My lady,' said the officer, 'the High Treasurer wishes to see you urgently.'

Aberia felt a frisson of pleasure. Knowing Khamudi, there must be exciting work in store. She hurried to Khamudi's office.

'Who are they, this herd of old men?' she asked as soon as she arrived.

'Dangerous rebels,' replied Khamudi.

'Dangerous? Them?' scoffed Aberia.

'Much more dangerous than you think. Those old men and women embody harmful traditions and are passing them on to younger generations. They cannot stay in Avaris, because they're setting a bad example. Their place is somewhere else, far away from here.'

The lady Aberia's interest was beginning to stir. 'And it would be my task to . . . see to it?'

'Near our rearward base in Palestine, at Sharuhen, there are marshy areas where a prison camp could be set up.'

'An ordinary prison camp, or a place of killing?'

'Whichever you wish,' said Khamudi.

The strangler now regarded her prisoners in a quite different light. 'You are right, High Treasurer. They are indeed dangerous rebels, and I shall treat them as such.'

The procession took the path that ran eastwards along the lakes. Seated comfortably in a chair carried by bearers, Aberia forced her team of slaves to march as fast as possible, and granted them only a short halt and a little water every five hours.

The stamina of these old Egyptians astonished her. Only a few had collapsed since the beginning of the journey, and Aberia had not allowed anyone else to take care of wringing their necks. Their remains would be feasted on by vultures and other scavengers. Only one prisoner had tried to run away, and he had been instantly killed by a Hyksos guard. The others kept on walking, step after step, under a burning sun.

If anyone weakened, the strongest supported him as best they could and helped him along. From time to time, someone's heart gave out. The corpse was abandoned beside the road, unburied and unmourned. The first man who asked for more water was whipped to death, so the old people kept on walking without complaint, watched delightedly by Aberia, who was already thinking of organizing other journeys like this.

'You must not lose hope,' said a seventy-year-old to one of his companions in misfortune. 'My son belongs to a network of rebels, and he told me that Queen Ahhotep is in command of an army of liberation.'

'She has no chance.'

'She has already defeated the Hyksos several times.'

'No one has said anything about that in Avaris,' retorted the woman.

'No one would dare – the emperor's soldiers and guards are everywhere. But the news will eventually get around, all the same. The Theban army has reached Qis and obviously intends to attack the Delta.'

'The Hyksos are too powerful, and the gods have abandoned us.'

'No, they haven't. I'm certain they haven't.'

Despite her reservations, the woman whispered in the ear of her neighbour, who passed on the information to the woman next to him. Little by little, all the prisoners learnt that Thebes had lifted her head once more and that battle had been joined. Even the most exhausted prisoners found new strength, and the way seemed less agonizing, despite the heat, the thirst and the mosquitoes.

After Avaris, Sharuhen was the most impressive fortress in the empire. High towers enabled look-outs to keep a close watch on the surrounding area and the port. The garrison town housed highly trained troops who could take rapid action in Syria and Palestine at any moment and nip in the bud the smallest attempt at sedition.

In accordance with Apophis's orders, the Hyksos carried out regular raids to remind the civilian population that the emperor's law was inviolable. A village would be burnt and looted, and the women raped and then used as slaves, together with their strongest children. It was the favourite pastime of the garrison at Sharuhen, whose port housed cargo-boats groaning with food supplies.

The fortress commander was surprised by the arrival of the pitiful procession and impressed by the lady Aberia's muscular frame.

'I am on an official mission,' she declared haughtily. 'The emperor wishes me to set up a prison camp near the fortress. He has decided to deport as many rebels as possible, so that they do not trouble the Hyksos order.'

'But these are old men!'

'They have been spreading dangerous ideas, liable to unsettle people's minds.'

'Very well, very well,' said the commander. 'You would do best to travel further into the interior, because it is very marshy around here, and—'

'That suits me perfectly. I want these prisoners to be within bowshot of your archers on the towers. If one of these bandits tries to break through the barriers we build, they are to kill him.'

Aberia chose the worst place she could find: a waterlogged area, infested with insects and buffeted by the wind. She ordered the prisoners to build themselves reed huts. From now on they would live there, hoping for the mercy of the emperor, who, in his great goodness, had granted them a daily food ration.

One week later, half of the old people were dead. Their companions buried the bodies in the mud, digging the graves with their bare hands. They themselves would not survive much longer.

Thoroughly satisfied, Lady Aberia set off again for Avaris. She would thank Khamudi warmly for his initiative. She would also prepare for the next deportation of rebels, who would cause the emperor no further trouble once they had sampled the delights of Sharuhen.

CHAPTER 8

Although he was almost twenty years old, Way-Finder was still head of all the donkeys in Thebes. He guided them along the tracks and oversaw the carriage of goods. He never balked at any task, so long as the humans did likewise and did not look down upon him. Without Way-Finder and the other donkeys, the military camp could not have seen the light of day. And the donkey continued working, with the same constancy and the same sense of a job well done.

And yet for Ahhotep this beautiful spring morning was touched with sorrow. At dawn Laughter, her unfailing guard and friend, had died. The huge old dog, his body worn out, had laid his enormous head upon the young woman's feet and gazed lovingly at her for the last time. Then he had given one final long, deep sigh.

Fortunately six-month-old Young Laughter not only had the same sandy pelt, black muzzle and amber eyes, but promised to be as strong and intelligent as his father. He could already detect his mistress's every intention.

Old Laughter was mummified and buried close

to Pharaoh Seqen. Beneath the bandages was laid a papyrus bearing the magical incantations needed to pass through the gates of the other world.

Way-Finder shared the queen's sorrow, and nuzzled her shoulder gently. She stroked his neck and asked him to grant his friendship to the young dog, who still had a great deal to learn.

The donkey shook his long ears, signifying his agreement.

Aberia's report delighted the emperor, who was in a foul temper after the failure of the lies about Ahhotep's death. He only wished he had thought earlier of deporting rebels to a camp where they would die? Khamudi's new idea was an excellent one, and Sharuhen was a total success. Little by little, Avaris would be emptied of possible opponents, even potential troublemakers, and the Hyksos would keep only the slaves needed to carry out the lowliest tasks.

'Majesty,' said Khamudi smugly, 'I have here a list of rebels whose actions or words merit imprisonment.'

'Keep back a few for the bull and the labyrinth.'

'Of course, Majesty. But I must warn you: there are others beside Egyptians.'

Apophis raised an eyebrow.

'A Hyksos scribe showed a lack of respect for me,' explained Khamudi, 'and there's an Anatolian gardener my wife dislikes. Don't they deserve to be shown the error of their ways?'

'Definitely,' replied the emperor. 'And I shall add a palace guard who made the mistake of sleeping with my loving sister, Windswept, and complaining of inconvenient working-hours. Such criticism cannot go unpunished. The camp at Sharuhen will correct his way of thinking. The lady Aberia shall take charge of this new consignment.'

The deportation of the widows and widowers had spread terror throughout the Egyptian population of the Delta. No one felt safe from the arbitrary decisions taken by the emperor and Khamudi. The rebel networks no longer dared take any action at all, and confined themselves to gathering snippets of information from the front, in the hope that it was true. But hardly anyone yet knew that the army of liberation had reached Qis.

Off the coast of Mycenae, Jannas had won victory after victory, but finding and pursuing the pirates' ships took a great deal of time. Moreover, he had to keep part of his fleet within sight of Minoa, which he suspected might otherwise intervene.

In Asia, Hyksos troops were imposing a bloody occupation, punctuated by summary executions. Despite this brutality, the tribal chiefs still persisted in taking up arms. None resisted for very long, and they and their families all ended up dead, but the irritating unrest meant that Apophis could not bring his regiments home and use them to attack Upper Egypt.

'Queen Ahhotep won't be able to make any

further progress,' observed Khamudi. 'Her miserable war-band will soon wear itself out. I shouldn't be surprised if she soon surrendered. Choosing a woman as a war-chief! What a ludicrous mistake! These Egyptians will never make real fighters.'

'Very true,' agreed the emperor. 'We know, of course, that the Thebans are just about capable of controlling a few distant provinces. Nevertheless, we can attack the root of the evil and eliminate the cause of this stupid rebellion without even resorting to battle. One of our good friends will take care of it.'

As he had vowed, Prince Kamose allowed himself no rest. He trained so intensively in handling weapons that his body became that of an athlete, and it took all the queen's authority to make him lie down for a few hours to prevent exhaustion. But Kamose hardly slept, for he was haunted by the face of his father, whom he so badly wanted to emulate.

From his mother, he was learning the art of governing. Together with his little brother, who was thoughtful and attentive, he read the texts of wisdom passed on by the pharaohs of the golden age. From time to time, he caught himself dreaming that Egypt was really free, that it was possible to move from one province to another and to travel peacefully along the Nile. But then reality hit home, and with renewed fire in his belly he continued his apprenticeship to become Pharaoh.

51

One morning, as Ahhotep was addressing the members of a detachment setting out for Kebet, Qaris informed her that an unexpected visitor was requesting an audience: an envoy from Titi, the governor of Kebet. He showed in a short, fat, bearded man.

The man bowed before the regent queen and said, 'Majesty, I have good news. Governor Titi has at last succeeded in liberating Kebet. The last Hyksos have fled, and we have seized a cargo-boat containing many jars of food. Here are a few of them, in advance of other prizes.'

They were indeed Hyksos jars, pot-bellied and painted brown.

'I and two soldiers from Titi's personal body-guard brought them here along country tracks,' explained the envoy. 'The region is quiet, and the peasants are regaining confidence. The inhabitants of Kebet await you, Majesty.'

'Is the governor sure of his success?'

'If not, Majesty, he would not have sent me to Thebes. Titi has suffered greatly from the occu-pation, and he is a cautious man.'

Ahhotep remembered her brief stay in Kebet with Seqen. During their meeting, the governor had told her that he was organizing resistance with the greatest caution, while all the time pretending to be an ally of the Hyksos who controlled his town.

Qaris beckoned to a servant and told him, 'Take these jars to the kitchens.'

'You will dine with us, envoy,' said the queen, 'and tell us all about the liberation of Kebet.'

The hungriest of all was Young Laughter. Had it not been for Ahhotep's stern looks, he would gladly have leapt at the dishes that the servants were laying on the royal table. The dog played for sympathy, as though he had not been fed for several days, and always managed to prompt some gullible person into giving him a titbit or two.

'Do the Hyksos still control the caravan routes?' the queen asked Governor Titi's envoy.

'No, Majesty, not for a long time now. But we shall have to dismantle the forts they set up in the desert, reaching as far as the Red Sea.'

'Has the governor a detailed map?'

'Yes, thanks to the caravan leaders, who are delighted to have escaped the Hyksos yoke at last. By using their information, we shall be able to mount surprise attacks on the enemy and dismantle his installations one by one.'

By using this strategy, Ahhotep could free more of the Theban province, which would once again be able to receive the goods it had been deprived of for so many long years.

'How many men has the governor at his disposal?'

While the little bearded man launched into rather involved explanations, the queen ate mechanically from a dish of beans and braised beef.

Suddenly, Laughter nudged her wrist with his nose.

'Laughter! You really are a bad—'

The dog knocked over the dish with his paw, and started barking at the envoy from Kebet.

The queen understood: her best bodyguard had saved her.

'Arrest that man,' she ordered.

The envoy jumped to his feet and ran towards the door of the dining-hall. Two guards barred his way.

'This food is poisoned,' said Ahhotep, 'and I have eaten some of it.'

CHAPTER 9

Queen Ahhotep had begun to feel ill, and was lying down on a low bed while her mother wiped her forehead with perfumed linen.

Heray, who had been interrogating the 'envoy' came in and bowed. 'The man has talked,' he said. 'He poisoned your food with castor-oil seeds and scorpion's venom. If it hadn't been for Laughter, Majesty, you would be dead.'

The huge dog lay at the foot of the bed. He had made up his mind never again to leave his mistress's side.

'Did he really come from Kebet?' asked Ahhotep.

'Yes, Majesty.'

'Then he must have been acting on Titi's orders.'

'He was. It was indeed the governor who sent the assassin, probably at Apophis's behest.'

'We must take Kebet as quickly as possible,' said Ahhotep. She tried to stand up, but her stomach pains were so fierce that she could not.

'We must go to the Temple of Hathor at once,'

advised Teti anxiously. 'The priestesses will know how to cure you.'

Despite taking a curative mixture of onion, carob, linen extract and a plant called 'serpent's wood', Ahhotep was seriously ill on the way to Deir el-Bahari. By the time they arrived she was unconscious, and Heray had to carry her to the temple.

Built by Pharaoh Montuhotep II,* the temple was truly remarkable. The vast tree-lined forecourt gave access to a portico. Its pillars were fronted by statues depicting the king wearing the Red Crown and the close-fitting white robe he wore during the Festival of Regeneration. The king's black face, hands and enormous legs made him almost frightening.

The pharaoh bore the three colours of the magic of resurrection, and was thus multiplied into the same number of guardians. These watched over the central monument: a representation of the primordial mound, the island that had appeared on the first morning of the world, and on which light had taken corporeal form.

Beside the shrine, priestesses of the goddess Sekhmet were worshipping a very ancient statue which stood before a vast stone-lined pool where, in cases of serious illness, certain patients were allowed to bathe.

*The Montuhoteps were one of the principal lines of the XIth dynasty (c2060–1991 BC).

Teti and Heray, the latter still carrying Ahhotep, went over to the priestesses.

'I am Teti the Small and I entrust the Queen of Egypt to your care. She has been poisoned.'

'Please read aloud the text written upon the statue,' said the most senior priestess.

'"Come to me, you whose name is hidden, even from the gods, you who created the heaven and the earth, and brought all beings into the world. No evil shall be done against you, for you are water, sky, earth and air. May healing be granted unto me."'

The water first rippled, and then began to bubble.

'The spirit of the statue accepts the patient,' said the priestess. 'Undress her and place her in the pool.'

While Teti and the other priestesses were doing this, the senior priestess poured water on to the hieroglyphs. One of her colleagues collected up the precious liquid, which was now imbued with a magical energy.

As soon as the unconscious Ahhotep was laid in the pool, the servant of Sekhmet sprinkled her throat with healing water. When she had performed this act seven times, she asked all those present to leave.

'Is my daughter going to live?' asked her anguished mother.

The priestess did not reply.

*   *   *

Kebet was celebrating. In return for his services to the Hyksos, Titi had been given permission to celebrate the Festival of Min. Of course, certain elements of the ceremonies were omitted, such as the procession of the statues representing the royal ancestors. The only pharaoh was Apophis.

By obeying orders, Titi had just ended a futile war which would have seen thousands of Egyptians die needlessly. For a long time now, the governor had realized that the invaders' power was going to continue growing and that his country had become a Hyksos province. By playing a subtle double game, he had preserved a few of his prerogatives and enabled his favourites to live reasonably well under the occupation. Basically, all one needed to do was renounce the old values and adapt to the emperor's demands. Consequently, this old festival of the god of spiritual and material fertility was to lose its sacred character altogether, and become a popular celebration accompanied by a glorification of Apophis, the benefactor of Egypt.

If it had not been for that madwoman Ahhotep and her insane husband, the Theban province would have continued to live peacefully. Fortunately, Seqen had been killed and his army was rotting at Qis.

The last danger was the queen. Having met her at Kebet, many years before, Titi knew that she would never give up the fight. She was too stubborn to face up to reality. Because of her, the

South was in danger of falling victim to terrible repression.

However, thanks to its governor, Kebet would be spared. By sending one of his most trusted men to Thebes to poison Ahhotep, Titi had become a hero of the empire. The queen's death would mean the end of the fighting. This was the excellent news Titi was going to announce to the people, who were so happy to be celebrating.

'Is everything ready?' he asked his steward.

'Yes, but the Hyksos guards insist on surrounding the procession.'

'That is quite natural: I would not wish there to be any unruly behaviour.'

Titi hurried to greet the commander of the local guards, a coarse-faced Syrian.

'At the first sign of trouble,' said the commander, 'I shall throw the rioters into prison and have half of them executed.'

'Don't worry, the inhabitants of Kebet are reasonable people. They will be content with enjoying themselves and will thank the emperor for these festivities.'

Priests carried in procession the astonishing statue of Min, wrapped in the white shroud of resurrection. With his eternally erect phallus, he embodied the creative power that enabled life to carry on in all its forms and that, in particular, gave life to wheat.

Desert prospectors, miners and caravan-traders were moved to see the statue pass by, for the god possessed the secret of the stones that were born in the belly of the mountains. With his arm raised, forming a secret angle known to temple-builders, and holding the three-skinned sceptre symbolizing the three births, celestial, earthly and underground, Min reigned over distant roads and guided adventurers.

A magnificent white bull walked placidly behind the statue. According to tradition, it was the queen who mastered its natural violence and transformed it into fertile power. But the last queen was dead, and Apophis forbade women to attend rituals.

Already a huge climbing-pole was being raised and stayed with ropes. The most agile men would try to be first to climb to the top and unhook the sought-after gifts. The competition never took place without incident, and there would be countless falls.

'There are too many temples in Kebet, Governor,' said the Syrian. 'You may keep one – that will be quite enough – and the others will be turned into barracks and weapons stores.'

Titi yielded. The emperor hated obvious displays of the former culture, and Kebet already enjoyed preferential treatment.

'Are you absolutely sure Ahhotep is dead?' asked the Syrian.

'Absolutely. The man who poisoned her has been executed, and Thebes is in mourning. Before long, all the rebels will lay down their arms. Ahhotep was their heart and soul, and without her they will have neither the strength nor the courage to continue. I know the Egyptians well: they will believe that their queen was punished by the gods because she acted wrongly. Shouldn't we encourage the spread of that idea?'

'I'll see to it, Governor.'

Most unusually, two taverns had been opened. Under close watch by the guards, they were selling bad beer which the revellers would have to be content with. At the first sign of drunkenness, troublemakers would be arrested and deported. The emperor would not tolerate any breach of public order, and Aberia would be delighted to increase the number of prisoners destined for the camp at Sharuhen.

'This beer is rubbish,' said the Afghan.

'Just like this pathetic so-called festival,' agreed Moustache.

'In other words, we've been robbed. I think we deserve compensation.'

'Shall we call the innkeeper over?'

'That coward? He's scared to death. What we need is someone with real authority. That armed guard, for example.'

Moustache went over to him. 'My man, my friend and I are thoroughly dissatisfied. The procession is mediocre, the beer is undrinkable and the atmosphere is depressing, all of which is absolutely unacceptable, don't you think?'

The guard was struck dumb with astonishment,

but soon got his voice back. 'You're both drunk! Follow me and don't argue.'

'We can't,' said Moustache.

'What the devil do you mean?'

'He's right,' said the Afghan, 'we can't. First, we're not drunk. Second, we're not here to have fun – still less to see the inside of one of your prisons.'

'And who the devil do you think you are?'

'A rebel who's going to kill a Hyksos guard, burn down this pathetic tavern – and so give the signal for the army of liberation to attack.'

CHAPTER 10

As soon as the flames roared up, Ahhotep's soldiers – half of whom had mingled with the crowd – charged at the Hyksos guards in charge of keeping public order. Well trained in close combat by the Afghan and Moustache, they had the advantage of surprise, and in a few moments they had killed most of their enemies.

The astounded Syrian commander told Governor Titi, 'Go to the palace, quickly! Order your men to join forces with mine.'

The terrified priests had taken refuge in the temple with the statue of Min. From the top of the climbing-pole, two youths were throwing pots at the Hyksos guards. Urged on by Moustache, the revellers turned on their oppressors. Several Hyksos were trampled underfoot by the inhabitants of Kebet, who were only too happy to express the hatred they had held in for so long.

The Syrian and Titi did not get far. Suddenly, there before them stood Ahhotep, at the head of Titi's personal bodyguard.

'These men now belong to the army of liberation,' declared the queen.

'Majesty, you . . . you aren't dead! No, it's a ghost – it must be a ghost. We must run to the Temple of Geb. They won't dare touch us there.'

Ahhotep prevented an archer from firing.

The two fugitives managed to force their way through the skirmish, which was turning definitively in favour of the Egyptians, and reach the forecourt of the Temple of Geb. The door was closed, and Titi hammered on it with his fists.

'Open up! It's the governor, and I demand safe haven!'

The door remained closed.

All at once, a heavy silence fell over the town: no more shouts of victory or cries of pain, no more voices, not even the bark of a dog.

Alone on the temple forecourt, Titi and the Syrian were gradually surrounded by the people of Kebet and by the soldiers of Ahhotep's army.

Ahhotep stepped forward. 'Hear these words, which are spoken in this place each time judgment is pronounced: "May the liar fear Geb, the creative power which loves truth. He detests falsehood. It is for him to decide."'

'Majesty, don't let there be a misunderstanding about me!' implored Titi. 'I pretended to be an ally of the Hyksos so that I could better protect my fellow citizens – without me, many would have been executed or tortured. In fact, I have been loyal to you ever since the beginning of your campaign. You remember our meeting, don't you? I realize now that I should have confided in you. Here are two proofs of my righteousness: first, the names of the sailors, caravan-owners and merchants who betrayed Egypt to the Hyksos – I'll tell you them all, I swear it! And the second proof is even more convincing.'

Titi plunged his dagger into the Syrian's back, rolled the wounded man over and finished him off.

Then he knelt down. 'I am your humble servant, Majesty.'

Ahhotep's eyes flamed. 'You are nothing but a coward, and you have violated this sacred place. This is my decree, which will be kept in our archives. Your title of governor is withdrawn, and it will not be conferred upon any of your descendants. Your goods will be given to the temples of Kebet, your writings will be destroyed, your name is to be accursed and forgotten for ever. Any pharaoh who granted you pardon would be unworthy of wearing the Double Crown and would at once be abandoned by the gods.'

At the trade-tax post outside Kebet, a guard said to his superior officer, 'Sir, I can see smoke.'

'Where?'

'It looks as if it's coming from the town.'

'Probably just some old building burning down. It's not our concern. We're here to collect taxes from anyone who passes through Kebet, charge them the maximum fee and keep the emperor happy. Nothing else matters.'

'Sir?'

'What is it now?'

'There are people coming.'

'You deal with it. My arm's aching from stamping my seal on all those documents, and I need a nap.'

'There are an awful lot of them, sir.'

'Merchants, do you mean?'

'No, sir. I think they're soldiers.'

The officer was jolted out of his apathy. He looked out of the tax-post and his jaw dropped. On the Nile, there were ten warships carrying many archers. On the road, there were hundreds of Egyptian soldiers, commanded by Moustache.

The soldiers soon reached the tax-post.

'This,' announced Moustache, 'is the choice I offer you: you can either surrender or be killed.'

Hollow-cheeked and sad-eyed, Heray bowed before the queen.

'Majesty, I offer you my resignation as Overseer of Granaries and of Thebes's security. I can only hope that you may one day be able to forgive my incompetence and lack of foresight. No one could have been more at fault, and I know it. The only favour I beg is not to be expelled from Thebes, but if you decide I must be I will accept your decision.'

Ahhotep smiled warmly at him. 'I have no reproaches for you, Heray.'

'Majesty! I let an assassin get near you – he

poisoned your food and you almost died. Because of me, the battle for freedom could have been lost. Dismissal is the very least I deserve.'

'No, Heray, because every single day you demonstrate the greatest of all virtues: faithfulness. Thanks to that, we shall remain united and we shall win.'

'But, M-Majesty . . .' stammered Heray.

'Do me the honour of continuing in office, my friend, and carry out your duties with the greatest vigilance. I myself have made serious mistakes, and I fear I shall make more in the future. Our enemies will continue to attack us in the most cunning ways they can think of, so there must be no weak points in our armour.'

The big man was moved to tears. He prostrated himself before the Wife of God, whom he admired more each day.

Ahhotep raised him to his feet. 'You have a great deal of work to do,' she said. 'Before he was executed, Titi supplied us with an impressive list of collaborators. But he mixed truth and lies, hoping that we will kill people who really are allies. So you must check each case with great care, to make sure that doesn't happen.'

'You can rely on me, Majesty.'

'Now, let us go and look at Qaris's model.'

Qaris had already, with profound joy, added Kebet and its surroundings to the liberated area on the model. No more Hyksos occupation, no more

67

arbitrary arrests, no more torture: the people were beginning to breathe more freely again.

'How happy Seqen must be,' murmured the queen. 'When we succeed in reopening the caravan routes, many of our difficulties will be solved.'

'Tomorrow,' enthused Qaris, 'we shall celebrate the true Festival of Min! And the Queen of Egypt will lead the ritual, paying homage to the ancestors' memory.'

Ahhotep's beautiful face was sombre. 'This is only a modest victory. It will lead nowhere unless we redouble our efforts.'

'Our weapons have improved a great deal, Majesty,' said Qaris. 'They'll soon be soon as good as you wish them to be.'

'If we are to extend the liberated area northwards, we need more boats. The Hyksos have chariots and horses, and know how to use them; we know how to make use of the Nile. We must open new boatyards straight away, and put as many craftsmen as possible to work.'

CHAPTER 11

Emheb, governor of Edfu, was a huge man. Everything about him was huge: his head, his nose, his shoulders and his girth. At first sight he looked like a man who enjoyed the good life, but his bull's neck and hard eyes gave the lie to that impression.

He was a staunch ally of Queen Ahhotep, and had been in the thick of the early battles of the war for freedom. He had pretended to submit to the Hyksos occupiers of Edfu, while quietly killing them one by one and replacing them with men from his own rebel network, until eventually he regained control of his city.

Seqen's death had affected him deeply, and he had never imagined that the young woman could withstand such a shock. And yet, with a courage that even hardened sceptics admired, she had decided to carry on the work her dead husband had begun. As the dawn sun rose, vanquishing the dragon of darkness, Emheb pictured Ahhotep's success. To have reached Qis was in itself an achievement, one which had restored a little of his countrymen's lost pride; and they owed that happy fact to a queen who was bold enough to attempt the impossible. Then the cold light of day had come to the front, which had not moved in months, and he had to face facts: Apophis, for whatever reason, was allowing the situation to stagnate. Either the emperor was convinced that the Egyptians would eventually give up, or he was preparing for a massive offensive.

Emheb knew very well that, even if he strengthened his positions, he would not be able to hold out for long against the full might of the Hyksos regiments. But Ahhotep trusted him completely, and he would not withdraw. He no longer asked questions. Ahhotep had ordered him to hold the line, and he would hold it.

His personal scribe showed in Ahmes, son of Abana, a young and extraordinarily brave soldier.

For once, Ahmes looked worried. 'Governor,' he said, 'we must reassure our men. Many of them still believe that Queen Ahhotep is dead and that it would be better to surrender before we're slaughtered.'

'I have just received messages signed by the queen herself. Not only is she alive but she has retaken Kebet. As for those who wish to surrender, have they considered what their fate would be?'

'That's precisely what I told them, sir, but rumours are like poison. We—'

Ahmes broke off as a lookout shouted, 'They're attacking! The Hyksos are attacking!'

They both rushed out to take up their battle positions.

As soon as he was in position, Emheb dispatched carrier-pigeons to Thebes with an urgent request for help. If reinforcements did not arrive in time, the front line would collapse and the enemy armies would overrun the South.

The port at Thebes had become a vast boatyard, where even the soldiers were set to work by the carpenters, so that as many boats as possible could be built in record time without sacrificing quality.

Several teams went off to find timber, mainly acacia and sycamore. Trunks and branches were trimmed with an axe, and split into planks. Hammers and chisels were used to cut out mortises, heavy mallets to force in the tenons, and a short-handled adze for finishing. No one counted the hours, for everyone knew their work was vital and that Egypt's future depended on it. Every time a boat neared completion, the men who varnished the planks with cedar-oil and beeswax rejoiced in the fact that they would soon see a new vessel launched on the Nile.

Ahhotep had set the weaving-women of Thebes to work making linen sails. Some consisted of one large sheet, others were made from strips of varying widths sewn together with great care. With these new sails, the Egyptian war-fleet would be much faster.

Always accompanied by Young Laughter, who

watched over his mistress as vigilantly as his pre-decessor, Ahhotep made constant inspections of the boatyard and encouraged the craftsmen. If a man seemed so exhausted that he was at risk of having an accident, she ordered him to take a rest. She made sure to check the oars, too. The steering-oar enabled an experienced helmsman to manoeuvre his boat with relative ease on a river which could be capricious, while the rowing-oars enabled the sailors to give of their best when the boat was trav-elling upstream or if there was no wind.

The queen had ordered the construction of several cargo-vessels, each capable of carrying enormous quantities of weapons, raw materials and foodstuffs. These would ensure that the Egyptian army was self-sufficient if it succeeded in breaking through into enemy territory. Even milch-cows would be taken on board, after prayers had been offered to Hathor to calm these precious animals. Calves and oxen would be tethered to rings fixed to the deck, but the cows that were good sailors could wander about freely.

The sound of running feet alerted Laughter, who bared his teeth but then, when he saw that it was Qaris coming, sat down in front of his mistress.

'Majesty,' panted the steward, 'we've had an alarming message from Emheb. The Hyksos are trying to break through the front, and he asks urgently for reinforcements.'

'Are enough boats ready to leave?'

'No, Majesty. If we take those that are, they'd

be so overloaded that they'd probably capsize. Besides, would it not be dangerous to leave Thebes unprotected?'

It was not the exhausted Rascal who made the return flight to the front but another pigeon, almost as experienced as its leader.

The traitor who had infiltrated the Thebans had at first thought of killing the bird, but soon thought better of it. Even an excellent archer could not be certain of success, unless he shot as the bird was taking off, and in that case someone was bound to see him.

He decided on a more reliable course of action: in the pigeon's food he'd put a poison which would not take effect until the bird was halfway through its flight. It would never reach Qis, Emheb would think he had been abandoned, and the emperor's army would smash the barrier that blocked its way to the South.

'Still no message?' Emheb asked Ahmes.

'No, sir, nothing.'

'The queen cannot just abandon us!'

'Either our birds have been killed or Thebes can't send any reinforcements. Either way, sir, we must manage alone. Our men are putting up strong resistance, and the Hyksos haven't yet launched an all-out attack. I think they may be testing our mettle before sending in their main body of troops.'

'We must lay more booby-traps,' decided Emheb. 'It's vital that the enemy waste a great deal of time dealing with them. And we must set up more concealed firing positions. The Hyksos may have a larger, stronger army, but they do not know this terrain. Despite our difficulties, all is not lost yet.'

'Indeed it isn't, sir,' agreed Ahmes.

The two men knew that they were lying to themselves, the better to overcome their fear and fight courageously to the end.

'I must go back to our forward positions,' said Ahmes, whose young face betrayed not a trace of emotion.

'As soon as you feel you're in difficulty, send me a footsoldier and I'll hurry to your aid.'

'May the gods preserve you, Governor.'

'May they also protect you, my boy.'

Emheb had no regrets. From the very beginning of this mad adventure, he had known that the Egyptian army was not strong enough to take on the Hyksos monster. And yet that was the only road they could have followed, even if it ended in the death of Ahhotep and the destruction of Thebes. At least these years of rebellion had wiped away the shame and bitterness of the past. The Egyptians had at last stopped behaving like cowards, and could appear before the court of the afterlife in the proud knowledge that they had done their duty.

A young officer came running up. 'Governor,

there are two Hyksos war-boats coming,' he said with a cheerful smile.

Emheb thought he must be having a bad dream. 'And you're actually pleased about that?'

'Oh yes, sir, because they've chosen their moment very badly.'

'What do you mean?'

'They're about to meet the most beautiful war-fleet I've ever seen: about twenty Egyptian boats from the south – with Queen Ahhotep at their head!'

CHAPTER 12

Wearing her mother's gold crown, and holding up the Sword of Amon before her, the Queen of Freedom stood at the prow of the flagship as the oarsmen rowed swiftly along.

The Hyksos boats reacted immediately. After hurriedly lowering their sails, they turned tail and retreated as fast as they could.

On the banks, the Egyptian footsoldiers gave shouts of victory. At last, the reinforcements they had awaited so long!

Emheb was amazed to see a few archers and hordes of peasants disembarking. They looked nothing like soldiers.

'Majesty,' he said, 'what joy to see you again! But . . . who are these people?'

'Citizens of Kebet and farmers from the liberated provinces. You shall train them, Governor, and they will help you to consolidate the front. I could not leave Thebes unguarded, but neither could I abandon you, as my message explained.'

Emheb's expression darkened. 'I have received no message, Majesty.'

The smile faded from Ahhotep's face. 'We sent you one of our best pigeons. The poor thing must have been killed on the way here.'

'No doubt by a bird of prey,' said Emheb.

'No doubt,' repeated the queen, though she did not believe it.

'The important thing is that you have come – and at just the right moment. Despite the denials, some of the men still believed you were dead.'

'I shall not leave here until I have met each and every one of your soldiers. You are to keep almost all the boats, three-quarters of which have brought supplies of weapons and equipment for you. If necessary, the others will enable you to travel back to Thebes. Thanks to their new sails, they are faster than the Hyksos boats.'

To see the queen, speak with her, celebrate with her the birth of the sun, hear her beseeching the gods not to leave the land of Egypt but to dwell in the soldiers' hearts: such things swept away all fears for the future.

Ahhotep gave a great banquet for the heroes who were holding back the Hyksos, and promised them future evenings of celebration once Egypt was liberated. She showed them the gift she was going to send to the emperor, and it made everyone burst out laughing.

The emperor dropped the limestone scarab on to the stone floor, as though it were a burning coal.

'Who received this abomination?' he demanded. 'And who dared send it to me?

'An Egyptian archer fired it over our front line at Qis, Majesty,' replied Khamudi. 'An officer picked it up and gave it to the army messenger.'

'Have those imbeciles executed! Have you read this text, Khamudi? Have you read the loathsome message that loathsome female dares send me?'

The High Treasurer picked up the scarab, which bore a clear inscription in beautiful hieroglyphs: *'Greetings to the vile Hyksos Apophis, who occupies my country. Queen Ahhotep is very much alive, and every Egyptian knows it. They also know that you are not invulnerable.'*

'It must be a forgery, Majesty.'

'Of course it isn't!' snapped Apophis. 'Now that damned woman is going to flood the country with scarabs like this, and wreck our campaign of false information. And the frontier at Qis is now firmly established.'

'Our surprise attacks have not been very effective, I admit, but they have shown us that that's where the Egyptians have massed the main body of their troops, and that they cannot advance any further. Also, the news from Asia is good: the local rulers are becoming less troublesome, and Hyksos order has been re-established. As for Jannas, he is pursuing the last of the pirates in the Mycenaean islands, where they think they are safe. Killing that scum was vital. All that remains is for you to say, Majesty, whether you wish him to destroy Minoa.'

'I'll think about it,' said the emperor, his voice even harsher than usual. 'Now tell me, doesn't one bit of this contemptible message surprise you?'

Khamudi read it again. '"*Every Egyptian knows it*": does that mean there are still rebels in the Delta, who might spread information from the South?'

The semblance of a smile added an extra touch of ugliness to the emperor's face. 'That vainglorious queen has made a grave mistake by trying to insult me. We have been too lenient with the the natives, Khamudi, much too lenient. I require interrogations to be made far more rigorous, and there are to be as many deportations as necessary. No town or village is to be spared.'

Her mother had been raped and beheaded, her father disembowelled by the emperor's bull. Because of her beauty, the young Egyptian woman had had the honour of being chosen to become one of the courtesans in the official harem at Avaris. These courtesans had to be ready, at any hour of the day or night, to satisfy the lust of Hyksos dignitaries.

It was barely survival, and each hour weighed more heavily than the last, but the young woman put everything out of her mind in order to fight in her own way.

By offering herself to one of her guards, who was not permitted to touch these beautiful girls, she had succeeded in convincing him that she loved him. The rough fellow was absolutely besotted with her and would do anything not to lose her.

One night, after enchanting the brute once again, she had begged an immense favour: a meeting with her brother, who was working as a carpenter on the outskirts of Avaris. The guard could contact him via a groom. Just to see him for a few moments, to embrace him, that was all she wanted.

The guard had hesitated for a long time. But then he wondered how his beautiful girl would react if he said no. She might refuse him her charms – and he would never find another woman like her.

The first meeting had been arranged for the middle of the night, at the entrance to the harem kitchens, which the girl had described in detail to her 'brother', a rebel friend of her parents who had contacts in the South. Unfortunately, she could do no more for him.

What he had told her was extraordinary: the army of liberation really did exist, and a queen called Ahhotep was leading the fight! Soon the news would spread throughout the Delta, and new rebels would swell the present meagre ranks.

She had passed on to him an idea which had been haunting her: to get a raiding-party into the harem, kill the guards and take hostage the high-ranking Hyksos who would be found there. Her 'brother' agreed, and had promised he would not not come to the second meeting alone.

Now the moment she had so longed for had at last arrived.

After lavishing sensual delights upon the commander of the imperial guard, the young woman left the room and slipped down a poorly lit servants' passageway. She was barefoot, and hardly dared breathe in case someone heard her.

At this hour of the night, the kitchens were deserted. Here, she would have to give herself one last time to the guard before he would open the door.

'Here I am,' she whispered. 'Are you there?'

There was no answer. Surprised, she let her eyes grow accustomed to the darkness, avoided bumping into a large spit on which geese were roasted, and crept past one of the ovens.

'I'm here. Where are you hiding, my love?'

Her throat dry, she stumbled over something on the floor. She crouched down and felt around. Her hand touched hair, a nose, teeth, and they were sticky . . . She cried out in fear.

Suddenly, a torch lit up the kitchen.

'I slit that guard's throat myself,' said the lady Aberia. 'I knew he was sniffing round you, even though it's strictly forbidden.' She ripped open the girl's dress. 'You have pretty breasts, and the rest isn't unattractive, either. Before he died, that pig told me that he had allowed you to see your brother, which is also forbidden. He has just been arrested outside, with two of his friends. You were going to let them in here, weren't you?'

'I . . . I have nothing to say to you!'

'Come, come, little one. The emperor has ordered us to identify all the rebels, and I think I have sniffed one out. You will tell me everything, otherwise your pretty body will feel the kiss of this torch.'

The young woman leapt forward and threw herself on to the roasting-spit, which pierced her throat. When Aberia dragged the body off the spike, she thought she saw a gleam of victory in the dead Egyptian's eyes.

CHAPTER 13

All day long, under the cruel sun. Queen Ahhotep herself brought water and food to the carpenters, who were working without a break. In spite of the heat, Way-Finder never balked at carrying heavy loads. Sure-footed and even-tempered, he was constantly alert as he followed her and Laughter.

Only the bustling presence of the queen prevented the Thebans from lapsing into gloom. True, they were free again, but for how long? The Hyksos' power had been barely scratched; sooner or later the dragon would react – and that reaction would be terrifying. But there was Ahhotep, with her beauty, her smile and her determination, which nothing could weaken. Seqen's soul lived in her and endowed her with his strength.

Only Teti the Small sensed that her daughter was beginning to have doubts.

'Should we not pull back the front line and be content with Thebes?' she suggested, as they ate their evening meal on the palace terrace.

'That would certainly be the sensible thing to do.'

'In other words, you don't think it appropriate.'

'It is not appropriate for Egypt, Mother. Partial freedom would simply consign us to an even worse prison than the one we have broken out of. By falling back to our little piece of ground, we would become easy prey for the emperor.'

'Then you are refusing to face reality, Ahhotep.'

'I shall never accept the reality imposed by Apophis, because it is against the Rule of Ma'at. If we accept the supremacy of violence and injustice, this world will no longer be fit to live in.'

'Then what do you plan to do?'

'We have only a few statues of the gods left, and we don't honour them enough, even though without their support we can never succeed. For ten days, I shall offer them the finest food and beg the ancestors to inspire my actions. I shall then consult the moon-god.'

Teti the Small looked long and hard at her daughter. 'Ahhotep, you have become a true Queen of Egypt.'

Once again, the ritual upon which the balance of the universe depended was being enacted: caught in a fishing-net, then reassembled by the gods Thoth and Horus, the full moon's silver eye shone with such intense brilliance that the spirits of seers were opened.

'You who know yesterday, today and tomorrow,' declared Ahhotep, 'also know that I will not surrender. My life no longer belongs to me: I have offered it to my people. To live in slavery is worse than death. Trace out a path for me in the heavens, and I will follow it.'

Hieroglyphs appeared on the silver disc, spelling out a name.

When she read it, Ahhotep realized that her heart must continue to bleed, for the gods had left her no choice.

'Don't flatter him, Heray, and don't hide anything from me,' ordered the queen. 'Is he ready, yes or no?'

'Majesty, your son is a true soldier, well capable of fighting in the vanguard.'

'What are his weaknesses?'

'He is as good as our very best archers, wins every bout of hand-to-hand combat and wields a sword better than anyone. And all this with virtually no sleep.'

'Do the soldiers respect him?'

Heray lowered his eyes. 'Majesty, I hardly dare tell you—'

'I want the truth.'

'The transformation has been astonishing. He grows more and more like his father. I have never seen such a young man show such qualities of leadership. He doesn't realize it himself, but all he has to do is make an appearance and he is obeyed.'

So the moon-god had spoken truly when he revealed Kamose's name to her: the hour of his coronation had arrived.

★   ★   ★

'I don't wish to offend you, Mother, but is it really urgent?' asked Kamose. 'I was planning to practise with my bow this afternoon, and then—'

'I am speaking to you as Regent Queen of Egypt.'

Ahhotep's solemnity made a deep impression on the young man. Together, they walked slowly beside the sacred lake at Karnak. The light was intense, the place peaceful.

'Everyone reveres you,' said Kamose, 'but I have one criticism: why do you insist on being only a regent? Why don't you become Pharaoh?'

'Because that office falls upon you, my son.'

'On me?' Kamose was astounded. 'But I have neither your authority nor your experience.'

'The moon-god has decided that my period as regent is coming to an end, and that your reign is beginning. You are only seventeen, Kamose, but you must succeed your father.'

His face fell. 'He is still my ideal. How can I possibly equal him?'

'If you want to show yourself worthy of him, by achieving more than he did.'

'May I refuse this burden?'

'You know the answer to that question.'

Kamose halted and gazed deep into the blue waters of the sacred lake. 'How far away the war seems,' he said quietly. 'Yet as soon as I am crowned it will be my prime duty. And I must not only deal with the present situation, but go further – much further. Do you think I can do it?'

'The gods demand that you do.'

'You're the incarnation of the goddess of Thebes, aren't you, Mother? You're the true pharaoh, and I shall be merely your strong arm.'

'I shall fight tirelessly at your side, and I'll never fail to support you. But you must reign in your own way, Kamose, and according to your own abilities.'

'There's a fire burning inside me, and it won't let me sleep. It frightens me sometimes. Because of it, I can neither wait on events nor withdraw from them. If power is given to me, this fire will force me to attack all the obstacles I face, even if they're impossible to break down.'

Ahhotep kissed him on the forehead. 'You are my son and I love you.'

Moustache wished he could have thousands more nights like this one. The shopkeeper's daughter was as beautiful as Hathor. With her high, round breasts, her deliciously flat stomach and her slender legs, who would not have been seduced by her? And it was him, a soldier, and not exactly a handsome one, whom she had chosen – at least for a few hours.

The war was not wholly bad. In ordinary times, this young beauty would have thought only of starting a family. Today, who could be sure of living long enough for that? Brief liaisons came and went; people enjoyed ecstasy and forgot their anguish in intense moments of pleasure.

Moustache was caressing his sleeping mistress when out of the corner of his eye he caught sight of a ray of sunshine.

The new recruits! They must have been waiting for him for ages. It was his duty, as senior officer, to greet them – and the queen did not look at all kindly on lapses in discipline. Not even taking the time to shave, he tied on his leather kilt and rushed out on to the training-ground.

It was empty. In fact, the whole base was deserted and silent, save for the sentries at their posts atop the watch-towers.

Moustache walked back to the officers' houses and went into the Afghan's.

He found his friend fighting a rather more amorous battle than usual, with a pretty brown-haired girl with heavily made-up eyes. It appeared that the shopkeeper's elder daughter was no more shy than the younger.

Moustache coughed. 'Ahem, it's me.'

'I can see that,' said the Afghan. 'Did you fall out of bed?'

'I don't understand. There isn't a single soldier on the parade-ground.'

'You were really drunk last night, but I told you quite clearly that the army was enjoying a week's rest in honour of Kamose's coronation.'

Moustache rapped his forehead with his fist. 'It's coming back to me now.'

'Would it bother you if I asked you to leave?'

'No, not at all. I've got some urgent business to finish, too.'

CHAPTER 14

At Seqen's coronation, the pharaoh had had to be content with a simple crown, because the priests at Karnak had neither the Red Crown of Lower Egypt nor the White Crown of Upper Egypt.

The latter was widely thought to have been destroyed by the Hyksos, but after consulting the archives the High Priest of Karnak had reached a different conclusion.

'Formerly, Majesty,' he told Ahhotep, 'the Red Crown was kept in a temple at Memphis and the White in the ancient city of Nekhen, on whose site Elkab was built, and unfortunately Elkab was looted and destroyed by the invaders. It would probably be no use for you to go there, but . . .'

'I shall go there at once,' decided the queen.

Since Emheb had liberated the region, Elkab had changed greatly. Life had returned to the narrow streets, and the little white houses had been rebuilt in the traditional manner, even though the town and its people faced an uncertain future. Like Edfu, Elkab housed a regiment of reserve troops, who could be mobilized at a moment's notice to beat off a Nubian attempt at invasion or a Hyksos attack.

Ahhotep's only companions on her journey were Laughter and the twenty men who made up her personal bodyguard, all carefully chosen by Heray. As soon as they arrived, she made her way to the ancient fort, whose imposing walls were still standing. Inside the curtain wall, the temple of the vulture-goddess, 'Holder of the Royal Title',* lay in ruins.

'Majesty, I beg you not to go any further,' said the town's mayor anxiously. 'This place is haunted – looters who dared go inside were found dead. We must wait until the goddess's anger is appeased.'

'I have no time. I cannot wait.'

'Majesty, I implore you!'

'Stand aside.'

When Ahhotep set foot on the stone pavement, several black scorpions scuttled away. Dark forces had indeed taken possession of the ruined shrine, where the King of Upper Egypt had formerly received the supreme insignia of his office. No, Nekhen was not yet free. And it fell to Ahhotep to appease the goddess, for the new pharaoh's future depended upon it.

When a vulture flew above the building, tracing

*The royal title, *nekhbet*, derives from the goddess's name, Nekhbet.

wide circles in the blue sky, the queen knew what was killing intruders and what she must confront. The crowns were protected by both a celestial creature, the vulture, which was the supreme incarnation of the Mother, and an earthly being, the snake, which embodied the flame that destroyed the king's enemies.

Darting out of a ruined inner shrine, a female cobra reared up in front of the queen.

Ahhotep raised her hands in a gesture of worship.

'I have come here not to steal,' she declared, 'but to have my son declared the rightful King of Upper Egypt. I bow before you, the great ancestor who existed at the very beginning of all things. You who touch the limits of the universe and cause the sun to be born, you who are at once god and goddess, wipe away impurity and misfortune, and rise once again on Pharaoh's brow.'

For a few moments, the cobra hesitated. Ahhotep was so close that it could have struck at her throat, but the queen's gaze remained steady.

The cobra stretched out on the flagstones, then darted down between them, like a bolt of lightning entering the ground. Where it had disappeared, the stone was burnt, and on it lay the royal cobra's legacy: a gold uraeus which would be attached to the royal crown.

Ahhotep knelt down and picked it up reverently. Without fear, she continued on her way towards the furthermost part of the shrine, which the snake-goddess had guarded so vigilantly.

Despite the fire that had ravaged the temple, one of the stones was still intact, and it shone with a strange light, as though it were lit from the inside.

Ahhotep laid her hand upon the granite. The stone pivoted, revealing a hiding-place which contained an acacia-wood box. Inside it lay the White Crown of Upper Egypt.

After being purified in the sacred lake, Kamose meditated before one of the statues of Pharaoh Osiris, the symbol of the twofold nature of the royal office, which belonged both to this world and to the world beyond.

Then the young man went through the same ceremonies his father had, with one notable difference: whereas Seqen's coronation had been kept secret for a long time, in order to prevent collaborators informing the emperor, that of his elder son would be celebrated openly and would mark a new stage in the liberation of Egypt.

As the new pharaoh had no wife, it was the Wife of God who must recognize in him the presence of Horus and Set, the two brothers who shared the universe and reigned, the first over Lower Egypt and the second over Upper Egypt. Indivisible and constantly in conflict, they could not be reconciled or appeased except within the symbolic person of Pharaoh, who alone was capable of forging solid bonds between the two gods and the Two Lands.

Ahhotep gave her son his coronation names:

'Horus Who is Complete and Makes the Two Lands Bow the Knee', 'He Who Nurtures the Two Lands', 'He Who Restores That Which Endures', 'He Who Appears in Glory upon His Throne', 'The Transformation of the Light Is Accomplished'.

At last his name, Kamose, had taken on its full meaning, 'Power is born'. That power, the *ka*, was displayed in the fighting-bull, nourished by the strength of the moon-god.

'May you make these names complete and may they guide you along the path to victory,' proclaimed the queen, placing the White Crown with its uraeus upon the head of her son. 'May your father's spirit live in you and may his courage strengthen your arm.'

The Hyksos would never understand that Egyptian society was not made up solely of human beings, but consisted also of gods and ancestors, who were present in every facet of daily life. Apophis believed Seqen was dead, but he was wrong. Brought back to life by the rites and the words of knowledge, his radiant spirit travelled between the stars and the earth, and he lived on in the souls of those who remained faithful to him. Thanks to the power of the Word contained in the hieroglyphs, Ahhotep had made the invisible presence of her dead husband real and effective.

'Mother, I would like . . .'

'I know, Kamose. You would like to stay a while in the temple and enjoy its inexpressible peace. But Egypt's peace has not yet been won, and you will have to fight unceasingly to conquer it and give it to our people.'

All trace of hesitation had vanished from the young king's eyes. Pharaoh Kamose went out of the Temple of Amon, that realm of light where war, evil and injustice did not exist. After experiencing unimaginable happiness, he must now confront Apophis and try to re-establish the Rule of Ma'at.

Both soldiers and civilians were gathered in front of the temple to hail their new pharaoh. When he appeared, the White Crown shone so brightly that it dazzled them.

Queen Ahhotep presented her son with the sacred curved bronze sword, covered with silver and inlaid with an alloy of gold and silver; its hilt was decorated with a golden lotus, the symbol of the rebirth of the divine sun at the end of its nightly ordeals.

'As your father did before you, receive the Sword of Amon, with which you will rend the darkness asunder. May you, Pharaoh Kamose, overthrow its empire and be victorious in the war of the Crowns.'

CHAPTER 15

By the light of an exquisite lamp dating from the days of Pharaoh Menuhotep II, Apophis drew magical signs on a new sheet of papyrus, to stifle Thebes by attacking it from all four directions. To the east and west, the fire of Set made the deserts uninhabitable. To the south, the Hyksos' Nubian allies would be only too happy to massacre any Egyptian fugitives. And what rose up from the north would be as formidable as any army. Without his raising a finger, the emperor's spirit would kill huge numbers of his enemies.

Those Theban madmen had dared to send him a little limestone scarab, announcing the coronation of Pharaoh Kamose. Behind that puppet king, he knew, stood the inexhaustibly stubborn Queen Ahhotep. This time, she would pay very dearly for her insolence. No matter how skilful she might be, she would have no recourse against the misfortune that was about to descend upon Thebes.

Struck by a sudden doubt, the emperor took the secret passageway leading to the Treasury of the citadel. He alone knew how to unlock the door of the strong-room, which contained huge piles of stolen Egyptian ritual objects. The most precious was the Red Crown of Lower Egypt, characterized by its spiral shape, symbol of the harmonious growth of vital forces.

Apophis had worried needlessly. The crown was safe. Without it, Ahhotep would never manage to reconquer Egypt. She was nothing but a little rebel adventuress, lost in a dream that would soon be transformed into a nightmare.

Windswept had wrapped herself in a wonderfully soft bed-sheet which Asiatic merchants had just delivered to the palace. It was made of a material called silk, which was unknown in the land of the pharaohs. Tany, the emperor's wife, considered it coarse and uninteresting, so Windswept had acquired the whole consignment.

'Come,' she said to her companion.

He was the head groom at the palace, a stocky, coarse-faced man of fifty who smelt of the stable. There was nothing seductive about him, but his strength had caught Windswept's attention. She was sure that in his arms she would experience new pleasures.

Fascinated by the luxury of the bedchamber, he dared not take another step forward. 'Is that me?' he gasped in astonishment, catching sight of himself in a mirror whose glass was less cloudy than usual.

'Shouldn't you be looking at me?' Windswept

suggested, taking off her wrap and lying down on the bed.

The groom recoiled, sure he must be seeing a mirage.

'Don't be afraid,' she said softly. 'Come closer.'

Her voice was so alluring that he obeyed.

The temptress slowly untied his kilt. 'How strong you are,' she murmured greedily. 'Let me prepare you.'

She picked up a hollowed-out bull's horn containing perfumed oil. Slowly she let oil drip on to her lover's muscular chest, then smoothed it over his flesh so caressingly that his nervousness vanished and he flung himself on her.

Although delighted by her new conquest's hunger for her, Windswept was soon disappointed; the brute had no stamina at all, and even seemed to have difficulty getting his breath back.

'You have an exciting job, haven't you?' she said when he had recovered somewhat.

'That's true. I love horses – and I hate people who mistreat them.'

'Is someone doing so?'

'I can't say anything about it.'

'I am the emperor's sister. And I can help you.'

'You would do that?'

Windswept gave a convincing smile. 'Since we are lovers, what could be more natural?'

The groom sat up and perched on the side of the bed. 'It's that monster Khamudi and his she-devil of a wife. They brought some young women into my stable and did the most horrible things. He is far, far beyond my reach. However, if the emperor knew . . .'

'He will know.'

The groom gazed at Windswept as though she had been sent from heaven. 'Then Khamudi will be punished and will never set foot in my stable again?'

'You can be sure of it. The emperor demands very high standards of morality.'

'Then I shan't have to do anything, after all.'

'What were you planning to do?'

'Lure Khamudi and his wife into an ambush. As she likes stallions so much, I was going to show her one who has a dangerous little trick: if anyone comes up behind him, he kicks viciously. That madwoman wouldn't have escaped a second time, and her vile husband would have been spitted on my pitchfork.'

'The emperor's justice will solve all your problems,' promised Windswept.

In view of the circumstances, she would save the life of the High Treasurer and his wife, whose peccadilloes Apophis knew and approved of. The groom, though, was destined for the labyrinth.

As for Windswept, she now had useful new information about the unsavoury couple, whom she hated and would attack when the right moment came.

'Get dressed and leave now,' she ordered the groom.

'Thank you,' he said, his voice shaking. 'Thank you for everything you have granted me.'

Scarcely had he left when Minos came in. Still naked, Windswept threw her arms round his neck and kissed him so passionately that she took his breath away. The Minoan artist was her true love, the only one she had not yet sent to his death. Strangely, Minos was not fomenting even the tiniest plot against Apophis, even though the emperor had condemned him to perpetual exile.

With surprising constancy, the Minoan devoted himself only to his art. Thanks to his talent, the palace at Avaris was now fully the equal of the palace at Knossos. Large painted murals depicted Minoan landscapes, acrobats leaping over fierce bulls and labyrinths in which only the souls of the righteous could find their way.

Despite his mistress's innumerable infidelities, Minos never complained. Being loved by the most beautiful woman in Avaris filled him with joy, and he did not see the dangers he ran in sharing her bed.

'That brute of a groom has left me unsatisfied,' she complained. 'Will you console me?'

Her gentle caress of his perfumed skin aroused his desire at once. Not once had their amorous exploits disappointed her. Minos was not like any other man, and knew how to give pleasure with the spontaneity of an adolescent boy.

But after they had made love, she saw that he was troubled.

'Is something wrong?' she asked.

'It's to do with Minoa. Rumour has it that the emperor has decided to destroy the island.'

Windswept curled up against him, moulding her body to his. 'Don't worry, my love. Jannas hasn't yet finished cleansing the islands and eradicating support for Minoan independence. When he has finished, the Great Island will find itself alone again and with no choice but to give absolute obedience to Apophis. Of course, it will have to increase the quantities of tributes it pays, because it didn't do enough to help Jannas, but that will be only a minor inconvenience.'

'Then Minoa will be spared?'

'The emperor will turn it into a submissive and devoted province.'

'Do you think I'll be able to go home one day?'

'On two conditions: that I persuade the emperor your work is finished, and that I go with you.'

The painter's blue eyes were like a child's. 'Those are just dreams, aren't they?'

Windswept ran her fingers tenderly through his curly hair. 'It will take time to turn them into reality, but don't give up hope.'

'You and I, in Minoa . . . Nothing could be more wonderful.'

'Make love to me again, Minos. And never stop.'

CHAPTER 16

The year was drawing to a close, and Thebes was celebrating its new pharaoh, the completion of a large consignment of new weapons, and the launch of some new war-boats. Ahhotep's reputation was such that the inhabitants of Thebes, Kebet, Edfu and Dendera no longer cast doubt on her beliefs. Yes, victory really was possible – hadn't there been several miracles already? And, since a pharaoh now reigned, the gods would come to his aid.

The army of liberation was about to embark for the North, strengthened by many young soldiers who had enlisted over the last few months. After so many months of intensive training, the troops had only one wish: to leave for the front and kill some Hyksos.

'I'm going too,' little Ahmose informed his mother, as they watched weapons and stores being loaded aboard the war-fleet.

'You're only seven,' Ahhotep reminded him, 'and that's too young to fight.'

'My brother is Pharaoh, and he needs me. If I

don't help him, he'll lose the war. I know how to handle the wooden sword.'

'And the small bow, too, I know – I've seen you. But surely a good strategist understands the importance of having a strong rear base? While your brother is at the front, you will watch over Thebes.'

Ahmose did not take these words lightly. 'Does that mean preparing the second wave of attack and making all the necessary equipment?'

'Exactly.'

The boy's face grew intensely serious. 'And I would be responsible for all that?'

'Yes, with me, if you think you can do it.'

'I can, Mother.'

Heray came hurrying up to them and said, 'I must speak with you alone, Majesty.'

Ahhotep entrusted Ahmose to the officer in charge of his weapons training. She hoped Heray was going to say he had identified and arrested the spy responsible for Seqen's death, but he broached an entirely different subject.

'We must postpone the embarkation, Majesty.'

'Whatever for?'

'Some of our best captains and many of the oarsmen are ill.'

'Is there an epidemic of something?'

'I don't think so, because they're suffering from different illnesses. But all the men are seriously ill.'

There was a sudden violent gust of wind, which nearly blew the queen's headdress off.

'What a disgusting smell,' she said. 'It's just like the stink of rotting corpses.'

Fear tightened Heray's throat. 'It's a plague sent by the emissaries of Sekhmet, who is enraged with humanity and determined to destroy it.'

'That ought not to happen except in the five last days of the year,' Ahhotep reminded him, 'during that terrible period when the old time is dead and the new has not yet taken form. There's still more than a week to go before the period of danger.'

'Then it must be a curse sent by Apophis,' said Heray. 'It makes it impossible for us to strike north.'

The plague wind caused panic. How, asked townspeople and soldiers alike, could they protect themselves against the appalling stench, except by shutting themselves away in their houses and barracks, or huddling in the holds of the ships?'

'Summon all the officers,' Ahhotep ordered Heray. 'Tell them to assmble their men and put an immediate end to this disorder. Next, incense is to be burnt in every building.'

'We haven't very much, Majesty. We'll soon run out.'

'Send a boat to Edfu to fetch a large quantity of terebinth resin, and ensure that the infirmary is constantly purified with its smoke.'

Kamose came ashore from the flagship, looking anxious. 'Shouldn't we move everyone out of the base, Mother?'

'It would be no use – this wind will blow over

the whole of the Theban province. The emperor is trying to suffocate us.'

It was Teti the Small who reminded them of the first precaution to take when Sekhmet showed her anger like this: the left eye must be closed, to prevent the disease-causing air from entering the body, and the navel must be carefully cleaned, because that was the point of exit.

For both soldiers and civilians, there was one vital instruction: strict cleanliness. Even Way-Finder and Laughter were washed and brushed, in order to prevent the stench entering their flesh. But the evil wind doubled in strength during the last five days of the year, and despite constant care several people died.

If the emperor's curse triumphed, there would be no further rebirth of the light, no more procession of priests and priestesses carrying the ritual objects up to the temple roof to celebrate their union with the sun-disc, no more rites bringing the statues to life, and the army of liberation would die with the dying year.

Kamose and Ahhotep were everywhere, urging everyone not to give up hope but to fight the plague. Little Ahmose's courage greatly impressed everyone. Sprinkling himself with a scented essence at regular intervals, he calmed those who, in his opinion, were panicking needlessly.

On the fifth day, the wind became even stronger, and the number of deaths rose.

According to the ancient texts, there were only

two remedies left. The first was to write 'These curses will not attack us' on a strip of fine linen, then tie twelve knots in the cloth, offer it bread and beer, and apply it to one's throat. The second was to light as many torches as possible, in order to illuminate the darkness.

During this terrible ordeal, which threatened to put an end to his reign almost before it had begun, Kamose was able to master his fears and behaved with a composure worthy of a mature man. It was the pharaoh himself who lit most of the torches, watched by the Afghan and Moustache.

'That lad has real spirit,' said the Afghan admiringly. 'In my country, he would be considered worthy to fight.'

'A barbarian like you has no idea of what a pharaoh can be.'

'You've known a lot of pharaohs, have you?'

'With Seqen and Kamose, at least two. Instead of criticizing, why can't you admire what's being done?'

'If this damned wind doesn't drop, there'll soon be no one left to admire.'

'You're too much of a sceptic, Afghan. How can you imagine for a second that a true pharaoh could be struck down by adversity?'

The smoke from the torches rose up and attacked the plague-ridden air. The sky was transformed into an immense battlefield, deserted by the birds. Tortured spirals were drawn there, shot through with the immense red arrows fired by Sekhmet's emissaries.

Ahmose held his mother's hand tightly. 'You aren't afraid, are you?' he asked.

'Of course I am, but what does that matter? We have acted in accordance with the rites and used all our weapons. Now it is for the moon-god to decide. Up there, he fights a never-ending war, and sometimes he seems to be on the point of death, but he always succeeds in regaining the upper hand.'

'Do you think he'll succeed again?'

'I am absolutely certain of it.'

Ahmose never doubted his mother's word. And when the silver disc of the full moon pierced the clouds, he knew that that word was the truth.

As the first dawn of the new year broke, the wind dropped at last and the plague ebbed away. Exhausted, the Thebans fell into one another's arms, aware that they had escaped from mortal danger. Many dived into the Nile to purify themselves of the last traces of sickness; others prepared a celebratory meal.

Young Laughter barked with joy and Way-Finder shook his long ears, while Ahmose fell asleep in the queen's arms.

CHAPTER 17

The emperor thoroughly enjoyed his meal of a leg of goose cooked in sauce. The report Khamudi had just given him, based on information provided by the spy in Thebes, contained much to rejoice about. Many enemy soldiers had died of the plague, and the morale of Ahhotep's army was shattered. Only the troops at Qis still had to be isolated, made vulnerable to a determined attack.

Apophis had devised a new, rather entertaining plan which would allow him to swell the coffers of Avaris still further. Wholeheartedly enthusiastic about this plan, Khamudi had been instructed to put the emperor's thoughts into practice, on the one hand by sending out hundreds of scarabs into Middle Egypt, and on the other by sending officials charged with spreading the good news.

The stinking cloud had killed many animals and depopulated vast areas of farmland. People were so afraid that the peasants were cowering in their reed huts beside the fields, as if that pathetic shelter could protect them from the arrows of Sekhmet's invisible minions.

★   ★   ★

Many people, in the first days of the new year, all but despaired as they tried to resume their normal lives. But not Big-Feet. He was one of those who cared more about their milch-cows than about themselves. Plague wind or not, he had gone on feeding and milking his animals, while at the same time grumbling about the poor quality of the grass.

When the first boat arrived, Big-Feet did not run away. He had to defend his cows, even against a Hyksos regiment.

A civilian came towards him. 'I am one of the officials in charge of the floodplains and pastures of the Delta,' he said in a friendly manner. 'Up there, in the North, thanks to Apophis's magic, we haven't suffered any evil winds.'

'That's all very for you,' grunted Big-Feet.

'We benefit from the emperor's generosity, which extends to all his subjects, including you.'

'Oh yes? How?'

'Dozens of boats will take your animals and the other herds – there's plenty of fodder aboard – up north to the area around Avaris. They'll be well fed there, and will soon get their health back. Then you can come home again.'

This ancient practice had been abandoned since the beginning of the Hyksos occupation. To see it revived was something of a cause for celebration. But there was one serious problem.

'How much is this going to cost me?'

'Nothing at all, my friend – the emperor's only concern is the well-being of his people. I tell you, the Delta pastures are incredibly lush, and its stables are well-built and welcoming. Go and tell your village about it, and tell them that our boats are here. But tell them to hurry. Although the Hyksos have sent a huge fleet, there may not be room for everyone.'

After long, noisy discussions, most people opted to go. The emperor's generosity was an unexpected windfall – those who accused the Hyksos of cruelty were wrong. True, the occupation had had its difficult periods, but this decision marked a major turning-point. Apophis was behaving like a true pharaoh, concerned for the welfare of his people. He had realized that this was the only policy that would win the Egyptians' trust.

So the villagers herded their half-starved cows and oxen towards the boats, forgetting that, not far away, the rebels still held the front at Qis. A few peasants regretted not being able to provide them with food any more, but the Thebans had surely been wrong to stand up against their true sovereign. In any case, cow-herds and farmers were not soldiers.

Like his companions, Big-Feet found the journey very agreeable. They had all the beer, bread and dried fish they wanted, and they were able to enjoy long rests, something they were not used to. The further north they travelled, the more luxuriant the countryside became. The cultivated areas grew wider, and there were more and more waterways. It was a veritable paradise for cow-men and their herds.

At last they arrived.

Big-Feet stroked his cows, which had coped well with the long journey. 'Come along, my beauties, you're going to have a lovely time.'

A heavy hand landed on his shoulder, and a black-helmeted Hyksos officer said harshly, 'You, peasant, come with me.'

'I'm not leaving my cows.'

'*Your* cows? That's rubbish. Don't tell me you didn't realize . . . ? These animals are on a boat belonging to the emperor, so they belong to him, too.'

'What are you talking about? They're just going to graze here for a while, and then I'm taking them back home.'

The officer laughed loudly. 'That's the funniest thing I've heard in all my life! Now, stop talking, fellow, and follow me – now.'

'I'm a cow-herd, and I'm not leaving my cows.'

The Hyksos slapped him hard across the face.

Although peaceable by nature, Big-Feet hated being hit. He punched the Hyksos, and knocked him out.

The officer's men were enraged, and reacted at once. The odds were one against ten, and Big-Feet's resistance didn't last long. His head bloody, his wrists shackled, he was chained to another peasant and forced to join a never-ending procession of prisoners.

'Where are we being taken?' he asked his companion in misfortune.

'I don't know anything.'

'My cows . . . What will become of them? And the people from my village?'

'The Hyksos killed anyone who tried to run away. The others are chained up, like us.'

A tall woman with enormous hands hailed them. 'You're good sturdy fellows,' exclaimed the lady Aberia. 'That's much better. The journey will be more entertaining. Usually I have too many old men, females and city-dwellers. They're used to a soft life and don't last the distance. You aren't afraid of the sun or the dust or hard work, I'm sure. Whatever you do, don't disappoint me.'

Still thinking of his cows, and the fact that he was the only person who could milk them properly, Big-Feet walked on. Beside the track he saw the corpses of some old women and children.

'I'm thirsty,' said his companion.

'We'll ask them for water. They can't refuse.'

Big-Feet hailed two soldiers who were passing in a chariot drawn by two horses. 'We need water.'

'You'll get it when we stop, all except those who are insolent – like you.'

The chariot moved back up the column, in a cloud of dust.

'I thought the emperor was a good, just man,' confessed Big-Feet, 'because he was looking after my animals. Why has he done this? We haven't done him any harm.'

'He wants to remove all the Egyptians from Egypt and replace them with Hyksos – only Hyksos. Being Egyptian is a crime now.'

Big-Feet still did not understand, but he kept on walking, even when his companion died of thirst.

When they reached the marshes that surrounded Sharuhen, he flung himself into the reeds and drank muddy water. A Hyksos guard hauled him up by his hair and clubbed him, and he had not the strength to fight back.

The guard took off the chains attaching Big-Feet to the corpse he had dragged for so long, then pushed him into a large enclosed courtyard, watched over by archers posted on wooden towers.

The first person he saw there was a young, naked girl with mad eyes, her body covered with sores. She threw herself repeatedly against a stake and managed to break her skull.

Sitting on a mound of filth, an old man held his wife's hand, not noticing that she had stopped breathing. Exhausted men with empty eyes walked past one another without exchanging a single word. Others were digging in the waterlogged earth for any kind of food.

Who could have dreamt up and imposed such atrocities, if not the Emperor of Darkness, that liar who had not hesitated to trick simple peasants? Big-Feet would never forgive him for stealing his cows.

'Cow-herd, get down on your face.'

A guard set his foot on the prisoner's neck, while another branded a number on his buttock with a red-hot bronze rod. The surviving inmates of Sharuhen did not turn a hair as Big-Feet, prisoner number 1790, screamed in pain.

CHAPTER 18

'I can do that, too,' Ahmose told Kamose. 'I can hit the centre of a target.'

'I have the feeling you're boasting a little bit.'

'Try me!'

'All right.'

Kamose took Ahmose to an archery practice area reserved for beginners. It was surrounded by palisades, so that stray arrows would not injure anyone.

'Do you draw your bow yourself?' asked Kamose.

'Of course!'

'I'll check that the target is fixed firmly in place.'

There was complete understanding between the brothers. The king regretted that Ahmose was too young to fight at his side, but he knew that, if the worst happened, his brother would take up his sword.

Just as Kamose reached the target, he heard a familiar whistling sound.

'Get down, quickly!' yelled Ahmose at the top of his voice.

★　★　★

'It isn't serious,' said Teti. 'The arrow only grazed your neck. And with honey compresses there won't even be a scar.'

'You saved my life,' Kamose told Ahmose, who was still shaking.

'Did you see who fired?' Ahhotep asked him.

'No,' said the child. 'I ran straight to Kamose and didn't think to look around. When I saw blood on his neck I was afraid – so afraid!'

'Come and wash,' his grandmother ordered. 'You really don't look like a prince.' The two of them left the infirmary.

'There's a spy in the camp,' said Ahhotep, 'and he tried to kill you.'

'I don't think so, Mother. Despite Ahmose's warning, I didn't have time to duck. If the archer had really wanted to kill me, he wouldn't have missed. This wound is a warning: either I content myself with ruling Thebes or else I shall die.'

Ahhotep considered his words. 'In other words, your future depends on the outcome of today's council of war.'

Queen Ahhotep, Pharaoh Kamose, Heray, Qaris, the generals and principal government scribes had assembled in the twin-pillared hall of the palace at the military camp. They were all aware that they were participating in a momentous decision, and the atmosphere was tense.

'The current situation is a stalemate,' said the pharaoh. 'The little kingdom of Thebes may have

114

its freedom, but it's an illusory freedom because we're imprisoned by the Hyksos tyrant in the north and the Nubian tyrant in the south. We have no access to caravan or mining routes, and our isolation is becoming more and more intolerable, and even dangerous. The Pharaoh of Egypt wears only the White Crown. He cannot allow the Emperor of Darkness to usurp his right to wear the Red Crown.'

'Indeed, Majesty, indeed,' agreed the oldest general, 'but, all the same, is it wise to hurl ourselves into an all-out war which we will undoubtedly lose?'

'How can we know that unless we try?' asked a scribe called Neshi, a thin, bald man with piercing eyes.

The general, who cordially disliked the scholar, stiffened and retorted, 'In his own sphere, Neshi the Archivist's skills are indisputable, but I do not think he is qualified to suggest military tactics. Unless I am much mistaken, he is only here because of the need to take notes and produce a report.'

Kamose intervened. 'If I understand you correctly, General, you are in favour of maintaining the current situation.'

'To be absolutely frank, Majesty, I believe that is the best solution. I am well aware that the Hyksos are occupying a large part of our country, but is that not a reality we shall eventually have to accept? The enemy army is at least ten times more powerful than our own: it would be madness to attack it. We should be content with what Queen Ahhotep's courage has brought us. Thebes is free, and we can live here in peace. Why ask for more and destroy this fragile balance?'

'So fragile that it is no balance at all,' countered Neshi. 'Stagnation leads to death: that is what Queen Ahhotep has taught us. In believing we are safe, we make ourselves easy prey for the emperor.'

The general grew angrier. 'This is intolerable, Majesty. Neshi ought to hold his tongue.'

'It is I who give the orders, General,' said Kamose coldly, 'and I say that each member of this council may speak his mind.'

The soldier moderated his tone a little, but went on trying to persuade the king. 'Do you realize, Majesty, that the Hyksos are not opposed to peace? They have just given us a shining example of their good will by allowing livestock belonging to peasants from Middle Egypt to graze in the floodplains of the Delta. And that isn't all: they have also given grain to our pig-farmers. Hasn't the time come to lay down our arms and start negotiating about trade?'

'How can you believe such lies?' said Neshi furiously. 'The Hyksos are past masters at spreading false information, and people who let themselves be taken in by it always come to a bad end. Apophis will never agree to yield a single cubit of his empire. The peasants who go to the Delta will be made slaves, and their animals will be confiscated.'

'This really is too much!' exclaimed the general.

'On the basis of what information does this scribe dare contradict me?'

'Neshi is right,' confirmed Qaris. 'The Hyksos have indeed enslaved the peasants they pretended to be helping.'

Another senior officer leapt to the aid of his colleague. 'If the Hyksos are indeed still ruthless and unified, Majesty, surely that is another reason not to provoke them. It is clear that the emperor accepts the present situation, because he is allowing our northern border to exist at Qis. Let us take advantage of his indulgence and keep what we have gained.'

Ahhotep rose to her feet and gazed sternly at the two generals. 'Do you believe that Pharaoh Seqen died merely to enlarge the Theban enclave, and that he would be content with this gain? The whole of Egypt must be liberated, not just part of it. Anyone who forgets that sacred duty is unworthy to serve under Pharaoh Kamose.'

'You are no longer members of my war council,' the king informed the two officers. 'But I trust you will prove yourselves worthy on the field of battle, at the head of your regiments.'

The two generals withdrew sheepishly from the audience chamber.

The king turned to Neshi. 'You are hereby appointed Bearer of the Royal Seal and Overseer of the Treasury. I also charge you with steward-ship of the army: ensure that every man is well armed and properly fed.

Neshi rose and bowed deeply to Pharaoh. When he was seated again, he said, 'Although our troops are ready to leave, Majesty, my first advice to you is to wait.'

Kamose was surprised. 'Surely you don't agree that it would be better to negotiate with Apophis?'

'Absolutely not, since the empire of darkness will not change. But you told me to ensure that our soldiers are properly fed, and if we wage war at this time of year there is a risk that we shall run out of food. Late spring would be better, because by then the harvest will be in.'

Heray and Qaris agreed.

'Before launching the offensive, Majesty,' added Neshi, 'it would be a good idea to bring home some of the soldiers from the front and replace them with fresh men. Between now and the offensive, strengthening the front should be our main priority.'

Kamose was convinced his new adviser was right. 'Then that is what we shall do.'

'I believe we should consider another course of action,' said Ahhotep.

The king and his council looked at her attentively.

'Engaging all our forces on the northern front would carry a risk we are too apt to forget: an attack from the Nubians, who would dearly like to capture Thebes. Apophis is waiting for us at Qis, not at Elephantine or in Nubia. The real priority is to reconquer the southern part of our

118

country and to make the Nubians realize that if they attack they will be heavily defeated. For that reason, when spring comes the major part of our army will march not north but south.'

CHAPTER 19

Yima, Kamhudi's wife, was a fat woman with dyed blond hair, who considered herself a ravishing beauty. Knowing how possessive her husband was, she was careful not to be too blatant about taking lovers, and when she tired of her fleeting conquests she instantly got rid of them with the aid of her confidante, Aberia, who was only too happy to kill Egyptian slaves. Aberia could strangle a strong man with one hand, and every day she exercised to strengthen her muscles and amused herself by killing any Hyksos soldiers who dared defy her.

Yima lived in perfect happiness with Khamudi. She could enjoy his fortune, torture as many servants as she liked, and satisfy her perverted urges in the company of a husband who was as depraved as herself. But a lurking shadow threatened this happiness: Tany, the 'empress', always treated her with contempt.

Perhaps Aberia would be able to help her, thought Yima. So she went to the barracks where Aberia lived. She found her wolfing a huge plateful of red meat and washing it down with wine.

'Would you like to to share my meal?' asked Aberia.

'Oh, no, thank you,' replied Yima. 'I'm watching my weight at the moment.'

'Then stop eating pastries. They're food for little girls, anyway.'

'I am worried, very worried.'

'Is someone upsetting you, my poor darling?'

'Yes, but not someone you can get rid of for me.'

'Can't I? Who can it possibly be?' Intrigued, Aberia stopped chewing. 'Tell me the answer to this puzzle.'

'It's Tany – I think she hates me.'

Aberia burst out laughing. 'Tany's too ugly to have any feelings!'

'Don't joke. I really am upset. I don't understand why she dislikes me so much, and I don't know what she has against me. Do you know?'

'I haven't the faintest idea, my poor dear – well, actually, yes, I have. That little barrel contains nothing but venom. She hates absolutely everyone: the only person she loves is herself. She has no intention of letting anyone else share the benefits of being Apophis's woman, so she drives away anyone who might get a little too close to him.'

'But I wouldn't do that, I promise!' protested Yima.

'Your reputation suggests otherwise, my little one. But I believe I can solve the problem for you.'

'Really? How?'

'Myself, I have no taste for men. They're insipid and they tire too quickly. Women, on the other hand . . . what a delight! If the empress thinks you, too, love women, you'll no longer be in danger.'

Yima looked like a frightened child. 'What you're asking of me . . . I'd never dare, I—'

'Yes, you would. In fact, being so perverse, you'll enjoy it, and afterwards you won't be able to get enough of it. Come, let's go to my bedchamber. It's even better after a good meal.'

'But the soldiers will know, and—'

'That's exactly what we want, little one. We want our liaison to be notorious. Who would ever dare lay a finger on my darling?'

A young Egyptian woman, the daughter of a scribe who had been deported, was massaging Khamudi's toes, one of the parts of his body he considered perfect. After he had tried her out, she would end up either in the harem or in Sharuhen, depending on his whim of the moment.

Yima was lying on a comfortable mat beside her husband, her face smeared with regenerative clay.

'You've done the right thing,' he told her. 'The emperor thinks a lot of Aberia, and your being on good terms with her will be very useful for both of us. The more deportations there are, the more important Aberia becomes. As soon as she returns from Sharuhen, the emperor will appoint her head of the guards.'

'Has he decided to kill all the Egyptians?'

'If we want to govern this country in our own way, it's the only answer. At the moment we still need them as slaves, but foreigners brought up in the Hyksos ways will gradually replace them.'

'What a wonderful world the emperor is creating for us,' said Yima. 'A single way of thinking, a single direction, a single policy, a single dominant class wielding all the power, and faithful subjects who will obey because the law of Apophis is the law of Apophis! But when is he going to get rid of the Theban troublemakers?'

'He wishes to leave that pleasure to Jannas, and I think he is right. What splendid slaughter there will be! The Thebans are so afraid that they no longer even dare leave their rear camp. At the front, they will eventually tear each other to pieces. Either they will surrender, and Aberia will have many, many prisoners to transport, or else Jannas will have a good many heads to cut off. That's what happens to fools who put their trust in a woman like Ahhotep.'

The pirate captain at last got his breath back. When Jannas's ship had rammed his own, he had thought he was hallucinating: the Hyksos couldn't possibly be faster and more cunning than he was.

With incredible stubbornness, the commander had grimly pursued each last one of the Mycenaean, Cyprian and Minoan pirates who, with Minoa's tacit support, were attacking the emperor's trading-fleet. They had hoped to sink so many Hyksos ships that Jannas would be forced to retreat, but he was a formidable sailor and had had an answer to every single one of his adversaries' tricks: little by little, they had become hunted animals.

They had been sure they would find refuge in the Mycenaean islands – only to be disillusioned again. Even there, Jannas pursued them without falling into any of their many ambushes. Patient and meticulous, he isolated each enemy boat before capturing it with his more heavily armed sailors.

The captain and ten of his pirates were good swimmers, and reached the coast of Thera. The island was dominated by a volcano, but its eruptions did not frighten them. They would hide their booty there and then withdraw, their fortunes made.

'They're following us, Captain,' said a pirate.

Five boats full of Hyksos archers were heading for the island.

'We'll climb up higher,' said the captain. 'They won't dare follow.'

The smoking mountain did indeed make a strong impression on Jannas's men.

'Need we really bother with these miserable fugitives, Commander?' asked one officer.

'Every task must be fully completed. The emperor has ordered us to exterminate the pirates, and exterminate them we shall. If we don't, this handful of rebels will only get another ship and begin all over again.'

'Isn't this mountain . . . dangerous?'

'Not as dangerous as my sword,' replied Jannas menacingly.

The officer did not press the point. One more word, and he would be dead.

Slowly, the Hyksos climbed the slopes of the volcano.

'They're coming after us,' warned one of the pirates. 'We must go faster.'

As soon as they were within range, the Hyksos archers felled almost all the pirates. But, hampered by the plumes of smoke, they missed the captain, who skirted the edge of the crater, hoping to run down the opposite side and so escape his pursuers.

An arrow plunged into his thigh. Despite the pain, he dragged himself onwards across the rocks until a Hyksos caught him and kicked him to the ground.

'Don't kill him yet,' ordered Jannas. He had just discovered a strange lake. It contained not water but bright-red fire, which constantly boiled and bubbled.

'Listen to me,' begged the pirate. 'I've got a lot of treasure hidden up here in a cave.'

'Where?'

'I'll tell you if you spare my life.'

'Why not?'

'Do you give me your word?'

'Take your chance, pirate. And don't risk annoying me any more.'

'It's halfway up this slope, opposite a rock with

a circle drawn on it. You will see, it's a real hoard! Thanks to me, you'll be a rich man.'

'It is the Hyksos emperor whose coffers you will fill. I'm here only to destroy the bandits who've been attacking us.'

'And you'll spare my life?'

'A promise is a promise,' said Jannas. 'But before that, a quick bath will do you the world of good. You're dirty and you stink.'

'A bath? But . . .'

'That red lake looks suitable.'

'No!' howled the pirate. No! It's the mouth of hell!'

'Get him out of my sight,' ordered the commander.

Four Hyksos picked up the wounded man and threw him into the lake of molten lava.

CHAPTER 20

The military camp at Thebes was buzzing with activity. After a mild winter, during which many new boats had been built, Neshi presented his report to Pharaoh Kamose and Queen Ahhotep.

'Food supplies have been sent to the front, and it has been reinforced with eager young recruits,' he said. 'The experienced soldiers await your order to embark.'

'In your opinion, how good is the troops' morale?' asked Ahhotep.

Neshi hesitated. 'Our men are brave and determined, certainly, but . . .'

'But they are afraid of the Nubians, aren't they?'

'Indeed, Majesty. The Nubians' reputation for ferocity frightens more than a few of our men. The generals and I have tried to explain that we now have effective weapons and that our combat training is excellent, but we are a long way from banishing their fears.'

'Anyone guilty of cowardice will be executed in front of his comrades,' decreed Kamose.

'There may be other ways of calming this

ancestral and understandable fear,' suggested the queen.

Goose-livers stuffed with figs, roast duck, grilled sides of beef, puréed onions, lentils and courgettes, strong celebration beer of a beautiful amber hue, a thousand and one honey-cakes: these were among the elaborate dishes the palace had prepared for the army of liberation.

In addition, each soldier had received two comfortable new mats, and ointments based on terebinth resin to relax the muscles, maintain the proper bodily energies and repel insects.

'The queen is a mother to us,' declared Moustache through a mouthful of fresh bread spread with goose-liver. 'I've never eaten so well in my life.'

'When your country reaches heights like these,' admitted the Afghan, 'I almost forget my own.'

A man at the next table, a veteran soldier, flung away the stripped carcass of a duck. 'Instead of marvelling like stupid children, you'd do better to think. This is the last good meal you'll ever eat. On the boats you'll have to make do with rations, and then you'll be killed by the Nubians.'

'Well, I have no intention of dying,' retorted the Afghan.

'You ignorant fool, it's obvious you don't know where you're going.'

'And you do?'

'I've never set foot in Nubia, it's true, but no

one can beat those tall black soldiers – they're ten times stronger than we are.'

'Yet they don't dare attack the Hyksos,' pointed out Moustache.

The footsoldier was silenced, but only for a moment. 'They will one day. The Nubians were born to fight, not like us. Not a single Egyptian soldier will come back alive from this expedition.'

'If you're so sure of that, resign and go home,' advised the Afghan. 'A man who's beaten before he even sets off is as good as dead.'

'Are you accusing me of cowardice, foreigner?'

'I'm telling you to think clearly, that's all.'

'No, you aren't. You're trying to make me look a fool!'

Moustache was about to intervene when silence fell.

Queen Ahhotep began to speak. 'The ordeal we are all about to undergo is likely to be very dangerous, for we shall face formidable enemies. Before we even encounter the Nubians, who are rightly feared as warriors, we must first capture one of the Hyksos' largest fortresses, Per-Hathor. If the garrison manages to alert the Nubians, we shall have lost our chance of defeating them, which is why our first objective is to take Per-Hathor. The Hyksos occupy our country, steal its wealth and make our people their slaves. The time has come to make them realize that Egypt will never submit to tyranny. The will to be free is our finest weapon. Eat and drink well, and may courage fill your hearts!'

The soldier helped himself to another duck and gulped down another cup of strong beer. The queen's speech had reassured him. Capturing Per-Hathor was impossible, so the army would simply make a very brief excursion south and then come home, abandoning all thoughts of Nubia.

Ahhotep kissed her mother's hand; Teti had been confined to bed for several days.

'Mother, I shan't leave with Kamose, I shall stay with you.'

'No,' said Teti. 'Your place is beside the king, your son. He is young and inexperienced. Without you, he might make fatal mistakes.'

'Without you, my beloved mother, our adventure could never have become reality. Now, when you are ill, my duty is to care for you.'

'An old woman must not prevent you leading your troops to victory, Ahhotep. Leave me to face this trial alone, and think only of the future.'

'A daughter who abandons her mother is unworthy to be queen.'

Teti smiled. 'I'm beginning to wonder which of us is the more stubborn. Help me up.'

'The doctors say you must rest.'

'You have entrusted me with a task, and I shall carry it out. Thebes must be governed in your absence, and every single man in the province mobilized in the event of a Hyksos attack. So my death will have to wait – at least until you return.'

Teti left her bedchamber. She was so frail that

Ahhotep was sure she would be unable even to stand up for very long, but the old lady welcomed the warmth of the sun and summoned her household.

'Lying in bed is doing me no good,' she said. 'Go to Per-Hathor with a quiet heart, Ahhotep. Ahmose will help me, won't he?'

Moustache attached handles firmly to the knives and daggers, using resin; mixed with powdered limestone, it made an excellent adhesive. The Afghan was sharpening the blades and checking the arrowheads.

Qaris was rushing all over the place, anxious to leave nothing to chance. He spoke with each captain, visited each ship, and inspected each storage-chest and each jar. It was the eve of their departure for the south, and no detail must be neglected.

Heray, however, had other things on his mind.

'Majesty,' he confessed to Ahhotep, 'my investigation has had no results. No one saw the archer who fired at the king. Of course, I have doubled the size of his personal bodyguard and am imposing even stricter security measures.'

'My son thinks it was merely an attempt at intimidation.'

'Whether he is right or wrong, the important thing is to ensure his safety. If the Hyksos spy remains in Thebes, the king will be in no danger, at least for the moment. On the other hand, if the

131

spy is a member of the expeditionary force, his only thought will be to make another attempt on the king's life.'

'Don't worry, Heray. I'll watch over the pharaoh.'

Way-Finder was the first to board the flagship, where he had been allocated a new mat, in the shade of an awning, which he would share with Laughter. Then came a long procession, led by King Kamose proudly bearing the Sword of Amon.

The Afghan began to beat a strong, regular rhythm on a strange instrument.

Moustache had never seen anything like it before. 'What's that?' he asked. 'Did you make it yourself?'

'It's a drum. Its music will give the men courage – you'll see.'

The Afghan was right. The stirring rhythm calmed many fears, especially among the youngest soldiers.

After kissing little Ahmose and telling him to help his grandmother, Ahhotep gazed upon her brave men, all of them ready to sacrifice their lives to liberate Egypt. Many would not return from this journey, and she would be responsible for their deaths.

The Wife of God thought of her dead husband, whose absence weighed a little more heavily upon her with each day that passed. In uttering the 'words of glorification' that had brought his name and his spirit to life, the queen had created an energy which was essential if she was to pursue her mad adventure. Seqen was there, close beside her, giving her his strength.

Up in the sky, the moon began to shine.

CHAPTER 21

'**B**y all the gods!' exclaimed Moustache. 'How beautiful my country is!'

'There is some truth in what you say,' acknowledged the Afghan. 'Your land may not have high, snow-covered mountains, but it does have charm.'

'What is snow?'

'Water from the sky, which hardens as it falls to earth and turns a beautiful pure white.'

'You mean . . . cold water?'

'Very cold. It burns your hands when you touch it.'

'How horrible. Put that ugly thought out of your mind and look at the Nile and its green banks instead.'

On board the flagship, which had just set off for the south, the two men were experiencing a moment of perfect happiness. There was no more war, no more danger, no more Hyksos, simply a boat gliding along the river, while ibis and pelicans soared overhead.

In the bows, a tall, wiry man was sounding the depth of the water with a long forked stick. His role was vital: he decided, according to the depth, how the boat should be handled.

'What is your name?' Ahhotep asked him.

'Moon, Majesty.'

'Moon? Then you and I are protected by the same god.'

'If you only knew, Majesty, how I have longed for this. I was afraid I would die before I could fight the Hyksos and their allies. Thanks to you, my life has finally gained meaning. I swear to you that I shall guide this ship safely to its destination.'

The young helmsman's open smile lifted the queen's heart. 'For the moment, Moon, we shall pause in our journey.'

Their sails furled, the boats of the war-fleet hove to in perfect order.

While the soldiers were eating, Ahhotep and Kamose gathered together the men who had volunteered for the attack on Per-Hathor.

'We have nearly reached the fortress,' said the queen, 'and their lookouts must not see our boats.'

'Faced with such a massive attack,' said an officer, 'they might surrender.'

'I have seen the fortress,' Ahhotep told him, 'and it looks impregnable. Besides, the Hyksos are far more afraid of the emperor than of an Egyptian fleet. Per-Hathor is the gateway to Upper Egypt.'

'What if we just sailed past it as quickly as possible?'

'Their archers would shoot fire-arrows, and most of our boats would be set alight. The Nubian and Hyksos troops at Elephantine would be warned by visual signals and would slaughter our men, and then they'd go on to destroy Thebes. If we are to be able to use the Nile, it is vital that we capture Per-Hathor and do not give its garrison time to ask for help. Do not forget that from the tops of the towers lookouts can see further than a day's march to the south.'

'In other words,' concluded the king, 'we can't attack using our footsoldiers, and we can't lay siege to the fortress. What other option is there?'

'Before taking a decision,' said Ahhotep, 'we must send scouts to observe Per-Hathor.'

'I shall take ten men and do it myself,' said Kamose.

'No, you must remain here to lead our troops. I shall undertake this mission.'

'Mother, it's much too dangerous.'

'The Afghan and I are used to this kind of expedition,' said Moustache. 'If Her Majesty will agree to have us at her side, she will be safe.'

'Then we shall set off at once,' decided Ahhotep.

'I must admit, it's very strongly built and damnably well positioned,' said Moustache grudgingly.

Lying flat in the long grass, the queen and her two companions gazed at Per-Hathor. Thick walls, square towers, ramparts, a vast gateway, protective ditches: the monstrous fort looked invincible.

'You're always an optimist,' said Moustache to the Afghan. 'What would you do?'

'This time, I don't feel optimistic.'

The morale of the two rebels had reached a low ebb, but Ahhotep did not despair. She told them, 'Watch closely. There must be a weak point somewhere.'

Ahhotep had first seen Per-Hathor when she and Seqen had stumbled on it; they had almost been caught by soldiers foraging for food. This time, too, Hyksos soldiers emerged from the fortress to patrol the area, and Ahhotep would again have been caught unawares if the Afghan and Moustache, who were experienced fighters, had not warned her to take cover. The patrol passed very close to the trio, but did not see them.

'Killing them would serve no purpose,' said the Afghan.

'We could get inside when they open the great gate a little way,' suggested Moustache.

'A few of our men might get beyond the outer wall,' replied the queen, 'but they would be massacred.'

A boat appeared, sailing up from the south. As soon as it docked, Hyksos soldiers surrounded the Egyptian slaves who began to unload it, struggling under their heavy loads. One slave stumbled on the gangplank and dropped the jar he was carrying. It shattered on the quayside, and a great lake of beer spilt out.

A soldier plunged his spear into the neck of the clumsy slave, who made no attempt to defend himself or run away. The murderer kicked the man's corpse into the Nile.

Ahhotep tried to leap forward, but the Afghan's strong arms held her where she was.

'With all due respect, Majesty, don't try to do anything. Moustache and I have seen many things like that. If we'd acted in anger, we'd be dead.'

The unloading proceeded without further incident, then the boat left again for the south.

'Couldn't we set the fortress on fire?' suggested Moustache.

'It would take a very, very long time for our soldiers to lay enough wood at the foot of the walls,' replied Ahhotep, 'and they'd be shot down by the Hyksos archers. And I'm not certain that fire would do much damage to such strong walls.'

'Per-Hathor really is impregnable,' muttered the Afghan angrily.

'I've never seen you like this before,' commented Moustache.

'Nothing has ever seemed impossible before. But this time . . .'

Night was falling, and the moon-god was beginning to shine with all his brilliance.

'He will give us the solution,' promised the queen. 'We must go on watching.'

Nothing of note happened the following day, just three patrols at the same times as before. The day after that, the supply boat arrived with an even larger cargo and even larger jars.

One of the slaves, a worn-out old man, buckled under the weight and put one knee to the ground. Unable to go on, he laid down his burden and looked straight into the eyes of the Hyksos soldier who slit his throat with his dagger. A youth managed to carry the jar to the fortress.

Watched by the emperor's soldiers, the gate was opened just long enough to allow food and drink to enter the fortress. Then the boat left again, and it was time for the last patrol before dusk.

Night and day, archers were stationed on the tops of the watchtowers. There were so many torches burning that they lit up the whole area around the fortifications, ensuring that there could be no surprise attacks by night.

At dawn, the trio left their hiding-place. Neither Moustache nor the Afghan had come up with any way, not even a risky one, to take Per-Hathor, so they weren't surprised when the queen ordered, 'We must return to the flagship.'

CHAPTER 22

Jannas, who was of Asiatic origin, always wore a pleated headdress shaped like a mushroom, closely fitted to his pointed head. His appearance was distinctly misleading. Of average height and almost sickly-looking, slow of speech and gesture, he gave the impression of an honest fellow in whom one might readily confide.

In reality, he was a ruthless warlord who, throughout his brilliant career, had carried out the emperor's orders to the letter and without question. Like Apophis, he was convinced that military might was the only key to power and that all those who opposed Hyksos domination must be exterminated.

Wiping out the pirates hiding in the Mycenaean islands had taken him several years, but Jannas never yielded to impatience. All that mattered was ultimate success. And that was precisely what was annoying him: the leader of the pirates could only be from Minoa, and the emperor – for reasons which eluded Jannas – was refusing to destroy it. Tomorrow, thought Jannas, the Minoans would arm other pirates, and they would immediately start attacking Hyksos trading-ships again.

However, there was one last opportunity to inflict on the Great Island punishment from which it would not recover, if it could be shown to be guilty of harbouring criminals. To this end, Jannas's ships had driven the last active pirate boat back towards Minoa, but had not intercepted it. They saw it enter a narrow creek, where the crew disembarked. Jannas's duty was therefore clear.

The Hyksos war-fleet was drawn up ready for a massive assault. This time, Minoa would not escape. Its towns and villages would be burnt, the countryside laid waste, and its wealth would revert to the emperor.

'An envoy is asking to speak with you, sir,' a junior officer told him. 'He has come by small boat, and he's alone and unarmed.'

The Minoan was around fifty years old, and his hair and beard were meticulously groomed. His face bore the marks of anxiety.

Jannas received him on deck, facing the Great Island.

'May I remind you, Commander,' said the envoy, 'that the Minoans are the emperor's faithful subjects?'

'Subjects who shelter and support our enemies! Do you take me for a fool?'

'If you are referring to those pirates, who thought they could hide among us, you are wrong. We have arrested and executed them. Their corpses are at your disposal.'

Jannas sneered. 'I don't believe a word of it. You've

simply killed a few peasants to deceive me, while the real culprits dine at your king's table. Without your help, they'd never have eluded me for so long.'

'Commander, I swear to you that you are quite wrong. Minoa is a province of the Hyksos Empire, and I go each year to Avaris to present the emperor with ever-greater tributes. Apophis is our beloved sovereign, whose authority no Minoan would dream of disputing.'

'What fine, diplomatic words – you lie more fluently than a sand-traveller.'

'Commander, I cannot allow you to—'

'I allow myself!' cut in Jannas furiously. 'I have hunted the pirates down, one by one. Before killing them I tortured them, and they talked. All of them said the same thing: they were attacking our ships on behalf of Minoa, to recover the goods given to the emperor. I took many, many statements, and they leave absolutely no doubt of the Great Island's guilt.'

'They lied to try to save their lives – that's obvious! Why should my country have acted so irresponsibly?'

'I've just explained that to you, Envoy. Are you deaf?'

'The emperor must hear me. Let me sail for Avaris.'

'That's out of the question. Minoa is a refuge for pirates and I must destroy it.'

'Do not do that, I beg of you! We will double our tributes.'

'It's too late, Envoy. For once, your tricks are useless. Go back to your island and tell your countrymen to prepare to defend themselves. I don't like winning without meeting at least a little resistance.'

'Is there no argument which could change your mind?'

'Not one.'

Jannas sat in his cabin, brooding. The destruction of Minoa would mark the summit of his career, proving to Apophis that the Hyksos Empire must continue to extend its borders as ruthlessly as ever. During the invasion of Egypt, it was strength and strength alone that had overcome. There had been no question of diplomacy, or concessions to the vanquished.

In believing that they could strike at the empire by using pirates and without suffering the consequences of their crime, the Minoans had made a fatal mistake. Once their army was wiped out, the Great Island would become the starting-point for other conquests.

Conquest: Jannas's life had no other meaning. Winning demanded sacrifices, courage and a sense of strategy. Failure would be worse than death.

From time to time, he wondered about the emperor's attitude. Was Apophis becoming too cautious as he grew older? True, the army was still everywhere in Avaris, but within the palace luxurious living seemed to hold sway. Egypt was a land of magical charms, where one might easily lose the taste for fighting. In Apophis's place, Jannas would have taken up residence in a much less comfortable country, like Syria, so as never to forget that any land not forcibly integrated into the empire remained a potential enemy.

But Jannas reproached himself for criticisms like these. Apophis saw further than he did, and certainly had good reasons for acting as he did. The High Treasurer, however, was definitely a bad influence on the emperor. Jannas loathed Khamudi, who was utterly corrupt, interested in nothing but his own personal gain. But in this matter, too, how could he oppose the will of the emperor, who had made Khamudi his right-hand man?

Jannas stood at the emperor's other hand, and would not allow him to be manipulated by the High Treasurer. Once back in Avaris, he decided, he must take measures to restrict Khamudi's influence, because Khamudi was extremely prompt in killing anyone he thought might become a rival.

The morning was fine, the sea calm. Ideal weather for attacking the Great Island, which was experiencing its last moments of freedom before paying the price for its hypocrisy.

Jannas's second-in-command, who was in charge of co-ordinating the attack troops, knocked on the cabin door.

'Commander, all the officers are in their fighting positions.'

'Any problems?'

'No, sir. The weapons have been checked, the boats arranged according to your orders.'

Jannas went on deck and looked towards the coast, to which the Hyksos fleet was very close.

'Not one Minoan soldier,' he noted. 'Anyone would think they were leaving the field wide open for us.'

'Might it not be a trap, sir?' asked his second-in-command.

'Of course it might, and for that very reason we're going to use our catapults to set fire to the vegetation. A lot of Minoans will be burnt to a crisp, and the others will run away. Any who try to resist will be killed by our archers. Next, we shall sweep the entire island, with one single instruction: no survivors.'

The men in charge of the catapults were waiting for his signal.

But at that moment something unexpected happened: a fast, light Hyksos boat was spotted, heading towards the flagship.

Curious, Jannas told his men to wait. What did this intruder want?

An officer climbed aboard and handed Jannas a large limestone scarab. 'Commander,' he said, 'new orders from the emperor.'

Jannas read the words engraved on the scarab. Because of a serious uprising in Anatolia, Apophis ordered him to ignore the last few pirates, leave the islands immediately, and sail east at full speed to put down the rebellion.

'I did not think I would find you so easily,' said the officer. 'It's lucky you're so close to Minoa.'

Jannas smiled enigmatically. 'Lucky? I never rely on luck.'

Before giving the signal to leave, he directed a last, furious glare at the Great Island. Still, he thought, there was nothing to lose by waiting.

CHAPTER 23

The commander of Per-Hathor was a sixty year-old Canaanite who owed everything to the emperor. In his youth, he had burnt many villages in Palestine and the Delta, raped a fine tally of women and slaughtered plenty of old men. Particularly pleased with his services, Apophis had crowned the end of his career by giving him command of this magnificent fortress, the gateway to the south of Egypt.

He was not worried about the Theban rebels. The fact that they had succeeded in massing troops at Qis had intoxicated them, but that derisory achievement would lead nowhere. Unable to make progress to either the north or the south, they would stay trapped in their little enclave, which the emperor could destroy whenever he chose.

The only danger was Nubia. But the chief who had united the tribes to form the kingdom of Kerma was a reasonable man. He knew very well that being the unconditional ally of the Hyksos was much better than defying them.

So all that remained was routine. To prevent the

garrison becoming complacent, the commander imposed an iron discipline, with rigorous standards in all military and domestic activities. Per-Hathor was ready at any time to contain an attack, which would inevitably fail, anyway. And if a Theban boat appeared, a rain of fire-arrows would send it to the bottom.

The only delicate operations were the morning and afternoon patrols, which might encounter a raiding-party. But Queen Ahhotep had never dared send one, knowing only too well that it had no chance of success. Hyksos archers atop the towers kept permanent watch on the surrounding area, and would kill anyone who tried to get near the walls.

Moreover, in the event of an attack Per-Hathor would signal to a watchtower a day's march to the south, which would in turn pass the signal on. The troops at Elephantine would soon be mobilized and would hurry down the Nile to Per-Hathor. They might even join forces with the Nubian soldiers stationed upstream of the First Cataract. Massacring a band of Egyptian rebels would be a welcome distraction.

'Commander, the supply-boat's coming,' an officer informed him.

It would be bringing fresh water, meat, dried fish, vegetables, fruit, good-quality beer: the garrison lacked for nothing.

'Is it the usual one?'

'Yes, sir.'

From his post high on the ramparts, the commander watched big two-handled, egg-shaped jars of Canaanite design being unloaded.

'It is the day when honey, olive oil and wine are delivered,' said the officer greedily. 'I also ordered some boxes of fabric to replace clothes and bedsheets. If the supply-officer has done his work properly, it will all be here.'

The commander never tired of seeing the Egyptians humiliated. His sturdy soldiers in their black helmets never missed an opportunity to beat them and make them well aware of their inferiority. Any slave who showed the slightest sign of resistance was executed on the spot.

The gate of the fortress opened to allow the heavily laden slaves to enter. Forced to hurry, most of them were on the point of collapse. The moment they had deposited their burdens in the storehouses, they had to run back to the gate, heads bowed, to get out of the fortress as quickly as possible.

Twenty archers stood in position on the ramparts and aimed at the slaves. Others aimed at the area immediately around the main entrance, in case madmen thought they could take advantage of the delivery to enter the great courtyard.

As usual, the security instructions were observed to the letter.

'I sense that we shall soon receive a message from the emperor,' prophesied the commander. 'When the front at Qis has been strengthened, he will order us to attack Thebes, together with the troops from Elephantine.'

The crew were raising the sail on the cargo-boat, which was to leave again for the south.

'Shall we sample the wine this evening?' suggested the officer.

'Certainly not. The men must have an early night, because tomorrow they have cleaning duties at dawn and an inspection at noon. If I find the fortress spotlessly clean, we might organize a small celebration.'

Although disappointed, the officer resolved to take this blow patiently. With the aid of a sentry, he would gladly have uncorked a jar for his personal use. But if the commander found out, he would receive thirty days in prison and a transfer to somewhere much less agreeable. So at dinner he would be content with ordinary rations.

Per-Hathor was asleep. Only a few sentries were on lookout, and some of them were having difficulty keeping their eyes open. It was just one more peaceful night in this stronghold, where nothing could harm them.

The silence of the storehouse was almost imperceptibly broken by a small, dry sound: the side of a jar being broken. Slowly, Moustache emerged from his uncomfortable mode of transport. Beside him, the Afghan followed suit. And so did the fifteen other members of the raiding-party.

The first part of Queen Ahhotep's daring plan

had succeeded: to seize the supply-boat, replace the Hyksos soldiers with Thebans, persuade the slaves to act out the charade before they were freed, and find volunteers who were mad enough to hide in the largest jars. If the Hyksos had checked the contents before storing them, the raiders would not have stood a chance. But habit and the soldiers' belief in their security had prevailed.

The Afghan and Moustache looked at each other, surprised still to be alive. Their comrades joined them, daggers in hand.

Moustache told them, 'The Afghan and I are going to scout around. As soon as we've located the sentries, we'll return for you, and then we'll kill them all. While one of us opens the great gate, the others are to kill as many Hyksos as possible in their beds. We must move fast and in absolute silence.'

'What if one of the sentries manages to sound the alert?' asked a Theban.

'Then we're all dead, so make sure it doesn't happen.'

Barefoot, as always when moving soundlessly in enemy territory, the Afghan and Moustache ventured out into the fortress. Their fear gave way to intense concentration and economy of movement.

The two first sentries, who were stationed in the inner courtyard, had their throats cut before they could make a sound. Their corpses were dragged into an outbuilding and stripped, and the two rebels put on their tunics, breastplates and black helmets.

The Afghan signalled to his companion that he was going to climb the main stairway to the battlements and that Moustache should take the other one. They reached the two main lookout posts simultaneously; each was occupied by two archers.

With odds of two against one, the operation would be a tricky one.

'What are you doing here?' asked one of the Hyksos when he saw the Afghan. 'You know the commander has forbidden us to leave our posts.'

The Afghan slit his throat, in the hope that his companion's first thought would be to defend himself rather than shout for help. Indeed the man did, and that was his fatal mistake.

Once his two sentries were dead, the Afghan turned to see if Moustache had had the same success. He saw only the silhouette of a Hyksos soldier, but was reassured when the soldier removed his helmet.

Moustache went back down into the courtyard to fetch the Thebans. He showed them where the other lookouts were posted and allocated each man a target.

'These young fellows aren't quite as clumsy as I thought,' he mused as he watched them move into action.

Eager and determined, they did not set a foot

wrong. Less than half an hour after they emerged from the jars, the raiding-party had killed all the Hyksos sentries.

'Now for the gate,' ordered Moustache.

Two Thebans opened it while the Afghan set fire to the top of one of the towers. At this signal, Kamose's first attack regiment would know it could move towards Per-Hathor without fear.

'Let's hope he gets here soon,' whispered the Afghan, 'or we may have problems.'

'We must get to the sleeping-quarters,' Moustache whispered back, 'and kill as many Hyksos as possible.'

'No, wait a moment. Look there, at the bottom of the main tower. Do you think that's the commander's quarters?'

'Let's go and find out.'

Protected by the friendly darkness, they pounced on the commander, who was sound asleep – at first.

'Order your men to surrender,' advised the Afghan.

'A Hyksos does not surrender.'

'I know you,' said Moustache. 'You were stationed in the Delta a few years ago, and you tortured several of our comrades.'

'Per-Hathor is impregnable,' said the commander. 'Lay down your weapons immediately.'

'You Hyksos bore me,' said the Afghan. 'It's impossible to have a discussion with you.'

He pushed the commander outside, forced him

to climb up on to the ramparts and, seizing his ankles, threw him over the edge.

'Now,' he said, 'we'll go to the sleeping-quarters.'

Fortune continued to smile on them. The Thebans managed to break down the doors of two of the chambers, using heavy beams as battering-rams. The soldiers in the third, awakened by the noise, came rushing out; they were killed one by one as they emerged.

Just as the members of the raiding-party were beginning to tire, the vanguard of the army of liberation poured into the fortress, with Pharaoh Kamose at its head.

Queen Ahhotep stood at the prow of the flagship, watching the impregnable fortress burn.

CHAPTER 24

As Hyksos envoy and a master spy, One-Eye knew everything that happened in Nubia. It was a vast region, populated by warlike tribes which had recently been united by King Nedjeh, a natural leader of men, and one whose methods were brutal.

One-Eye was a former infantry general and expert killer. Officially, he had lost his left eye during a heroic fight from which he had emerged victorious. Actually, it had been put out by a Nubian girl he was trying to rape.

For a long time, he had worried that Nedjeh might be so full of his own importance that he would dare to attack Elephantine. But the Nubian had contented himself with his rich domain of Kerma, and declared himself a faithful vassal of Apophis, to whom he sent regular tributes.

This sensible behaviour had made One-Eye suspicious. Was Nedjeh secretly preparing to capture Elephantine, the great city that lay at the southern tip of Egypt, beside the First Cataract? Fortunately, the information provided by his spies gave no cause for concern. Several of them indicated that Nedjeh was growing fat and was interested only in consolidating his position locally. After travelling the length and breadth of Nubia to reassure himself that no trouble was brewing, One-Eye had come to Elephantine for a few weeks' rest.

The Hyksos garrison here led a peaceful life. They had a perfect understanding with the few Nubian soldiers stationed upstream of the cataract, and, being so far from Avaris, some of the officers were beginning to forget their people's warlike vocation. Anyone could see that discipline was growing less and less strict, and that the main barracks housed more and more women, whose presence had previously been forbidden. Little by little, the mild winters and hot summers had softened even the hardiest souls, and the men were more interested in having good food and comfortable living-quarters than in keeping their weapons in proper order.

The garrison had neither chariots nor horses, which were reserved for the army of the North. Its boats were ancient and in need of major repair. As for the fortress itself, though it looked as impressive as Per-Hathor it suffered from faults in its construction. Moreover, its great gate was often left open, and the sentries were not as vigilant as they might be.

'But who would ever dare attack Elephantine?' the town's governor asked One-eye, whose initial anger had been softened by the Nubian girl he had found in his bed and the excellent meal he and the governor had just finished.

'Are there any problems with the Nubians?' asked One-Eye.

'Not a single one, dear friend. As allies they are a little hot-tempered, but they're perfectly loyal. The mere name of the emperor brings them to heel, and so it should. Between ourselves, I hope I shall not be recalled to Avaris. Leaving this little paradise would be a wrench.'

A cup-bearer hurried up to the table and handed the governor a shard of limestone. 'An urgent message, my lord, very urgent!'

'What is it now? I'll wager the officers are complaining about the quality of the local beer. All the same, we mustn't—' The governor stopped dead as he read the message, which was written in a sailor's clumsy hand. '"*Per-Hathor has fallen.*" What's that supposed to mean, "*Per-Hathor has fallen*"?'

'Someone has captured it,' said One-Eye.

'But who on earth could do that?'

As the two men looked at each other, stunned, they heard shouts rising up from the Nile.

'We may not have to wait long to find out,' said One-Eye grimly.

They hurried up to the top of the fortress's highest tower. From this vantage-point, they saw the Theban war-fleet, its sails bellying out in a strong north wind.

Taken by surprise, the Hyksos boats were already

sinking. In a few minutes, the army of Kamose and Ahhotep would reach land and attack the citadel. Panic overtook the Hyksos soldiers, contradictory orders flying about in all directions.

'The gate . . . the archers . . . the barracks . . . Quickly – we must act quickly!' exclaimed the governor, rushing down the stairway.

In his hurry, he missed a step and fell. On the long way down, his head hit the wall several times. By the time he reached the bottom of the stairway, he was dead.

One-Eye had only one objective: to get out of Elephantine and reach Kerma, to warn King Nedjeh.

For the first time, Moustache and the Afghan did not have to join battle themselves during the final, victorious attack. Although disorganized after their commander's death, the Hyksos defended themselves fiercely, but the Thebans' zeal was so great that it swept away the enemy within a few hours.

'Our young lads gave a good account of themselves,' observed Moustache.

'Hard work always pays off,' replied the Afghan. 'Today they're reaping the benefits of the training the queen demanded of them.'

As he spoke, Ahhotep emerged into the square before the Temple of Khnum, the patron god of Elephantine; beside her was Pharaoh Kamose, who wore the White Crown. Holding a bow in her left hand and an ankh, the sign of life, in her right, she embodied Thebes the liberator.

Kamose had never felt so happy. Thanks to Ahhotep's plan, which had been executed with breathtaking speed, all the land between Thebes and Elephantine was now free of Hyksos. In the streets and squares, the people were honouring the soldiers of the army of liberation, and already banquets were being prepared which would last late into the night.

A very old priest emerged from the temple. He walked with difficulty, leaning on a stick. 'I wish I could bow before Your Majesties, but my back is too stiff. What happiness to welcome you here! I was right to resist death, in the impossible hope that I would see this town set free.'

'Take my arm,' said the queen.

'Majesty, I . . .'

'Please. You are the guardian of the potter's wheel, are you not?'

The old man's lined face lit up. 'In spite of all their searching, the Hyksos did not find it. In this temple, the first steering-oar was made, enabling the ship of state to be guided. Also here, the god Khnum fashioned all living beings on his potter's wheel. I shall reveal these mysteries to you, and then I shall be able to die in peace.'

Dozens of gazelles had come out of the desert, to invade the gardens of Elephantine and play with the children. Once again, the people could celebrate the festival of their patron goddess, Anukis, represented by a very pretty woman wearing a white crown decorated with the slender horns of a gazelle.

While the town was expressing its joy, the old priest reopened the entrance to the the temple's vaults, which lay under the paved floor of the inner shrine. A hundred times the Hyksos soldiers had profaned this place, never suspecting that the treasures they coveted lay beneath their feet.

The acacia-wood steering-oar was so heavy that Kamose had to summon several men to lift it out of the depths. From this day on, it would steer the flagship.

Then the young pharaoh took in his hands the potter's wheel with which Khnum had positioned the celestial vault, raised up the firmament and shaped the cosmos so that light might shine through every part of it. One by one, the gods, animals and men had emerged from this matrix.

The old priest, the queen and the king climbed up to the temple roof. There, they would expose the wheel to the sun so that it would be able to function once more.

'Life begins again,' intoned the priest, 'and breath brings matter to life.'

When the night sky was unveiled, the old scholar showed his guests how to use the sighting-instruments that had helped the ancients to understand the movements of the sun, the moon and the stars. They had known that the so-called 'fixed' stars in fact moved, and that the centre around which they seemed to move also changed position because of the precession of the world's axis.

Kamose was fascinated and could have listened enraptured for nights on end as the old man happily passed on his knowledge.

'First thing tomorrow,' promised the pharaoh, 'you shall begin training your successors. Many priests, servants and craftsmen will be appointed so that this temple may regain its former activity and splendour.'

The priest smiled. 'Then my death will have to wait a little longer, Majesty.'

Ahhotep gazed out at the First Cataract, which marked the border with Nubia. She shared her son's joy at the taking of Elephantine, but it was only a stage in the war and their victory, though dazzling, was very fragile. Beyond the barrier of rocks illuminated by the moon-god lay the enemy. An enemy quite capable of wiping out the army of liberation.

CHAPTER 25

Queen Ahhotep and King Kamose spent a long time meditating on the isle of Biga where, according to tradition, both the body of Osiris and the sources of the Nile were located. The waters of the river divided as they sprang forth from a cavern, one branch flowing north while the other flowed south. The source of the spring lay so deep that no one had ever reached it.

There was absolute silence on the island. Even the birds forbore to sing there, so as not to disturb the rest of the reborn god whom Isis had snatched back from death. By and in Osiris the souls of the righteous were reborn, the beings of light among whom Pharaoh Seqen now dwelt.

Aboard the boat taking them back to Elephantine, the young king could not hide his profound emotion. 'This town is the head of the country, the capital of the first province of Upper Egypt, and it safeguards the sacred origins of the Nile. By controlling it again, we make the river our invincible ally. Like Osiris, the land of the pharaohs is reborn. Shouldn't we forget

162

the Nubians and leave immediately for the North?'

Ahhotep shook her head. 'No, because we must slacken the noose once and for all by making sure that King Nedjeh will never again wish to attack us. And there is only one way to do that: we must reconquer Buhen and so cordon off the whole of Nubia.'

Kamose unrolled a papyrus on which a simple map was drawn. 'So we must sail almost as far as the Second Cataract. On such a long journey, isn't there a risk that the Nubians will ambush us long before we reach Buhen?'

'It is a possibility,' agreed Ahhotep, 'but I believe he has blind confidence in Buhen's ability to repulse any attack. It is as powerful as Per-Hathor and Elephantine put together. If its Egyptian governor had not betrayed us to the Hyksos, the Nubians would certainly not have succeeded in taking it.'

'Are you planning to use the trick with the jars again?'

'I'm afraid that's impossible.'

'Then we must expect a long and painful siege, with an uncertain outcome. And during that time, there is a risk that the front at Qis will collapse.'

'That is another possibility,' admitted the queen. 'If you think my plan is wrong, you are free to reject it.'

'I'd never dare oppose you, Mother. You're the liberator of Egypt.'

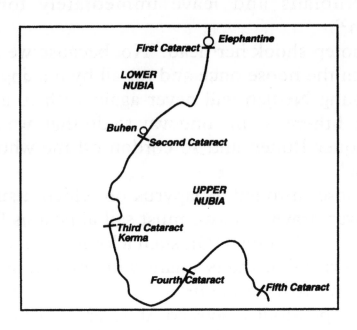

'And you are Pharaoh. I shall always obey your orders.'

Kamose gazed out over the Nile. 'By becoming the Wife of God, by giving all your love to this country, which you rightly revere, you are following an earthly path which was born in the heavens. I am only a young king and I do not yet have your clarity of thought and vision. Sometimes, I wonder if you are completely of this world or if part of you dwells beyond the visible, leading this army safely to its goal. I shall never give you an order, Mother, and I shall follow wherever you lead.'

The festival was over, the town silent, and the gazelles had returned to the desert. Although most of the soldiers had dreadful headaches, all those who were to leave for Nubia had gathered on the quayside. They envied their comrades who were to form the new garrison at Elephantine.

Neshi went up to the pharaoh and bowed. 'All is ready, Majesty. We have taken on large supplies of foodstuffs and weapons. I checked each consignment myself.'

'You look worried.'

'Our men are afraid, Majesty. The inhabitants of Elephantine have told them about the black warriors, who are as dangerous as wild beasts. Everyone knows that Nubia is full of evil spells which no one can eradicate. After all, the creator's eye fled into those burning deserts, to destroy all forms of life. If you were to give up this expedition into the unknown, everyone would be relieved.'

'Including you, Neshi?'

'I would be disappointed and anxious. Disappointed by our leaders' inconstancy, and anxious about the process of liberation.'

'That is not a very diplomatic thing to say.'

'I am not a diplomat, Majesty. I am the Bearer of the Royal Seal, who ratifies and makes known Pharaoh's decisions. If I find them bad, I must be honest. And if that honesty displeases you, dismiss me and replace me with someone more tractable.'

Kamose smiled. 'Whatever else you do, Neshi, don't change.'

'Our troops' fear is a setback, and I don't know how to counter it.'

'My mother has asked the craftsmen of Elephantine to make some unusual weapons which should reassure them.'

Dazzlingly beautiful in a long green gown and floral headdress, Queen Ahhotep went out into the square to address the army. She was followed by several craftsmen carrying heavy baskets.

'We are about to face formidable enemies,' she acknowledged. 'Before we even reach Buhen, we shall have to defeat Nubian warriors who will fight ferociously. But there is a magical means of weakening them: using these objects covered with powerful symbols.'

She reached into one of the baskets and took out a curved throwing-stick engraved with an eye, a rearing cobra, a griffin and the head of a jackal.

'The eye will enable us to see danger,' she explained, 'and the cobra to dispel it. The griffin and the jackal will ward off the destructive forces of the desert. Officers and their deputies will be equipped with these weapons in order to protect the men under their command. And one made of ivory, bearing the same signs, will ensure that our voyage is peaceful.'

The queen had never lied to them, so the men were persuaded that, once again, she would succeed in protecting them from evil. With enthusiasm, the sailors hoisted the sails and yards with the aid of halyards on which they heaved with all their strength. The manoeuvre was a difficult one, even for professionals. But nothing went wrong, and the sails fluttered free, watched attentively by the captains.

On the flagship, seven sturdy fellows hoisted the topsail using two halyards, while an eighth climbed to the top of the mast to help them. His clambering amused a young monkey, which proved swifter than he and teased the crew with little cries.

Laughter barked, warning the monkey to behave itself. Perched on the top of the mainsail, the animal did not have to be told a second time.

Pharaoh himself took charge of the steering-oar when the boat headed into a channel which would enable it to avoid the rocks of the First Cataract and rejoin the Nile.

Using his long forked stick, Moon measured the depth of the water; there was no scope for error. And slowly the boat continued on its way. Moon had an uncommon capacity for concentration; he was one with his craft. With all his being, with all his senses, he experienced each movement of the water and detected all its many snares.

Ahhotep saw that Moon's brow was deeply furrowed, as if the dangers were growing greater by the moment. She looked down into the channel, which sparkled in the sunshine, and offered a prayer to Hapy, the life-energy of the river, asking him not to hinder the war-fleet's progress.

On the poop of the flagship, Moustache noticed that the Afghan looked ill at ease: his face was taking on a strange green tinge. Moustache grinned and said, 'I have a feeling you don't much like sailing.'

'Turn away. That'll make me feel better.'

'Be sick in peace, Afghan. We only have a few weeks' travelling ahead of us, interspersed with murderous battles. Let's hope for your sake that some of them will be on dry land.'

The Afghan's stomach was heaving so much that he couldn't reply.

'Don't worry,' said Moustache. 'I hear the river is rather calm in Nubia. That's better for delicate constitutions like yours, isn't it? Oh, watch out! We're going over some rapids, and that might shake us up a bit. Just don't look. I'm not even sure if our boat can withstand the shock.'

Little by little, the lines on Moon's brow relaxed and disappeared. Although watchful as ever, he handled his measuring-staff less apprehensively.

Queen Ahhotep stopped gazing at the water and instead looked at some clumps of palm-trees sparkling in the sun.

'Good news, Afghan!' exclaimed Moustache. 'We've just entered Nubia.'

CHAPTER 26

The riverbed was narrower than in Egypt, and lined with palm-trees which had their roots in the water and their crowns in the sunshine. Most of them lived for a hundred years, and the best gave up to thirty clusters of dates. Ripening with the flood, between July and September, they were a useful source of food during the hot season. The doum-palms were as tall as ten men and had one special feature: their trunk forked twice or more, and each branch ended in a sort of crown. Apart from their red-brown fruit, with its soft, sweet flesh, they provided welcome shade, and their kernels contained a refreshing liquid which Moustache was fond of.

'Are you feeling better, Afghan? I think the boat is pitching a bit less.'

The Afghan was still greenish, and hardly eating anything. 'One day,' he said firmly, 'I shall take you into my mountains in the middle of winter. We'll see how proud you are when you have your feet in the snow. From what I know of you, you'll have an attack of vertigo and won't be able to climb up or down. And don't rely on me to help you.'

'At the moment we're in Nubia, and you'd do better to look straight ahead. We have visitors.'

They were very black-skinned, very tall, very strongly built, and were armed with spears and bows. They wore only a simple kilt, while their faces and torsos were painted with warlike insignia.

Ahhotep gave orders for the flagship to halt and for the gangplank to be put out.

'Mother,' said Kamose anxiously, 'don't leave the boat.'

'These are warlike men, but they have a sense of honour. They will not kill a woman who comes to meet them alone and unarmed.'

Moustache was not so sure.

The Afghan laid a hand on his shoulder. 'Don't threaten them, and let her do as she wishes. She knows what she's doing.'

'Those brutes will slaughter her.'

'People don't kill a woman like her. Look at them. It wouldn't take much to make them prostrate themselves before the Queen of Egypt.'

Surprised by Ahhotep's actions, a tall man wearing gold bracelets pushed through the ranks of his soldiers to confront this unexpected adversary.

'I am Ahhotep, Queen of the Two Lands, and I am travelling with Pharaoh Kamose, at the head of his army.'

'I am the chief of the Medjai tribe and I thought the only pharaoh was Apophis. What do you seek to do on my land, Queen of Egypt?'

'To fight the allies of the Hyksos, who are occupying my country, and to retake the fortress of Buhen, which was handed over to the enemy by traitors and collaborators.'

'Have you decided to wage war against the King of Kerma?'

'Since he is the faithful friend of the Emperor of Darkness, I shall destroy him.'

'King Nedjeh is invincible.'

'Pharaoh will vanquish him.'

The chief looked troubled.

'What do you Medjai desire?' asked Ahhotep, whose serene beauty fascinated the Nubian.

'The Medjai inhabit a large part of this land, between the First and Second Cataracts. For a while, we thought that Nedjeh would be our liberator. In reality, he is nothing but a tyrant, and he wanted to turn us into slaves. When we resisted, with the aid of the Hyksos he killed many of us and destroyed many of our villages. We took refuge in the desert and only re-emerged a few days ago, when we learnt that a fleet from Thebes had liberated Elephantine and entered Nubia. We killed the soldiers of King Nedjeh who were preparing to attack you. We want to fight at the side of the Pharaoh of Egypt.'

While Kamose, Moustache and the Egyptian soldiers looked on in astonishment, the Medjai prostrated themselves before Queen Ahhotep.

The Afghan was only modestly triumphant, for he had not really believed his own prediction.

171

'That woman is a miracle in herself,' he murmured.

Soped, the Egyptian commander of Buhen fortress, listened attentively to One-Eye. The Hyksos knew Nubia better than anyone, and scaremongering was anathema to him, so his warning was not to be taken lightly.

'So, One-Eye, an army from Thebes has taken Elephantine. A serious blow to the Hyksos, I agree, but it's only a temporary reverse. You know as well as I do that the emperor's reaction will be terrifying. He will raze Thebes and Elephantine to the ground and station garrisons there to prevent any future unrest. Now, I am a loyal servant of the King of Kerma. I have washed my feet in my master's water,* and I belong to his entourage, so I am safe and sound.'

'I'm sure you're right, Commander, but nevertheless you should strengthen your defences.'

'Buhen is impregnable.'

'So was Per-Hathor,' said One-Eye drily.

'The comparison does not hold water. Buhen is a small town, and I have a large enough garrison to resist an attack. Besides, the troops of King Nedjeh and the Medjai tribe must already have sunk most of the ships belonging to that ridiculous pharaoh Kamose. Believe me, my friend, no enemy boat will reach Buhen.'

*An Egyptian expression denoting absolute loyalty.

172

'Probably not,' conceded One-Eye, 'but Queen Ahhotep is a formidable force.'

'A woman! Are you joking?'

'This woman seems to be in league with the gods.'

'The gods didn't protect Egypt during the Hyksos invasion, and they won't protect her today.'

'I shall go to Kerma to alert King Nedjeh and ask him to send you reinforcements.'

'He will simply laugh in your face.'

'I think it advisable to take every precaution,' said One-Eye.

'Why are you so worried? These are just the last efforts of a Theban faction which is mad enough still to believe in Egyptian freedom.'

'I shall feel less worried when that woman Ahhotep is dead.'

'She's probably dead already, even as we speak. Take your time in Kerma and give King Nedjeh my greetings. It seems his palace grows more beautiful by the day and that his court will soon shine more brightly than that of the pharaohs.'

With some relief, the commander watched the Hyksos leave for the south. One-Eye was beginning to fall prey to an old man's fears, and was no longer capable of dealing with new situations. The emperor would not leave him in office for much longer, and would replace him with a younger, more dynamic man who was not afraid of his own shadow.

One-Eye's advice had not pleased Soped in the least. Nobody knew the fortress's capacity for resistance better than its commander! That very evening, he would write a highly critical report about One-Eye's behaviour and send it urgently to Kerma, so that the king could demand that the emperor dismiss him.

Commander Soped could be proud of his achievements. As a junior officer, he had quickly realized that the Hyksos were the new masters of Egypt and that their work must be facilitated as much as possible. So he had denounced all his superiors as accomplices of the Thebans.

The emperor had proved not ungrateful: in exchange for this spontaneous collaboration, he had appointed Soped commander of Buhen fortress, charged with turning it into an impregnable bastion and beheading anyone suspected of opposing the Hyksos, even in thought. Soped had taken advantage of this to kill everyone he disliked, in full agreement with his assistant, who had come from Kerma to keep watch on him. From time to time, the Nubian was obliged to restrain the commander, whose thirst for executions seemed never-ending.

Today, Commander Soped was the unchallenged ruler of the stronghold, which provided shelter for caravans, acted as a tax-post for goods, a workshop for washing gold and a postal centre. Obeying orders from both the emperor and the King of Kerma, Soped succeeded in annoying neither. And if things were quiet for too long he could always torture a civilian, who would duly be forced to confess that he was conspiring against Apophis.

By appropriating small amounts of gold during each washing operation, the commander was, little by little, amassing a modest fortune. His only worry was the possible emergence of a rival who might try to oust him; but he was so vigilant that it was a very small worry indeed.

'Dinner is served,' announced his cup-bearer.

Another quiet evening lay ahead.

CHAPTER 27

Nedjeh, all-powerful King of Kerma, was being massaged with oil of shea made from the fruit of the 'butter tree', which contained an oily nut. In the last two years, the handsome, athletic Nubian had gained a lot of weight and he was becoming almost fat. But he could never resist the sauces and desserts prepared by his cooks.

When he seized power in the fertile region of Dongola, just above the Third Cataract, Nedjeh had been a warrior hungry for conquests. Ruler of an extensive river basin where cereal crops grew in abundance and livestock thrived, Nedjeh had thought he would be able to take Elephantine, then Thebes, and so conquer Upper Egypt. But Emperor Apophis's clear-sightedness had decided matters otherwise, and the Nubian felt it preferable not to go to war with the Hyksos.

By remaining their faithful ally and sending tributes to Avaris, Nedjeh ensured his lands were left in peace, and he was able to rule despotically and mercilessly.

He had made spectacular improvements to his

capital by having a fortified brick temple built in the very centre, as tall as twenty men. A monumental staircase led to its summit, which looked out over the whole city. To the south-west of the city a vast circular hut served as an audience chamber; to the east there was a burial-ground, whose principal tombs were decorated with bulls' heads. Defensive earthworks, watchtowers and heavy gates ensured the security of Kerma, where slaves were sacrificed as readily as rams.

Nedjeh's latest whim was glazed porcelain tiles and friezes depicting lions. Thanks to the gold mines, the prince's wealth continued to grow, and he took advantage of it to make Kerma magnificent, in accordance with his taste. Apophis, with whom he communicated via inscribed scarabs borne by the imperial messengers, had sent him some undeniably talented carpenters. So his palace was filled with refined furniture in the Egyptian style.

The inhabitants of the new capital lacked for nothing. Trading-relations with the Hyksos were good, and consignments of Minoan and Cyprian jars arrived regularly at Kerma, where the tribal chiefs came to pay allegiance to Nedjeh.

Other people, too, had noticed that the king had put on weight, but no one complained. Good food and luxury made him forget his warlike ambitions in favour of comfort. The price to be paid was only an unconditional alliance with the Hyksos, but would those predators be content with exterminating the Egyptians? Nubia's gold was so tempting . . .

Nedjeh reassured himself by increasing, each year, the quantity of gold he presented to the emperor. In this way Apophis kept a tight rein on far-off Kerma, which did not threaten him in any way.

When the king's steward announced the arrival of One-Eye, Nedjeh frowned. The Hyksos was a master of trickery and manipulation, and it would not be easy to lie to him. He had probably come to demand more gold, so the king would have to persuade him that the miners had already produced all they could.

'You look very well, One-Eye,' he said.

'Appearances are sometimes deceptive, my lord.'

'Come, come. Surely you aren't the bearer of bad news?'

'The Theban army has taken Per-Hathor and Elephantine.'

'I know; I received your messages. It's annoying, of course, but they'll both soon be retaken by the emperor's soldiers, won't they?'

'That is a certainty.'

'Then why worry?'

'Because Ahhotep and Pharaoh Kamose have entered Nubia.'

Nedjeh burst out laughing. 'A woman and a boy! Their folly has condemned them to death.'

One-Eye seemed depressed. 'I am not so sure.'

'But how can you doubt it? I have troops

stationed close to the First Cataract, and they and the Medjai tribe will make short work of your Thebans.'

'Lately, the Medjai have seemed less and less reliable. Your men have bullied them, and I know they are resentful.'

'They would never dare disobey me. You can be sure that the Theban army has been wiped out.'

'But what if it hasn't? Wouldn't it be sensible to strengthen the defences at Buhen?'

'Buhen cannot be taken. If Soped hadn't betrayed his own kind, I'd have had to besiege it for an eternity – and even then I might not have taken it.'

'I believe we would be making a grave mistake by underestimating the Thebans. Ahhotep is a true war-leader. For an army regarded as of no account, is it not a remarkable achievement to take Per-Hathor and then Elephantine?'

'Don't exaggerate,' said Nedjeh scornfully. 'They took advantage of favourable circumstances, that's all.'

'My lord, I strongly advise you to send reinforcements to Buhen.'

'To be frank, that seems pointless.'

'I very much regret it but, as representative of the Hyksos emperor, I find myself obliged to order you to do so.'

Hiding his anger, Nedjeh bowed. 'As you wish. But I think you're being very alarmist.'

'If the Medjai have turned against your troops,

Ahhotep and Kamose have had free rein. Their main objective can only be Buhen. If they retake it, they will pin you down in Kerma.'

'This is all merely conjecture.'

'My instinct rarely deceives me. I know that that woman Ahhotep is dangerous and that you must take action.'

'You need say no more. The emperor's orders shall be carried out, as usual. Has Apophis ever had cause to complain about me?'

'Never,' agreed One-Eye, satisfied with the outcome of the interview. 'And you, the King of Kerma, shall have the privilege of crushing the Theban rebellion. Of course, you will acquire important privileges by doing so. In the report that Apophis will demand, I shall write about you in glowing terms.'

'You will always be welcome in my town, One-Eye. Do you think the emperor will be satisfied if his envoy takes him the heads of Ahhotep and Kamose on the ends of spears?'

'He would certainly appreciate that kind of homage.'

'Then it is agreed, my friend. Now, shall we go and amuse ourselves a little?'

Nedjeh's favourite entertainment, after lavish banquets, was women. And in that respect One-Eye felt capable of rivalling him, especially since Kerma housed some splendid, hot-blooded creatures.

One of the vast bedchambers at the palace was

reserved for the prince's new conquests; despite his plumpness, he remained a vigorous lover. There were four of them, all young, pretty and smiling.

'I shall leave the choice to you, One-Eye.'

'My lord, you are too generous!'

'Please: it is a gift to celebrate our perfect understanding.'

What the Hyksos liked best about Nubia was its girls. At once challenging and docile, disturbing she-panthers and languorous cats, they fascinated him. If he had an attachment to this rough, sun-scorched land, he owed it to them.

And One-Eye took great delight in the King of Kerma's sumptuous gift.

Night was falling when Nedjeh shook One-Eye awake. 'You have had a good sleep, my friend. Before we dine, I should like to show you my latest project.'

One-Eye stretched. Two Nubian girls had drained every last drop of moisture from his body, and he would gladly have lapsed back into restorative sleep. But he could not displease the king.

Accompanied by two bodyguards, Nedjeh led the envoy to the burial-ground, where vast tombs reserved for officials were hollowed out.

'I am going to grant you a new privilege, One-Eye: to visit my tomb, which will be worthy of a great pharaoh. You, the Hyksos, attach little importance to your final dwelling; here, it is different.

I have a palace in my lifetime, and I want another for my death.'

The two men set off along a long, sloping corridor which ended in an antechamber. Beyond it was a vault filled with statues, vases and furniture looted from Elephantine. But the most impressive item was the carpet of human skulls covering the beaten-earth floor.

'I don't like being annoyed,' confessed Nedjeh. 'Anger takes hold of me and makes me kill anyone who contests my power. And you have annoyed me a great deal, One-Eye.'

The Hyksos retreated a pace or two, crushing the bones beneath his feet. There was no way out.

'Listen to me, my lord—'

'Anyone who angers me does not deserve my pardon. But I shall grant you one favour: your skull will remain in this tomb with those of the slaves I killed with my own hands.'

One-Eye tried to force his way out, but he was not strong enough to fight the Nubian, who hurled him to the ground, then broke his neck with a violent blow from his heel. Officially, the envoy would have met a peaceful death in the good city of Kerma.

The emperor would not easily find a Hyksos who knew the region as well as that unbearable lesson-giver. How could vain One-Eye have thought that Nedjeh would tolerate being told how to behave?

CHAPTER 28

A violent hammering on his door awoke Commander Soped in the middle of the night. Irritably, he got up and opened the door. Outside stood the officer in charge of the night watch.

'What is it?' demanded Soped.

'A patrol has just found a curse not far from the main gate.'

'A curse?'

'An ivory throwing-stick with magical signs. Two soldiers tried to pick it up, but it burnt their fingers. The men are very anxious, Commander. They are waiting for you to do something.'

Soped dressed in haste. In the heart of Nubia this kind of event could not be dismissed lightly, because the black sorcerers had real powers. For reasons as yet unknown, one of them had decided to harm the fortress. The urgent thing was to destroy the basis of the curse.

Soped strode across the courtyard and left the fortress by the great gate. He found dozens of Nubian and Hyksos soldiers gathered around the throwing-stick.

'Stand aside,' he ordered.

The moonlight lit up the ivory, on which signs had been drawn – signs which terrified the soldiers of Buhen, especially the rearing cobra and the griffin with its menacing beak.'

'This is nothing,' declared Soped, who was shaking like a wind-tossed palm-tree.

'If it's really nothing,' objected a Nubian, 'pick it up and break it.'

'I'm told it burns. I don't intend to burn myself in order to dispel this magic.'

Everyone realized that he was afraid. The sentries had left their posts and joined their comrades, who could not take their eyes off the mysterious object.

'The cobra's eyes . . . they're glowing red!' one of them exclaimed.

'And so are the eyes of Anubis,' gasped his neighbour.

'Bring me a hammer,' ordered Soped. 'I'll smash the ivory.'

The man who went to fetch the hammer did not return. He was strangled by one of the Medjai who had just entered the fortress through the great gate, which had been left open and unguarded. The attackers would have taken the risk of scaling the walls, but Ahhotep's magic spared them this perilous climb. Swift and agile, they slaughtered the guards in the courtyard, then climbed to the tops of the watchtowers, where they soon dispatched the archers.

'Where is that hammer?' demanded Soped impatiently. He was standing at a respectful distance from the magical ivory, which was still lit by the rays of the moon-god.

The sound of the great gate slamming shut made them all jump, and they swung round in shock.

'The imbecile who did that will be thrown into irons,' promised Soped.

From the tops of the towers volleys of arrows rained down, most of them finding their targets. Soped saw many of his garrison falling around him.

'The Medjai!' roared a Hyksos. 'It's the Medjai – they'll slaughter us to the last man.'

'To the river!' shouted Soped. 'We'll get away on the rescue-boats.'

The survivors ran to the riverbank, but there they were halted in their tracks by a detachment of the army of liberation, commanded by Kamose himself.

Abandoning his men, Soped turned on one of his own officers and killed him, to make it look as if he was fighting for the Egyptians. Then he slunk off towards the Nile. He planned to swim with the current, reach a boat and distance himself from Buhen as swiftly as possible.

The plan would have succeeded had Moustache not foreseen it. He threw himself into the water at the same time as Soped and grabbed him round the neck. 'You're in a big hurry, my friend.'

'I am the commander of the fortress and I have

185

gold, well hidden. Spare my life and you'll be rich.'

'Where is it hidden, this gold?'

'Over there.' Half choking, Soped managed to point to a reedbed. 'In a boat moored in the reeds.'

'We shall go there. But no tricks, or I'll rip out your throat.'

Soped checked that he still had a dagger hidden in a fold of his kilt. That precaution had saved his life more than once. Pretending to be defeated, he swam slowly to the boat.

'There are several bags of gold tied to the hull,' he said. 'All you have to do is dive down and untie them.'

'Well, go on, then.'

The commander dived down into the water, but almost immediately darted up again behind Moustache and tried to stab him in the back. Used to hand-to-hand fighting and this kind of trickery, the rebel seized his attacker's wrist and turned his weapon against him.

'You traitor and coward! It gives me real pleasure to kill you.'

As the blade ripped open his flesh, from belly to heart, the commander's eyes grew glassy.

He was already dead when Moustache cried out in pain. The jaws of a crocodile had closed on his left leg. As the great reptile dragged him towards the bottom, the Afghan jumped on to its back and plunged his dagger into its eye. Maddened with pain, the crocodile let go of its prey and swam away.

With the aid of two Egyptian soldiers, the Afghan got the wounded man back to the riverbank.

'Luckily for you, it was a young crocodile. All the same, the wound is not a pretty sight. We'd better get you back to the fortress straight away.'

On the first day, the military doctor applied meat to the wound. On the second, he used a poultice of bull's fat and mouldy barley-bread, whose medicinal qualities were well known. A drug made from extracts of mandragora, jujube and opium ensured that Moustache felt no pain. Honey and myrrh, used to prevent infection, would eventually heal him.

'Be honest, Afghan. Will I be able to walk again?'

'With no problems at all, and you'll have only a minor scar – it won't even enable you to show off to the girls. Getting yourself bitten by a crocodile is hardly a daring exploit.'

'Without me, that filthy Hyksos would have escaped.'

'Pharaoh Kamose has decided to decorate you for that; and he's decorating me, too, for saving you. What's more, we're being promoted and we're going to lead two attack regiments. Because of your exploits, we're destined for the front line.'

'That's the only thing that interests you, isn't it?'

'Stop thinking for me. It wears me out.'

'Who'd have thought that damned traitor could lure me into a trap with his lies about gold hidden under a boat?'

'But it wasn't lies,' said the Afghan. 'There really was a fine haul of it there, and a share of it will come to you when the war is over.'

'If it ever is over . . .'

A young Nubian girl with a slender body entered the bedchamber where Moustache was being treated.

'This is your nurse,' explained the Afghan. 'She belongs to the Medjai tribe, and knows wonderful herbs which will speed your recovery. Right, I shall leave you now. Looking at sick people depresses me.'

When he saw the girl take off her tiny kilt before preparing a potion for him. Moustache thought he must have a fever.

'It's hot here,' she whispered in a luscious voice, 'and I love being naked. Let me take care of you, brave warrior. You won't be disappointed.'

Queen Ahhotep and Pharaoh Kamose stood at the top of the main watchtower and gazed out over Nubia. The reconquest of Buhen meant that all river traffic was now barred to King Nedjeh. Moreover, the goods transported by the caravans that halted near the fortress now came within the scope of the Thebans, not to mention part of the gold production, which was washed on-site.

'Mother,' said Kamose, 'by persuading the Medjai to become our allies and using that magic ivory, you enabled us to win a great victory, and without losing a single man.'

'It won't always be so.' Ahhotep was silent for a moment, then went on, 'You must appoint a new fortress commander, and administrators who will manage the wealth of the region, and then choose a governor for Nubia.'

'Does that mean that we're turning round and going back to the northern front?'

'Not yet. Even when he learns that we have recaptured Buhen, King Nedjeh will think he is perfectly safe, because he thinks we'll never be able to get past the Second Cataract. He is wrong.'

CHAPTER 29

Even the Medjai did not venture into the Miu region, between the Second and Third Cataracts. Proud that they now belonged to the army of liberation, they were placed under the authority of the new governor of Nubia, and would take on all guard duties in the reconquered territories.

The general opinion was that it would be best to be content with what had been won, and not to provoke the anger of King Nedjeh, who up to now had been silent. By violating his shrine, the Thebans would provoke a ferocious response.

And yet, when the council of war met, Neshi strongly opposed those senior officers who recommended a strategic withdrawal.

'When are you going to stop behaving like frightened women?' he said. 'And how many victories will it take for you to believe at last in our troops' abilities? Our enemies' magic has proved ineffective in the face of Queen Ahhotep's, hasn't it? To make Buhen our new southern frontier would be a grave mistake, because sooner or later Nedjeh would attack it. So let us create a barrier across our enemy's domain and isolate him, as the pharaoh and the queen recommend.'

'But what if nearly all our men are killed?' asked the oldest general, worriedly.

'We are at war,' King Kamose reminded him, 'and we cannot always make progress without losses. Queen Ahhotep's plan is the only feasible one. Tomorrow we shall cross the Second Cataract.'

The two new commanders of the attack regiments were proudly wearing their decorations, a little gold griffin attached to their linen tunics. They met at the foot of the flagship's gangplank.

'All the wounded are to stay here, in the infirmary,' said the Afghan firmly.

'I'm all right,' retorted Moustache. 'But as a precautionary measure I'm bringing my nurse with me. The moment my scar starts hurting, she knows just how to soothe it.'

It was the first time Moustache had spent so much time with a woman. At first, he was afraid he'd be lulled into a tranquil state of mind and forget about the war. But he underestimated the fighting abilities of his young mistress, who practised the games of love as though they were themselves a contest. With her, there was no question of wasting time on endless preliminaries or pointless debate. So the patient had not been allowed very much rest, particularly since the plant remedies prescribed by this sorceress markedly increased his vigour.

From time to time, Moustache shivered. If the crocodile had been a little larger, or the Afghan had acted a little more slowly, he would now have only one leg. If he hadn't been able to fight any longer, he'd have killed himself.

'Stop thinking dark thoughts,' advised the Afghan.

'And you stop reading my mind. You mountain folk are really unbearable! By the way, how did you occupy your time while I was convalescing?'

'Do you think you're the only man who knows how to seduce Nubian girls?'

On the prow of each boat large eyes had been painted, enabling the Egyptian warships to see both the visible and the invisible. Moon appreciated this magical assistance, because he had to stay alert for hours on end in order to ensure that the fleet travelled safely. Ahhotep often stood beside him. She had ordered ivory throwing-sticks to be fixed to the ships' rails, so that their signs of power could drive away evil spirits.

The queen's presence both intimidated and reassured the helmsman. Without her, the army of liberation would long since have dispersed, for fear was strong within their bellies. The simple fact of seeing the Queen of Freedom, feeling her so close and yet inaccessible, gave courage to the most timid.

Moreover, young Pharaoh Kamose was gaining more confidence by the day. Like his father, he had an innate sense of leadership, and during attacks he always fought in the vanguard of his men, refusing to heed his mother's orders to be careful.

In accordance with the pharaoh's orders, Neshi ensured that rigorous cleanliness was practised on board the boats. The decks were washed several times a day, the cabins were carefully cleaned, and everyone smeared their skin with ointment to repel insects. To combat eye irritations, they used the froth from good-quality beer, which was also effective against stomach upsets. Each soldier had two mats wound round with a red leather cord, which he assembled to form a comfortable sleeping-bag. Each meal included onions, which were to be chewed, so that the smell would drive away snakes and scorpions.

'Majesty, we are coming to a village,' said Moon. 'Shall I slow down?'

'Not yet,' replied Ahhotep.

The queen wanted to observe the first reactions of the inhabitants of Miu who were under King Nedjeh's yoke.

At first stunned, the villagers hurriedly grabbed their bows and slingshots. The first arrows fell into the water, but the stones almost hit the prow.

'Take shelter, Majesty,' begged Moon.

'Stop the boat,' ordered Ahhotep.

Already, several soldiers were jumping on to the riverbank, at the risk of broken limbs. But the months of training proved their worth, and

the young Egyptians were able to position themselves so as to strike down their opponents. As
soon as the gangplank was put down, Kamose
joined them and led them to the village, whose
resistance was soon overcome.

A lone Nubian had succeeded in escaping by
diving into the Nile, just in front of the flagship.
He scaled the prow, furiously intent on killing the
sorceress who had opened up the way to the
Egyptian army. He leapt on to the deck and rushed
at Ahhotep.

Pushing past the queen, Moon shattered the
attacker's skull with his long stick. Ahhotep had
not moved, trusting to the helmsman's skilled and
steady hand.

Moon knelt. 'Forgive me, Majesty. I might have
hurt you.'

Ahhotep raised him to his feet. 'I appoint you
to command our naval forces. From now on,
Commander Moon, you shall take all decisions
regarding our ships and boats, and all the other
captains will obey you.'

On dry land, the brief battle was ending. Not a
single Nubian warrior had agreed to surrender,
and two Egyptians were dead. On Kamose's order,
the women and children were allowed to leave.

The conquest of Miu province had begun.

After slitting the throats of a ram and a slave,
whose bones would join those of the Hyksos
envoy, Nedjeh was preparing for a celebratory

feast. There were no fewer than ten dishes, including poultry and an enormous Nile perch. While he was eating, two serving-girls fanned him. As soon as he had finished a dish, one of them washed his hands while the other anointed him with perfume. Nedjeh hated having greasy fingers and liked to smell nice.

The white wine came from the great Khargeh oasis, in the Western desert, and was excellent. Nedjeh never drank less than two large jugfuls with every meal.

'More,' he ordered his cup-bearer. 'Can you not see my cup is empty?'

How pleasant life was at Kerma! Thanks to the region's agricultural wealth, one could live as well there as in the most beautiful Egyptian provinces.

The king's personal scribe arrived at the threshold of the dining-chamber. 'My lord, may I interrupt your meal?'

'What can possibly be so urgent?'

'The Thebans have crossed the Second Cataract and are invading Miu.'

Nedjeh's appetite abruptly vanished. 'Is this information reliable?'

'Unfortunately, yes, my lord. And that is not all.'

'What else?'

'The Thebans have destroyed only one village, but—'

'That's excellent news! So the others have resisted successfully.'

'No, my lord. Queen Ahhotep has spoken to

each village chief and persuaded them all to change sides. From now on they are to be under the protection of the Egyptian troops stationed at Buhen and of Medjai guards. We thought we had subjugated these tribes once and for all, but they now form the first line of defence against us. And also . . .'

'Also what?'

The scribe bowed his head. 'And also there is no reason for the enemy army to stop when it is making such good progress.'

'Do you mean that this woman Ahhotep and her damned pharaoh might dare attack Kerma? That would be a fatal mistake.'

Maddened as a fighting-bull, Nedjeh abandoned several very tempting dishes and ordered the city's officials to be summoned to the vast round council-hut, abandoning their daily business.

Nedjeh did not hide the gravity of the situation from them. This time, it was no longer possible to regard the Theban army as of no importance.

'Ahhotep will establish herself in Miu,' he said, 'and consolidate her position in the hope that we will leave our territory to attack her. But we shall not fall into that trap. On the contrary, we shall lay one for her. The best strategy is to strengthen our town's defences and to mass our troops north of the Third Cataract. The Egyptians will eventually become impatient and advance towards us. Thanks to our knowledge of the terrain, we shall easily wipe them out.'

Appealing to the Hyksos was out of the question. If they intervened, they would use the opportunity to seize Kerma. So Nedjeh must resolve the situation himself. He was beginning to realize what it was that prompted Queen Ahhotep to take so many risks: the taste for conquest.

Seeing that Nedjeh was not reacting, she would think he was at bay and attack his capital like a famished beast. A beast which would fall into a deadly trap.

CHAPTER 30

The sound of drums thundered throughout Miu, but they were not the drums of war. Nubians from every village in the region had laid down their weapons before Pharaoh Kamose and Queen Ahhotep.

The reputation of the great, invulnerable sorceress had spread quickly, and the tribal chiefs had chosen submission in preference to annihilation, particularly since the pharaoh had promised to pardon them, so long as they became faithful allies of Egypt. And every tribe had suffered great cruelty at the hands of Nedjeh, that unscrupulous predator.

Long days of debate proved necessary to establish a clear hierarchy, acceptable to everyone. Several times, Ahhotep's skilful diplomacy averted a split between rival factions, and they were eventually happy to stand together beneath the banner of the young king who would ensure their safety.

'The queen is truly an extraordinary woman,' said the Afghan to Moustache as they gazed at incredible scenes of Egyptian soldiers and Nubian warriors fraternizing: instead of killing each other, they were celebrating, drinking beer and date-wine.

'The only problem,' Moustache pointed out, putting an arm round the nurse who took such good care of him, 'is that the conquest of Nubia isn't our goal. They're waiting for us up there in the North.'

'You are never happy about anything! Take your time, because no one knows what tomorrow will bring. Or rather they do: we shall have to face Nedjeh.'

'You're right. Let's not talk about that tonight. Let's have another drink.'

'What is the situation?' Nedjeh asked the official in charge of defences.

'You should be pleased, my lord. We have dug many ditches, which are perfectly hidden. At the bottom, we have placed well-sharpened stakes. Hundreds of Egyptian footsoldiers will be impaled upon them.'

There was still much to be done, but the work was going well. The Egyptian army would meet only feeble resistance on the outskirts of Kerma and, blinded by its successes, would think that the great Nubian city was defeated in advance. Nedjeh would sacrifice a few men who would fight to the death to defend the main road.

At the head of his troops, Pharaoh Kamose would charge towards a new triumph, and all the Nubian traps would be sprung simultaneously.

The Egyptian advance guard would fall into the ditches, and the rear guard would be wiped out by Nubian archers hidden in the trees and fields. As for the main body of the army, it would be trapped by Nedjeh's footsoldiers. Terrified by this ferocious attack, the Thebans would seek salvation in flight and would be wiped out to the last man.

The skulls of Kamose and Ahhotep would end up in the prince's tomb, and Apophis was certain to congratulate him.

At the thought of the joyful times ahead, the fat man moved with more ease than usual. Ahhotep was wrong if she thought her magic was stronger than his. If he had the good fortune to take her alive, he would make her suffer unspeakable tortures before granting her the mercy of death.

The celebration were still under way. The Nubians rivalled each other in magnificence, wearing red wigs which contrasted with their black skin, gold earrings and kilts decorated with floral patterns. With their necklaces of many-coloured pearls, and bracelets at their wrists and ankles, the Nubian women were irresistibly seductive.

Only Moon and Neshi did not yield to the intoxicating atmosphere. Moon inspected boat after boat, while Neshi was permanently preoccupied with supply matters. Both were perfectionists and thought only of the next battle, which was bound to be terrifying.

This was not the case with Moustache, who had fallen in love with the province of Miu and almost forgotten the Delta of his birth.

'You should settle here and start a family,' suggested the Afghan.

'Me, have children? Are you serious? Live idly here while the Hyksos occupy my country? Sometimes you don't know what you're talking about.'

'Enjoy the rest of the evening and try to have a clear head tomorrow morning. The senior officers have been summoned to the flagship.'

Kamose and Ahhotep listened attentively to the detailed reports given by Moon and Neshi. Moon's appointment had been well received by all the troops, who were also delighted with Neshi's efficiency. Neither man had any problems to report. The war-fleet was ready to set sail for Kerma and attack its ruler, the Hyksos' ally.

This time, most of the soldiers had no fear of the coming battle. Per-Hathor, Elephantine, Buhen, Miu . . . the growing list of their victories gave rise to a solid feeling of comradeship, sustained by Queen Ahhotep's magic.

Kamose himself dreamt of coming face to face with Nedjeh and killing him in his own palace. All that remained was to gain the agreement of the queen, who had consulted the moon-god for a large part of the night.

All eyes turned towards the Wife of God.

'We are retracing our steps,' she declared.

'But, Mother, why not deliver the decisive blow?' asked the king in astonishment.

'Because Nedjeh has set a trap for us and we would not escape unharmed. We would be wrong to think he will not fight back, and that he is resigned to submitting to us. On the contrary, he thinks only of destroying us by means of trickery. We have achieved our objective: Nedjeh is isolated in Kerma. If he tries to leave it, he will come up against our forces in Miu, together with the Medjai and Buhen. What matters most is to make him believe we do indeed intend to capture his kingdom.'

Kamose could not oppose her argument. And he was burning to drive north at last.

'However,' added Ahhotep, 'there is one last thing we must accomplish in Nubia.'

The fleet halted near Aniba, to the north of Buhen. Immediately a caravan was formed and it set off into the western desert, to a quarry begun by Pharaoh Khafra, builder of one of the great pyramids on the Giza plateau. The queen had asked her son to remain on the flagship, and she was accompanied only by fifty men guided by Way-Finder.

As they neared the quarry they saw grey and green stones lying here and there; they also saw unfinished stelae and statues. Warned of the Hyksos invasion, the sculptors had abandoned the quarry, which had lapsed into sleep beneath the burning sun of the Great South.

Seeing that their goal had been reached, Way-Finder halted. Ahhotep gave him and Laughter water to drink. His thirst slaked, the giant dog ran around in all directions, then returned to his mistress.

Ahhotep had obeyed the moon-god and come here, but she did not yet know why. She looked wonderingly upon the unfinished masterpieces and promised that she would reopen this quarry as soon as Egypt was liberated. One day, Nubia must be covered with splendid temples so that the gods might dwell in this proud, burning land.

Alone with her dog at the heart of this overheated stone world, the queen gazed at the seams that had been so carefully cut. They reminded her of the necessary steps that separated her from the final triumph, which was still so far away and unattainable. She would surely need the patience and solidity of stone to wear down the emperor's terrifying strength.

Laughter growled. A royal cobra had slithered out of a crack in the rock and was coming towards Ahhotep. The dog was well aware of the danger, so, despite his courage, he kept his distance while he looked for an angle of attack.

'Stay away, Laughter,' said Ahhotep. 'This is the lord of the quarry. I have come to meet him, so I have nothing to fear.'

Only half convinced, the dog remained wary.

The cobra did not rear up as if to strike. On the contrary, it stretched itself out flat on the ground.

Ahhotep seized it firmly behind the head.

'Look, Laughter! The power that runs through the earth agrees to become my weapon.'

The snake had been transformed into a staff of cornelian, stiff and light.

The dog sniffed it for a long time. Then, satisfied with his examination, he led the queen back to the encampment.

CHAPTER 31

After a night disturbed by his itching skin and one of his wife's bouts of hysteria, which he had cured with a slap, High Treasurer Khamudi got up much earlier than usual.

It was the time of day when one of his Egyptian slave-girls cleaned the rooms, making not a sound so as to avoid disturbing the couple.

What Khamudi saw took his breath away. Unaware that he was there, the slave slipped into a cloth bag a valuable mirror the emperor's wife had recently given him. The slave was actually daring to steal from him in his own home!

'Curse you, what do you think you're doing?'

The girl was so frightened that she dropped the bag. As it hit the stone floor, the precious mirror shattered.

'Forgive me, Master, forgive me! I wanted to sell it so that I could take care of my parents. Believe me, I beg of you!'

Khamudi grabbed a wooden stool and smashed it down on the girl's head. She collapsed to the floor. Maddened with rage, he trampled her underfoot, shouting so loudly that the whole household was aroused. The other servants watched, powerless, as he killed a young woman born of an excellent family in Sais. She had escaped deportation only to die by the hand of an enraged torturer.

'Stop, Khamudi, stop!' shouted Yima, trying to pull him back. 'She's dead!'

Eventually he emerged from his frenzy and calmed down. 'Have hot branding-irons brought to me and summon all my staff.'

Terror-stricken, the slaves were herded into a corner of the room by Hyksos guards.

'The thief who tried to steal my mirror has been suitably punished,' declared Khamudi emphatically. 'So that no one else will try the same thing, I am going to brand everything that belongs to me, whether slaves or objects. You, come here.'

The assistant cook Khamudi pointed at tried to run away, but two guards pinned him to the ground. As Khamudi branded him on the back, the young man let out a heart-rending cry of pain.

Although he usually had a hearty appetite, Khamudi merely toyed with his food.

'Are you ill, my darling?' asked Yima.

'No, of course not.'

'But . . . you're all yellow.'

'Don't talk nonsense.'

'Look at yourself in a mirror, I beg of you.'

Khamudi had to face facts: he did indeed have jaundice.

★   ★   ★

Emperor Apophis was eager to examine an interesting discovery made in the library at the temple in Sais: papyri devoted to geometry, mathematics and medicine. He enjoyed nothing more than the world of figures and calculations, which excluded all human considerations. A thousand deportees, a hundred executions . . . It was so simple and so entertaining to write these quantities on a papyrus, which took on the force of law without his having to listen to cries or protestations. Reducing people to numbers, and manipulating them in the tranquillity of his palace: that was surely the summit of power.

Life, divided up geometrically; the state, directed by mathematics; the economy, subject to equations: that was the goal the emperor had attained. Egypt, the supreme land of the gods, was his own private workshop, where he could experiment as he wished.

The festering stalemate at Qis amused him. Little by little, the army of liberation was rotting on its feet, wondering when the Hyksos troops would at last launch a major offensive. Without the support of Queen Ahhotep and Pharaoh Kamose, the rebels would eventually turn on their leaders.

Apophis's only real concern was the rebellion by the Anatolians, tough fighters whom Jannas was tracking in their mountains, where they had innumerable hideouts. As ever, Jannas was proceeding patiently and methodically: he was quartering the terrain and advancing step by step, avoiding the ambushes the enemy laid. In view of the difficulty

of the operation, Apophis had sent him reinforcements taken from the regiments stationed
in Palestine. Just like the pirates in the Mycenaean
islands, the Anatolians would be wiped out to the
last man.

As he was preparing to attend his Great Council,
the emperor was informed that the High Treasurer
was suffering from severe jaundice. He was
vomiting and unable to take any food.

Was this the moment to rid himself of
Khamudi and replace him? Carefully doctored
medicine would send him discreetly to the tomb
before his charming wife was entrusted to the
tender care of the lady Aberia. But whom could
he find who would be more servile and more
skilful? No one knew more secrets than the High
Treasurer, who managed the empire's interests
– and therefore the emperor's – supremely well.
Khamudi had no wish to take the place of
Apophis, who allowed him to indulge his corrup-
tion and depraved vices and never censured him
for them.

No, the emperor could not find a better right-
hand man. So he consulted an old treatise on
Egyptian medicine.

Lukewarm water and oil injected into the anus
with an ivory horn: these were the only remedies
Yima would allow, fearing her husband would be
poisoned. But Khamudi was fading away under
her very eyes and complaining of pains all over.

'Lady Yima,' a frightened servant informed her, 'it is the emperor!'

'You don't mean . . . The emperor is here, in my house?'

'Yes, my lady. He has just arrived.'

The servants rushed to open all the doors to Apophis, whose dragging gait seemed to embody heavy threats. Whenever she saw him, Yima could not prevent her stomach gurgling ridiculously.

'Majesty, I am deeply honoured.'

'Your husband is fond of luxury,' said Apophis in the harsh voice that froze the blood of even the bravest man. 'But that is normal – my High Treasurer should be a rich man. Khamudi must be cured quickly, so I have brought him a remedy prepared at the palace. It is composed of wine, powdered sisyphus, figs, lotus-leaves, juniper-leaves, fresh incense and sweet beer. The proportions recommended by the doctors of the Old Kingdom have been strictly adhered to. Have him drink it immediately.'

As she took the phial, Yima was rooted to the spot. It was impossible to oppose the emperor's will, but she could not help but realize that he was forcing her to kill her own husband.

Up to that moment, she had believed that Khamudi was so vital to the smooth running of the empire that Apophis would not move against him. But a plotter must have sprung up in the shadows, like a poisonous plant, and it was too good an occasion not to get rid of the current High Treasurer.

'What are you waiting for, Yima? The sooner

Khamudi drinks that remedy, the sooner he will recover.'

'Must he drink all of it?'

'Of course. According to the old papyrus, four days' treatment are necessary. The three other phials will be delivered to you tomorrow.'

Yima was covered in gooseflesh. Not only would there be no other phials but she would be accused of murder and executed.

'Now hurry up, and come back and tell me what the effects are. You know very well that I have no time to lose.'

Biting her lip, Yima entered Khamudi's chamber, where he lay almost unconscious. With a trembling hand, she opened his mouth and poured in the reddish, odourless liquid.

Supporting himself on the shoulder of a servant, Khamudi entered the vast reception chamber. The emperor, who disliked the light, stood in the darkest corner.

Yima walked behind her husband, still not believing her good fortune. Khamudi had drunk the potion, and not only was he not dead but he had immediately felt so much better that he had insisted on getting up to greet his illustrious guest.

'I am still rather weak,' he said, 'but I have my appetite back. Majesty, you saved my life.'

Apophis's satisfied smile did not reassure Yima at all.

CHAPTER 32

Nedjeh was putting the finishing touches to his pitfalls. Soon, the Theban army would advance on Kerma, confident of an easy victory and never suspecting that they would scarcely have time to fight at all. After killing Ahhotep and Kamose, Nedjeh would take back Miu and Buhen. Should he then continue North and recapture Elephantine? Yes, but only to give it straight back to the emperor, in order to win his good graces and prove to him that his faithful ally was content with his own kingdom.

The whole city was on a war footing, and everyone was certain that the enemy would be struck a fatal blow, thanks to Nedjeh's strategic skill.

A scout came in and bowed. 'Majesty, I have just returned from Miu. All the tribes in the province have submitted to Ahhotep, and several times I was almost caught by Egyptian patrols.'

'I should have slaughtered the tribes!' roared the fat man. 'Because of me they have all the food they can eat, yet they betray me in favour of those damned Thebans! When are they going to attack?'

'Soon, or so it would seem. They are strengthening

their positions and fortifying the villages while preparing for the attack. It will not be easy to get more detailed information, but Kerma must be their next objective.'

'Let them come,' murmured Nedjeh hungrily. 'Let them come, and we shall give them the welcome they deserve.'

The young man was proud to be a member of the army of liberation which, although pinned down in one place, was managing to hold off the Hyksos. Despite a few fierce attacks, the enemy had not succeeded in breaking the Theban line.

Born in Qis, the son of peasants, and a peasant himself, the lad had learnt how to fight where he stood, beside Ahmes, son of Abana, who had taught him to dodge aside before crushing an enemy's skull with a heavy wooden club. True, Hyksos helmets were strong, but the young peasant's arm was even more so. Together with his comrades from his village, he could boast of having halted a murderous assault.

'Duck down,' advised Ahmes, who was crouched at the foot of the earthwork he had just built.

'I'm not afraid of anything.'

'The Hyksos are excellent archers. And they handle the slingshot very well, too.'

'No better than we do,' protested the young man, sending a large stone whistling on its way towards the enemy camp.

'Get down!'

It was the last order Ahmes gave the young

recruit. Hit on the forehead by a pointed flint, the peasant died instantly.

A deluge of missiles rained down on the earthworks protecting the main entrance to the Egyptian camp. From time to time the Hyksos unleashed an onslaught like this, pursuing a war of position which went on for ever. But did they know how the Theban forces were dwindling? It was a miracle that they had held out for so long. The messages brought by the carrier-pigeons gave the rebels some comfort, but they were no substitute for fresh troops.

When the slingshots fell silent Ahmes went to the army's headquarters, where Emheb was slowly recovering from a wound in his thigh.

'The pressure is increasing, Governor. We need reinforcements.'

'Every young man from Qis and the surrounding countryside has already joined us. We have no more reserves.'

'Should we not fall back on Thebes with the survivors, before it is too late?'

'And abandon Qis? That would be the start of defeat.'

'It would be a tactical retreat, Governor, nothing more.'

'You know that is not so.'

Ahmes sprinkled his brow with tepid water. 'You're right, I know it isn't. But victories in Nubia are no use to us. It is here that we must fight.'

'You are very young, my boy, and you do not

yet see far into the distance. Queen Ahhotep's decisions are vital for our future, but you won't understand them until later.'

'Later? When we are dead? Our men are exhausted – they have given everything. Leave me here with the bravest, Governor, and go. We'll hold back the Hyksos for as long as we can.'

Emheb got to his feet with difficulty. 'My old leg will soon be better, and I shall hold our position myself.'

'Queen Ahhotep doesn't want us all to die, does she? So let us do what is necessary.'

'The queen is much more remarkable than you could ever imagine,' declared Emheb with feeling. 'Since she embarked upon the liberation of Egypt, she has not made a single mistake. Soon, I am sure, a new message will come from the gods.'

Ahmes wondered if the governor had not also been wounded in the head: whether he liked it or not, Qis was on the point of collapse. 'Let us both try to put on a brave face,' he advised, 'and boost our troops' morale.'

As they left the governor's tent, the sound of fluttering wings made them look up.

'Rascal!' exclaimed Emheb. 'Come here quickly.'

The pigeon alighted gently on the governor's shoulder. A tiny papyrus bearing the royal seal was attached to his left leg.

The message was short and to the point: '*Hold fast. We are coming.*'

*   *   *

The Great Council of the Hyksos was held in the Temple of Set. The emperor was last to arrive. As he passed, everyone bowed low, including the High Treasurer, who had recovered completely, much to everyone's surprise. He must indeed be an important man for Apophis to have treated him instead of killing him.

Swathed in a brown cloak, the emperor was even more sinister than usual. If his eyes lingered too long on an official, death was certain. Today, though, he seemed content to listen to Khamudi's financial reports, without glaring at anyone in particular.

The empire's wealth was continuing to grow, and the temporary loss of Anatolian tributes was not going to reverse that growth. Commander Jannas, at the head of a powerful army, was even now crushing the rebellion, which would undoubtedly be the last.

'We have just received a long message from the King of Kerma by . . . by the usual route,' said Khamudi; he would not reveal the secret means of communication used. 'He pays homage to Emperor Apophis, thanks him for his goodness, and rejoices in the calm that reigns in Nubia. The tribes are obedient, the country is prosperous, and gold will continue to be delivered to Avaris.'

The emperor deigned to smile faintly.

This demonstration of good temper prompted one of the officials to ask the question that was on everybody's lips: 'Majesty, when will the rebels at Qis be wiped out? Their very existence is an insult to Hyksos greatness.'

Apophis's expression hardened. 'You miserable imbecile, don't you realize that it is only by my consent that the front at Qis exists? The Theban puppets are exhausting themselves there for nothing, and the survivors will soon be forced to retreat to Thebes. We shall pursue them and reduce that rebel city to ashes.'

'Do you not fear, Majesty, that Queen Ahhotep may eventually decide to help them?'

Apophis's eyes burnt with an evil flame. 'The emperor of the Hyksos fears no one. That woman Ahhotep is nothing but an upstart whose horrible death will serve as an example to anyone who might think of trying to imitate her.'

As Apophis had received no alarming messages from his spy, whom even Ahhotep could not identify, he knew that the last rebels at the front would obtain no more help.

'I should add,' said Khamudi, 'that Qis has no economic importance. Trade continues as normal through the great control-post at Khmun, which is beyond the rebels' reach.'

The emperor rose, signifying the end of the meeting. With an irritated wave of the hand, he indicated to Khamudi that the insolent man who had dared doubt his omnipotence was to be killed. The man was rather portly, so he would probably be a poor performer in the labyrinth, but he would amuse Apophis for a few minutes.

As he left the Temple of Set, the emperor felt his legs grow so heavy that he gladly sat down on a chair borne by slaves – a chair which the pharaohs of the Middle Kingdom had used before him.

Apophis shut himself away in his secret room at the heart of the citadel. Then he laid his hands delicately upon his blue-glazed flask, on which a map of Egypt had been drawn. When he placed his index finger on Avaris, then on Memphis and Khmun, each glowed bright red.

Reassured, he touched Elephantine. At first the red glow appeared. But very soon it flickered, and in its place appeared strange images: an eye, a rearing cobra, a griffin with a pointed beak, and a jackal's head. By using every bit of his magic, the emperor managed to make the vile things disappear, but Elephantine remained a blue dot on the map. That meant Apophis could no longer win back control: the Thebans had seized the great city and neither Nedjeh nor the Hyksos spy had been able to warn him.

Nedjeh was playing his own game, the spy had been caught and killed, and Ahhotep had won back all the land between Thebes and Elephantine. That was the new reality. There was no longer any question of waiting for Jannas to return before breaking through the front at Qis.

CHAPTER 33

Ahhotep had fixed the ivory throwing-stick bearing the signs of power to one of the highest battlements of the fortress at Elephantine. The eye would blind the emperor, the cobra would extinguish his destructive fire, the griffin would confuse his perception, and the jackal's head would fill his mind with anxiety. At least, that was what the queen hoped. She was convinced that Apophis had cast many spells on Egypt in order to hold it in a prison of curses, whose bars must be broken one by one.

Several boats and crews had remained in Miu, others at Buhen and the rest at Elephantine. Of the army that had originally set sail to conquer the South, barely half remained.

'Is it wise to lose so many soldiers?' asked Kamose worriedly.

'Holding the South is vital,' said Ahhotep. 'But it is true that we shall be short of men to attack the North.'

'In other words, Mother, our attack is bound to fail.'

'Certainly not, my son. Since the beginning of

this war, the situation has always been the same: we are fewer in number and our weapons are inferior, but we are endowed with the energy of the royal cobra that adorns Pharaoh's crown. You must make yourself many, breathe courage into those who lack it, and act with the strength of Horus – but also with that of Set.'

'You can rely on me, Majesty.'

With a pang of nostalgia, Moustache thought of the pretty Nubian girl to whom he had had to bid farewell. Her jet-black, enchantingly soft skin, her breasts, so firm and yet so soft to the touch, her legs, as long as a gazelle's . . . He never stopped reliving the charms of that sorceress, with whom he had almost fallen in love. But he was a warrior, who had no right to become attached to a woman.

Depressed, he headed for the stern of the boat to drink a jar of beer.

Suddenly he stopped in his tracks. A heap of baskets next to the jars had moved. Dagger in hand, Moustache crept closer: there must be a stowaway on board.

'Come out of there!' he ordered.

The baskets moved again, and the Nubian girl's face appeared.

Moustache gaped. 'You, here?'

'I didn't want to leave you, so I hid. I want to go with you, wherever you're going.' She wriggled free and threw her arms round his neck.

'You are just like a panther, a she-cat.'

'She-cat . . . I like that very much. From now on, that is what you must call me.'

'Listen, you have no right to travel on a war-boat and—'

'You're a war-hero, aren't you? Besides, I can fight. All you have to say is that I am your Nubian soldier.'

Moustache sensed that he would not win this particular fight. And as he really had fallen in love, he went to see Moon, who with his usual skill was guiding the fleet towards Thebes.

As they neared Thebes, Ahhotep's heart skipped a beat. This was where she had been born, where she had loved and where the desire for freedom had lit up her life. No other landscape could ever replace the splendour of the Nile, the great Peak of the West, the peaceful fields interspersed with palm-groves. Normally dedicated to peace, this enchanting place had nevertheless been transformed into the home of war, since that was the only language that could be used when dealing with the Hyksos.

She relived the Nubian expedition in her thoughts. It was evident that the Hyksos spy had not harmed it in any way. The conclusion was inevitable: he had stayed in Thebes. The names she was compelled to think of were those of people beyond suspicion. And yet Seqen had indeed been betrayed.

Hailed by cheering crowds, the boat reached its moorings. In accordance with tradition, the queen presented Hathor, patron of boat travel, with an offering of incense to thank her for her protection.

The first to rush up the gangplank was little Ahmose, who leapt into his mother's arms.

'Have you worked hard?' she asked.

'Grandmother and I never stopped. You shall see how beautiful and clean the houses are. We've cleaned everything, even the weapons.'

Teti the Small looked ten years younger. Anyone who had forgotten that the fragile old lady was the queen's mother, charged with watching over Thebes in the absence of Ahhotep and the pharaoh, had been forcibly reminded. Angered by the Thebans' easygoing attitude, Teti had re-established strict rules of cleanliness and, with Qaris and Heray, had seen that they were obeyed. Not a single home or storehouse had escaped being cleansed and purified. Each house was now equipped with jugs and basins for washing thoroughly in the morning, and with a supply of natron, the best of all mouthwashes. The weaving-workshops had produced many tunics for both men and women, who were delighted to renew their clothing.

In the shade of fabric canopies stretched between four stakes, barbers shaved the soldiers each morning and washed their hair, while the ladies' hairdressers worked hard to make them as pretty as possible, not forgetting to anoint them with perfume – it was admittedly still rather basic but it spoke of better days to come. By means of curling-tongs and spatulas for spreading wax, wigs were put back to work. The craftsmen were still a long way from achieving the masterpieces of yore, but they were once again making model wooden heads and slowly regaining their forgotten skills.

Even the most modest of houses was now furnished with mats, storage chests, cooking-pots, ladles, grain-bins, jars for oil and beer, and an amulet representing the god Bes, whose hearty laughter drove away evil spirits. Sturdy brooms, made from long, stiff palm-fibres, enabled house-wives to banish dust, while teams of washermen ensured that linens were kept clean.

The military base had become an attractive small town. Each morning it was filled with the scent of fresh bread. Young Ahmose had not exaggerated: Teti the Small really had been busy.

The most surprised person of all was She-Cat, who marvelled at the sight of the pretty white houses and their well-kept gardens. 'This is not a place to make war,' she said. 'Are we going to live here?'

Moustache smiled. 'You are. I have to leave again.'

'I've told you I won't leave you, and I'm very stubborn.'

'She-Cat, I—'

'Take me into one of those houses and give me a fine tunic. Then we shall make love.'

The closed council meeting took place on the terrace of the royal palace, bathed by the setting sun. The evening was so delightful that, for a few moments, Ahhotep wished she could forget past and future battles, persuade herself that the goal had been attained and there was no need to go any further.

But to yield to that illusion would have been the worst kind of desertion. Besides, she had to hear Qaris's report.

'Majesties, Rascal has returned from Qis. Emheb received your message and awaits you with impatience. Unfortunately, there is a danger of another front being opened up at Kebet. Our lookouts fear a counter-attack by the last supporters of the Hyksos in the region, aided by the garrisons in the forts on the desert road.'

'The safety of Thebes must be guaranteed,' said Kamose. 'Before leaving for the North, we must resolve the problem of Kebet.'

'Emheb and his men must be at the point of exhaustion,' objected Ahhotep. 'We cannot make them wait any longer. You, the wearer of the White Crown, must sail quickly to their aid. I and two attack regiments will take care of Kebet.'

'Mother, that's madness.'

'With respect, Majesty,' put in Heray, 'I agree with Pharaoh.'

'Perhaps, my son, acts of madness are all we have left.'

CHAPTER 34

After embracing his mother, whom he feared he might never see again, Kamose set off for Qis at the head of a reduced fleet, his heart in turmoil.

It took Ahhotep some time to console Ahmose, who was furious at not being allowed to accompany his brother. At last he stopped sulking and agreed to continue training, particularly since Teti had promised not to give him preferential treatment.

'Mother,' asked Ahhotep, 'did you notice anything unusual in Thebes during my absence?'

Teti thought, then shook her head.

'Nothing about Qaris's or Heray's behaviour caught your attention?'

'No. But you can't mean you suspect them of—'

'Be very watchful, I beg you.'

'You aren't really going to venture on the road to Kebet, are you? You said that to reassure Kamose, but you mean to stay in Thebes, don't you?'

Ahhotep smiled. 'You know me so well. Why ask?'

★   ★   ★

The queen had chosen the two regiments commanded by Moustache and the Afghan for a specific reason: their experience of quick, effective raids; she did not have enough men for a frontal assault on the enemy. The little troop would have almost no time to rest and would have to summon their last reserves of strength, especially if they suffered heavy losses.

Ahhotep addressed the soldiers, hiding nothing of the hardships they were about to endure. Not a single man withdrew.

'It's fear, not courage,' explained Moustache. 'They know that the Afghan and I break the backs of deserters. Grant me one favour, Majesty: She-Cat wants to carry my water-skins.'

'Does she know the dangers she'll be facing?'

'A Nubian girl fears neither snakes nor wild beasts. And this one is more stubborn than all other women put together! Oh forgive me. Majesty, I did not mean to say that—'

'We leave in an hour.'

The leading citizens of Kebet gathered in the forecourt of the temple to discuss the future. They dreaded the Hyksos so much that they were planning to change their allegiance, turning their backs on young Pharaoh Kamose, who would never be able to consolidate his power. True, Thebes was holding its head high again, but for how long? It was no good thinking about it: this rebellion would not last long, and only those who collaborated with the emperor would escape his vengeance. Voices in favour of rallying officially to the Hyksos cause were beginning to ring out when the Queen of Egypt made her appearance.

Attired in a gold diadem and a simple white dress, Ahhotep was more beautiful than ever. The crowd fell silent and bowed.

'The wounds of the occupation are still far from healed,' she said, 'and Kebet needs many repairs. Instead of debating idly, you should be at work.'

'Majesty,' said the High Priest of Min, 'we are your faithful servants and—'

'I know that you were preparing to betray me because you do not believe in Thebes's final victory. You are wrong.'

'You must understand, Majesty, the Hyksos are threatening us.'

'I am here to liberate the desert road for ever, and to guarantee Kebet's safety. If you show any more signs of cowardice, you will have me for an enemy.'

The queen's actions gave Kebet renewed life. She set out a programme of urgent works and appointed new administrators who would be responsible directly to her. The common people could approach and speak to her, and that simple contact brought hope to life again.

As always, the Afghan and Moustache looked on admiringly.

'She really is extraordinary,' said the Afghan yet again.

'Be content with obeying her,' advised Moustache, 'and don't waste time on crazy dreams. Every man in Egypt is in love with her, except me, now that I've got my Nubian girl – and even that's not certain.'

'There isn't a woman like her in the world. Even the most battle-hardened war-leader would have lost heart long ago, but she hasn't. The fire in her is not of this world.'

'But we are. This may be our last night on this earth, Afghan, so let's make the best of it.'

The queen had granted leave to all her men, and the taverns of Kebet welcomed them warmly. Everyone preferred not to think of the coming day.

While talking to a caravan-owner, the Afghan, although he was tipsy, had an idea which might save many Theban lives.

'Come on, Moustache, we must speak to the queen.'

'She'll be asleep.'

'Never mind. We'll wake her up.'

Heavy-footed, the two men headed for the governor's palace, where Ahhotep was staying. Not only was she not asleep, but she was actually implementing the plan – which she had thought of long before the Afghan did.

The first Hyksos fort stood about two hours to the east of Kebet and held absolute control of the road. No caravans could reach the city, because the emperor's soldiers intercepted them and stripped them of their goods.

This plunder made the difficult desert living-conditions bearable, but the Hyksos had not given up the idea of retaking Kebet. Soon the garrisons of the five forts between the town and the Red Sea would unite to attack the city. It had been sent an ultimatum: either it recognized the emperor's supremacy, or its entire population would be slaughtered.

'Caravan in sight!' shouted a lookout.

The commander of the fort joined him at his observation post. It was indeed a caravan, and a sizeable one, but it was not coming from the desert.

'It's coming from Kebet,' said the commander, 'and they must be important people. They're surrendering! Look at them, all those frightened people, and all the riches they're going to lay at our feet. Let's run the mayor through and decapitate the others.'

'I'd like to keep the donkey,' said the lookout. 'I've never seen such a fine one.'

'I'm the commander here, and I'll decide who gets what from the booty. Forget that donkey and think of the Kebet girls – they'll lick your feet and beg for mercy.'

Laughing heartily, the Hyksos let the donkeys approach, with the dignitaries and their servants. The governor of Kebet and his retinue were trembling, afraid they would be shot by the archers before they had even reached the gate of the fort. But they were so pitiful that the emperor's men didn't bother to waste their arrows. Torture would be much more amusing.

'Lie face down in the dust,' ordered the commander.

The dignitaries did so, looking more and more terrified.

Way-Finder gave the signal for the attack, by charging the officer and butting him hard. The Theban soldiers stopped pretending to be servants and threw their double-bladed daggers with deadly precision.

Meanwhile, Moustache, the Afghan and ten men arrived by means of a minor road shown on a map which had belonged to the traitor Titi. Taking advantage of the enemy's slackness, they scaled the watchtower and killed the archers.

In less than a quarter of an hour, the Hyksos garrison was wiped out. The Egyptians had suffered only two casualties, and they were minor wounds which She-Cat was already treating.

'You played your part well, Governor,' said Ahhotep, 'and so did your people.'

The governor was still shaking. 'Majesty,' he begged, 'may we go home now?'

'We still have four more forts to capture,' replied the queen with a broad smile.

CHAPTER 35

The last Hyksos attack had been murderous. With a courage bordering on foolhardiness, Ahmes, son of Abana, had managed to whip up the bravery of a hundred terrified youths and they had fought off a raiding-party of black-helmeted footsoldiers, the very sight of whom scared them out of their wits.

Once the attack had been repulsed, only ten exhausted survivors were left. Covered in enemy blood, Ahmes did not even take the time to wash before speaking to Emheb.

'It is finished, Governor. We can no longer hold the line.'

'The message Rascal brought was perfectly clear,' Emheb reminded him.

'The Thebans have been delayed or killed – either way, they won't come. If we don't fall back, we'll be wiped out.'

The governor did not protest: Ahmes was right. 'Give me one more day.'

'If the Hyksos launch another attack, we won't be able to hold. It would be playing with fire.'

'As a general rule, they take their time – sometimes a lot of time – before they attack again.'

'As a general rule, yes. But this time they saw that the front was no thicker than a sycamore leaf. In their place, I'd attack in the next few hours.'

'We'll organize our defence as best we can, and prepare to retreat.'

Emheb had spent the night burying corpses in simple, hastily dug trenches. There were no sarcophagi, no papyri bearing the words of resurrection, not even an ordinary protective amulet. The governor could do nothing but speak an ancient invocation to Osiris, beseeching him to welcome into paradise these young men, who had not hesitated to give their lives in an attempt to vanquish the empire of darkness.

And then dawn rose over an Egyptian camp which had no strength left. Two seriously wounded men died before the first rays of the sun were seen. Emheb buried them, too.

'You must get some sleep,' urged Ahmes.

'Have you slept?'

'I haven't had time. We strengthened an earth bank, positioned defensive stakes and rebuilt low brick walls behind which our last archers will shelter. But it's all useless . . .'

'The boats are ready to leave. See that the wounded are embarked.'

It was more than a dream crumbling, much more. Once the front at Qis had given way, the

Hyksos would pour south and put Thebes to fire and the sword. After Ahhotep, no one would take up the torch. The invaders' barbarity would become the common law, and the empire of darkness would grow ever larger.

On the Hyksos side, all seemed quiet, and that was even more worrying. The enemy was probably awaiting the order from Avaris to launch the final attack and sweep away the rebels.

Emheb ordered most of the soldiers to leave their posts and board the boats. Only the front line, made up entirely of volunteers, would remain in position.

'Your cabin has been cleaned, Governor,' said Ahmes. 'You can go aboard.'

'No, I'm staying here. You are to take command until you reach Thebes.'

'But, sir, you'll be needed there.'

'Our world is on the point of death, my boy, and "there" no longer exists. I'd rather fight to the end with these lads. They're half dead with fear, but they refuse to give in.'

'Then I shall stay as well. I'm the best archer in the Egyptian army, and I shall slow the Hyksos down a bit.'

The two men embraced.

'Take the left flank,' ordered Emheb, 'and I'll take the right. When we can no longer hold the line, the survivors will regroup on the hill.'

Ahmes knew only too well that they would not have time.

Emheb had one final fear: that the Hyksos attack would begin before the boats left and that the whole flotilla would be sunk before they could get away. So they were cast off quickly, at the risk of causing an accident. Fortunately nothing untoward happened. The north wind swelled the sails and the voyage to Thebes began.

Without a word, Emheb and Ahmes moved to their combat positions.

'Sir,' said Ahmes disbelievingly, 'they're coming back.'

He stood up, but with a firm hand Emheb forced him down on to his belly again.

'The boats – I swear to you, they're coming back!'

Emheb crawled up to a small hillock from which he could see the Nile but was out of range of Hyksos arrows.

The youth had good eyesight. But why were those who could escape death returning to Qis? There could be only one explanation: enemy vessels had forced them to turn back.

Nothing. Emheb could do nothing more to save them. He and the front line were caught like rats in a trap. He decided to order the footsoldiers to disperse. But one thing puzzled him: on the decks of the boats, there was not a single sign of commotion. He even thought he saw sailors dancing for joy.

A light shone from the powerful warship that seemed to be pursuing them.

At first Emheb was dazzled, then he realized that the sun's rays were glinting off the 'Resplendently Bright One', the White Crown of Pharaoh Kamose.

In his last report, the Hyksos general commanding the front at Qis had fully reassured the emperor: the war of attrition had proved effective, and the Egyptians were at their last gasp. It was therefore pointless to move an army from the Delta. One last attack would suffice to destroy the last remnants of the front.

'Is everything ready?' he asked a member of his staff.

'Yes, General. Your orders have been given to the officers.'

'This will be almost too easy,' thought the general.

After this wretched war, which had been at stalemate for so long, the Hyksos would take delight in disembowelling the last rebels. And the general's victory would be in Avaris, where he would certainly receive promotion. His boat would sail proudly up the main canal, with Governor Emheb's severed head at its prow.

Suddenly, a strange noise made him jump. 'What's that?'

'I've never heard it before,' said the assistant, his stomach turning over.

No Hyksos, indeed, had ever heard the maddening beat of the drums. Made in Nubia, they gave out fierce resonance, which put the fear of death into the Hyksos' hearts.

'It's a new curse from Queen Ahhotep,' exclaimed the assistant.

'The Hyksos will never retreat because of some damned music!' swore the general. 'Prepare to attack.'

A lookout ran up, his body dripping with sweat. 'General, the Egyptian front line has been re-inforced. There are at least three times as many soldiers there now, and more are still arriving.'

'Where are they coming from?'

'From boats arriving from the south, sir. I've even seen Egyptians congratulating each other, as if they're no longer afraid.'

Shaken, the general decided to check for himself. He followed the lookout up to a promontory from where he could see the enemy front line. What he saw took his breath away.

On the highest hillock fluttered a standard bearing the emblem of Thebes, a bow and arrows. And the man who was holding it firmly in his right hand was young and strong, and wore the White Crown of Upper Egypt, which seemed to give off powerful rays of magical light.

CHAPTER 36

The din of the Thebans' night-long celebrations, which were accompanied by drums, plunged the Hyksos into uncertainty.

Roasted lamb, bean paste, soft cheeses . . . With their bellies and hearts full of the joy of the feast, the Egyptians had the strength to believe in victory again. Now that supply-boats could get through, they were regaining the strength they would need to fight the emperor's troops.

Kamose was less optimistic. He did not hide the reality of the situation from Emheb. 'The messages brought by the carrier-pigeons inform me that my mother has taken the Hyksos forts on the road from Kebet to the Red Sea. But she has had to station Egyptian soldiers there as garrisons, and we have left many others in Nubia and at Elephantine, to hold our positions. I hope that she will soon join us, but with how big an army?'

'In other words, Majesty, we need more men.'

'We cannot mass all our forces at Qis. The Nubians would counter-attack from the south, and Thebes would be in danger.'

'Then we shall resort once again to a war of trenches and attrition. If the Hyksos repeat their savage attacks, how often will we be able to repel them?'

'I don't know,' confessed the pharaoh, 'but we shall not withdraw.'

'All is ready, Majesty,' declared the High Priest of the Temple of Set, as the bearers set down the emperor's chair and he stepped out.

Unlike the pharaohs, Apophis did not begin his day by celebrating a ritual. Usually he came to the shrine only to head a Great Council meeting, which often ended with the killing of an official who had become too insipid for his taste. This time, though, he was alone.

'You and your fellow priests, leave us,' he ordered.

There was such menace in the emperor's eyes that the High Priest scuttled away.

Apophis entered the temple. The oil-lamps had been extinguished, but he moved easily through the shadows. On an altar at the far end, the priests had laid a beautiful statuette of Hathor. The face was so finely sculpted that it quivered with life. The curves of the body expressed at once love, nobility and tenderness.

On another altar lay five daggers.

'Obey me, Set,' commanded the emperor. 'Help me to destroy those who oppose my will.'

Thunder rumbled overhead. Thick black clouds

massed above the temple, and dogs bayed at the moon. There was only one bolt of lightning, but it was so fierce that it tore open the whole sky. It struck the daggers, whose blades became incandescent.

With the first, Apophis decapitated the statuette and cut off its feet. He plunged two blades into its breasts and two more into its belly.

'Die, accursed Ahhotep!'

After halting beneath a carob-tree with thick foliage, and savouring its honey-sweet fruits, the queen headed for the temple at Dendera, which was surrounded by tall sycamores. By means of raids organized by Moustache and the Afghan, the Thebans had liberated, one by one, the villages still controlled by the Hyksos. The peasants had been swift to lend their aid to the army that had delivered them at last from unbearable tyranny.

Suddenly, Ahhotep felt a sharp pain in her chest. Ignoring it, she walked on towards the Temple of Hathor, which she feared she would find laid waste. But fire flowed into her feet, and she had to stop.

'Are you unwell, Majesty?' asked the Afghan anxiously.

'I'm a little tired – it's nothing serious.'

The next pain, in her stomach, was so bad that she could not breathe, and had to sit down. When her thoughts began to become confused, she realized what had happened.

'It's a curse. The emperor – it must be him. Take me into the temple.'

Moustache and the Afghan ran to fetch a small boat from the canal where it was moored, and laid the queen in it. Twelve men lifted it up, ran to the great, crumbling gateway, and hurried through it.

In the great courtyard lay broken stelae and statues. The likenesses of Hathor framing the entrance to the covered temple had been decapitated and mutilated.

Three frightened priestesses, two young and one very old, greeted them on the threshold.

'Do not violate this sacred place,' said the old one. 'To enter, you will first have to kill us.'

'We are with the army of liberation,' declared Moustache. 'Queen Ahhotep is ill and needs your help.'

The boat was set down upon the flagstones.

Queen Ahhotep! The old priestess remembered her visit to Dendera with her husband, Pharaoh Seqen. She had given them the *heka*, the magical power that conferred the ability to influence the course of destiny. Today, though, its force seemed to have run dry.

'The Emperor of Darkness is trying to seize my soul,' said the queen. 'Only the Golden Goddess can tear me from his grasp.'

The priestess laid her hand on Ahhotep's forehead. 'There is not a second to lose, Majesty. The fire of Set has already invaded most of your energy-channels. One of you men, help the queen to move.'

With Moustache's agreement, the Afghan lifted

her in his arms, carrying his precious burden with anguish and reverence. Fortunately, the priestess walked slowly, and he was able to follow her without stumbling.

Despite the Hyksos' threats, the High Priestess of Dendera had not revealed the hiding-place where Hathor's sacred objects were kept; even under torture, she had kept silent. Today she was being rewarded for her courage. She opened the sliding door of the secret room where the crown, sistra, necklaces and water-clock belonging to the Golden Goddess had been hidden. On the walls were painted scenes which She alone might see.

'Lay the queen on the ground,' she told the Afghan, 'and leave.'

When the door closed, a light sprang forth from a strange painting, an oval surrounded by a broken line, the first wave of creation, which had passed through matter and brought it to life. The vibration made the wall and Ahhotep's body tremble.

'The queen's soul is immersed in the *duat*, the starry matrix where the many forms of life are ceaselessly born,' explained the High Priestess. 'She must remain there for seventy hours, in the hope that the energy of Hathor will be more powerful than that of the Emperor of Darkness.'

'Aren't you certain?' asked Moustache worriedly.

'I don't know what kind of forces Apophis has used. If he called upon Set, who causes tumult in the universe, all Hathor's love will not be too much.'

'But surely the queen is in no danger of dying?' whispered the Afghan.

'May the Golden Goddess welcome her into her ship, which cuts through the darkness.'

At the end of the seventieth hour, the High Priestess of Dendera opened the door of the secret room. For what seemed an eternity, 'there was nothing but silence. Moustache bit his lip, while the Afghan stood still as a stone.

Eventually, Ahhotep appeared on the threshold of the little room that could so easily have been her tomb. Very pale, and walking unsteadily, she emerged from the darkness of the *duat*.

Seeing her sway, the Afghan offered her his arm.

'You must eat, Majesty,' urged Moustache.

'Before she does so, I must ensure that the queen is protected,' decreed the High Priestess. 'Wearing the goddess's necklace, she will be safe from another attack.'

The priestess entered the crypt and emerged with a *menat*. It was a strange object, formed from a necklace of gold beads and turquoises linked by two short cords to a gold counter-weight which ended in a disc, which was to be placed on the nape of the neck.

'With this symbol, the goddess transmits the magical fluid of life, which enables mothers to give birth and sailors to reach port safely. When it is held before the statue of Hathor, sadness and turmoil are dissipated. Harmful waves will break upon it.'

She placed the *menat*-necklace round Ahhotep's neck.

'It is thanks to you, Majesty, that the province of Dendera has been liberated. But how can Egypt be reborn while the temple at Abydos is still under the Hyksos threat?'

CHAPTER 37

Kamose's passionate speech had reassured the Egyptian soldiers. Apophis, he said, was a 'weak-armed man whose empty heart boasted of false victories'. With such a pharaoh to lead them, the Thebans would never retreat. And when Queen Ahhotep joined forces with them, they would at last strike northwards.

There was another reason for hope: the new weapons with which the front-line troops were now equipped. Strengthened with bronze strips, the wooden shields would protect them much better from Hyksos arrows and spears. Their own spears, which now had longer, sharper bronze heads, would kill the enemy more easily, as would their sharper swords; and their new axes were easier to handle. The new helmets and breastplates, which were covered in bronze plates, would be invaluable in hand-to-hand fighting.

With this new equipment, the soldiers of Kamose and Ahhotep felt almost invulnerable. True, the fear inspired by the black-helmeted warriors was far from gone, but every man felt able to face them.

And yet, out of sight of his men, the young king's expression was sombre.

'The news is good, Majesty,' announced Emheb. 'Rascal has just brought a message saying that Queen Ahhotep has liberated the province of Dendera. She is heading for Abydos.'

'Even if she manages to join us, she'll bring no reinforcements. And if we don't take action, the Hyksos will eventually crush us.' What, he wondered, would Ahhotep have done in this situation? He was determined to prove himself worthy of her, and not merely be content to hold the ground that had been gained. He said, 'Since we're so short of volunteers, we must persuade the reluctant men to fight on our side.'

'Are you thinking of the sailors, caravaneers or mercenaries the Hyksos employ in this region?'

'We must win them over.'

'These are men without faith or honour, Majesty.'

'Then we had better give them some.'

The caravaneers unloaded the donkeys under the protection of mercenaries paid by the Hyksos. So close to the front, this kind of precaution was a necessary one. According to the latest rumours, a young pharaoh wearing the White Crown had even reached Qis. True, there was talk of a forthcoming offensive which would inflict final defeat on the Thebans, but there was still a risk that the rebels would attack convoys of goods. Only the presence of Apophis's armed men would deter them.

As usual, the animals were unloaded without incident.

Just as the Hyksos were leaving, Ahmes, son of Abana, let fly his first arrow, which killed their commander instantly. With his usual calm and precision, he decimated the enemy's ranks, assisted by other elite archers.

Frozen to the spot beside their wares, the traders saw their protectors being massacred but dared not run away. And they were in no way reassured when they saw Kamose, wearing the dazzling White Crown.

'You have been collaborating with Apophis,' he declared, 'and are therefore enemies of Egypt.'

The traders' leader fell to his knees. 'Majesty, we have been oppressed! Understand us and forgive us. Egypt reigns in our hearts.'

Kamose smiled. 'I am happy to hear that. Luckily for you, the time has come for you to prove your allegiance.'

The man's expression changed. 'Majesty, we are peaceful men and—'

'We are at war,' the pharaoh reminded him, 'and every man must choose sides. Either you stand on the side of the Hyksos, in which case you will be executed for treason, or you will fight with us.'

'But, Majesty, we have no experience of fighting.'

'My instructors will assign you tasks within your capabilities.'

Since there was no way out, the merchant tried to gain an important advantage for his fellow traders. 'The trade-tax control-post at Khmun is choking the life out of us, Majesty. The officers are Asiatics and sand-travellers who steal vast quantities of goods. Are you planning to make changes?'

'That tax-post exists only because of the occupation.'

'So if you are victorious, it will be removed?'

'If *we* are victorious, it will.'

A broad smile lit up the man's face. 'We are your loyal subjects, Majesty, and we shall fight to the best of our ability.'

When they saw the detachment commanded by Kamose coming towards them, the villagers fled in terror and hid in their adobe houses. Like many tiny villages to the east of Qis, this one was under the thumb of a mercenary called Large-Knees, assisted by twenty rough fellows; they imposed a reign of terror by applying every one of the Hyksos decrees. Every man had his vocation, and Large-Knees had never lived better than he had since he entered the emperor's pay. He bled the population dry, enjoyed women who would otherwise have been out of his reach, and beat anyone who dared show him disrespect.

'Sir,' shouted one of his men, 'we're being attacked!'

Somewhat fuddled by beer, Large-Knees took several moments to realize that the incredible was happening. Of course, the front at Qis existed, and some people even spoke of the army of liberation's determination. But he had never believed in it. And now here was a band of Thebans, daring to attack his domain!

Although sceptical about the Thebans' ability to advance, Large-Knees had nevertheless foreseen this show of strength. If they thought they could make him submit, they were going to have a nasty surprise.

'Have you done what is necessary?'

'Have no fear, sir.'

Large-Knees got a shock when he emerged from his quarters. The attackers' leader was an athletic young man, wearing a crown so white that it hurt the eyes to look at it.

'Lay down your weapons,' ordered Kamose. 'My men outnumber yours, and you have no chance of winning.'

'The King of Thebes is not wanted on my territory,' retorted Large-Knees with a sneer.

'You have betrayed Pharaoh by selling yourself to the Hyksos. Bow before me or you shall die.'

'My only master is Apophis. If you don't withdraw at once, you will be responsible for the deaths of all the children in this village. You see that barn over there? They have all been gathered in there, and my men won't hesitate to cut their throats as soon as I give the order.'

'What kind of person could commit such an atrocity?'

Large-Knees sniggered. 'The Hyksos have schooled me well. You're nothing but a weakling, because you still believe in the existence of Ma'at.'

'Surrender – you still have time.'

'Leave my land, or the children will be executed.'

'Amon is my witness that not a single villager will die,' declared Kamose, turning to Ahmes.

The archer's arrow plunged into Large-Knees' left eye, and he toppled backwards, dead.

Deprived of their leader and cowed by Kamose's resolution, the mercenaries threw down their swords and bows. They had no wish to die.

'The hostages are safe,' said Large-Knees' second-in-command.

'To make amends for your deeds, there is only one thing you can do: obey me and swear to fight the Hyksos. If you break your word, the Soul-Eater will devour you in the afterlife.'

The soldiers took the oath. Only too happy to have emerged unscathed, they were not unhappy to place themselves under the command of a true leader.

'You will go to the neighbouring village with a detachment of my men,' Kamose ordered his new soldiers. 'There, you will urge the leader of the local guards to do as you have done and join our ranks. Otherwise he will suffer the fate of a bandit who subjugated you.'

CHAPTER 38

Abydos lay north of Dendera and south of Qis, and was consecrated to Osiris, master of eternal life. Although the sacred city had no economic importance, it housed the stelae of those people 'of just voice' who had appeared successfully before the two courts of earth and heaven.

The queen and her soldiers had pitched camp a good distance from the temple, which was plunged in silence. There was no trace of a Hyksos presence in the surrounding area. After several raids, which had enabled them to liberate the villages between Dendera and Abydos, the Thebans were grateful for a few hours' rest.

'There's no one left here,' said Moustache. 'As soon as my men have recovered their strength, shouldn't we head for the front with all due speed?'

'The Hyksos have replaced life with death,' said Ahhotep. 'At Abydos, Osiris transforms death into life, and we must first make sure that only radiant spirits reign there. Once Egypt is free, Abydos will once again become a magnificent, prosperous

249

temple. The stelae of the just will be raised up again, and priests and priestesses will celebrate the cult and the mysteries of the god, as in days gone by.'

Ahhotep's words made happiness seem more than an illusion. And her voice continued to awaken hope, even in those who thought they had lost it for ever.

Like the other soldiers, Way-Finder and Laughter forgot the war for a whole day. The donkey feasted on delicious thistles, while the dog sprawled in the shade of a sycamore tree and gnawed a bone.

Towards the middle of the following morning, the party approached the temple, which was partially hidden by wild grasses.

'I could swear I hear someone mourning,' said Moustache.

'So can I,' agreed the Afghan.

On the ancient processional road leading from the shrine to a little wood appeared ten priests, whose funereal chants related the murder of Osiris by his brother Set. They seemed profoundly moved by the drama they were re-enacting, and moved extremely slowly. At their head walked a tall fellow, his head covered by a hood, and the two who brought up the rear carried clubs to strike down the followers of Set, the enemies of Osiris.

So the ancient cults were still being celebrated, even if only in token fashion.

Just as Ahhotep was approaching the priests,

Way-Finder charged forward and knocked over the man in the hood, who fell heavily.

Leaping angrily to his feet, he took a dagger from a pocket of his tunic and tried to plunge it into the donkey's chest. But he had not bargained on Laughter, who leapt at the attacker and sank sharp teeth into his arm.

The priests armed with clubs ran at Ahhotep, intending to shatter her skull. The queen dodged the first blow, but she would not have escaped the second if the Afghan's powerful hand had not first blocked the assailant's wrist, then broken it. A second attacker could not escape Moustache, who head-butted him, smashing his nose.

'They are Hyksos!' declared one mourner, as he and the other true priests prostrated themselves at the queen's feet. 'They forced us to lay this ambush.'

Before trusting their words, the Thebans interrogated them at length. It emerged that they had indeed been taken hostage by three Hyksos, who were determined to kill the queen, even if they died in the attempt.

With tears in her eyes, Ahhotep wandered through the dirty, dilapidated temple; almost nothing remained of its ancient splendours. After meditating before the defaced scenes depicting the stages of Osiris's resurrection, she ventured into the desert, where houses of eternity had been created, far from the cultivated lands. These simple, long, narrow brick-walled chambers bore witness to the crucial period when which Upper and Lower Egypt had formed a single country for the first time. The Hyksos barbarians had taken no interest in these modest tombs.

Although the place was not imbued with sadness, Ahhotep felt so alone that the force of her will was shaken. True, the Egyptians' successes far exceeded even their wildest hopes. But was it possible to go further? On reflection, the wounds they had inflicted on the monster were only superficial. No doubt the emperor had allowed the queen to rush about like an insect, which would be easily crushed when the time came.

To go beyond Qis was a foolish dream. Beyond Qis began the true territory of the Hyksos, whose weapons were still far superior to those of the Egyptians. The tyrant would never allow Pharaoh Kamose to impinge upon his domain. But not to continue northwards, not to re-unify the Two Lands, meant losing the war and accepting once and for all an occupation which would only grow worse and worse.

Ahhotep halted before a tomb. On the offertory table before the entrance stood a small wine-jar, dedicated to Pharaoh Aha.

Aha's name meant 'the Fighter', so this must be a message from the pharaohs who had ruled at that time. She had to fight. There was no other way. She would fight to the death if necessary, and never give up the supreme goal: reunification.

When Ahhotep walked once again through the

Temple of Osiris, all traces of doubt had disappeared. The spirit of the ancient kings had entered her, demanding that she look beyond the horizon of Thebes.

Under the watchful eyes of Moustache and the Afghan, a priest approached her and presented a request.

'Majesty, our High Priest is still alive. He knows the incantations needed to celebrate the rites once again, and bring back life to the names of those judged righteous by Osiris. So that his wisdom is not lost, we have hidden him in a nearby village. Since you have liberated us from the Hyksos, will you bring him back here?'

Moustache frowned. 'It looks like a trap, Majesty.'

'A trap?' protested the priest. 'What do you mean? We wish only to bring our High Priest back to his home.'

'It looks more and more like a trap.'

'We shall go to the village,' decided Ahhotep.

'Majesty, at least take one precaution,' advised the Afghan. 'Make this priest walk in front of us and serve as a shield.'

The village nestled on a mound overlooking a canal. The Hyksos guard-post, which lay below, had posed no problem for Moustache, who had needed only two men to destroy it.

A handful of small children ran up, shouting for joy. A little boy jumped into the queen's arms and kissed her on both cheeks. Anxious mothers joined them, watched suspiciously by Moustache. Then the men dared to emerge from their houses, raising their hands high to show that they were unarmed.

'Is our High Priest still here?' asked the priest anxiously.

'He is, and he's safe and well,' replied the village headman.

Despite his advanced age, the High Priest was a vigorous man. Overcome with emotion, he bowed before the queen. 'I cannot believe it, Majesty! Is Abydos truly free?'

'You may return to the temple. Erect a stele in honour of Pharaoh Seqen, who is of just voice, and ensure that it is glorified each day.'

'It shall be done, Majesty. Forgive my curiosity, but have you decided to establish the border at Qis or to reconquer the North?'

'Egypt will survive only if she is reunified.'

'You speak words of gold, Majesty! But to have any hope of success, you must know the contents of the Jar of Predictions, which reveals good and evil days. Without that list, you will make mistakes and suffer heavy losses.'

'Where is the jar?'

'At Khmun.'

CHAPTER 39

As labourers unloaded the boxes sent from Asia, guards surrounded the port of Avaris. Khamudi had ordered that no one was to go near the boat, and that its cargo must be brought immediately to the palace.

As soon as it arrived, the High Treasurer abandoned his work to gaze upon the many ceramic vases. Admittedly they were rather vulgar, but their contents were priceless. As soon as he was alone in the huge cellar, he opened one of them.

It contained opium, which would be sold at a very high price to senior Hyksos officers and citizens of Avaris and the Delta cities. With the emperor's agreement, Khamudi had embarked upon the development of this new trade, which promised to be exceptionally profitable. While trying it out on some of his own entourage, he had found that users quickly became addicted to the drug and demanded more of it. Since it was the state's responsibility to ensure the well-being of those it administered, it should also derive the maximum benefits, the major part of which would go – quite rightly – to swell the emperor's fortune.

There was another, not inconsiderable benefit: many people would become dependent upon the supplies provided by Khamudi, and prices would therefore continue to rise. In a few months, the drug would have swamped all the provinces of the empire, and he would reap colossal profits. But he must first ensure that the opium was of high quality.

Taking with him a pretty, slender red vase, he returned to his house, where he found Yima having her body waxed.

'Back already, my darling?' she said.

'I have a nice surprise for you.'

'As soon as my servant has finished, I—'

'Send her away.'

Afraid of being beaten, the servant-girl hurried away.

Khamudi lit an incense-burner and heated some small balls of opium. 'You are going to sample this for me, my sweet.'

'What is it?'

'A delicacy.'

Yima enjoyed the gift. To judge from her reaction, which was of excitement punctuated with moments of apathy, Khamudi's customers were sure to be delighted.

Minos added a touch of pale blue to the pillar in the audience chamber at the palace, one of the details of the great wall-painting he was working at with meticulous care. He was a perfectionist, and painted the same figure several times before he was satisfied with it.

When a hand caressed his shoulder, he laid down his brush slowly. 'Windswept? You must let me work.'

'You've spent hours wearing yourself out, trying to make this dreary room more agreeable. It's time to enjoy yourself, don't you think?'

She pressed herself against the Minoan. The curves of their bodies fitted together perfectly, as if they had been created for each other.

'You're mad,' he said. 'Someone might catch us.'

'How exciting that is,' she whispered, untying her lover's kilt and revealing his obvious arousal.

'Windswept, no—'

'I'm in love with you, Minos, truly in love. Nothing should be forbidden to us.'

Although she was still a formidable carnivore, and still devoured the emperor's enemies by extracting bedroom confessions, she was sincerely in love with the painter, whose innocence had touched her heart. The more bored she grew in the arms of her fleeting lovers, the more intense was the pleasure she felt each time she gave herself to him. She could no longer do without him. She would never allow him to return to Minoa, even if she let him believe otherwise.

'Your paintings grow more and more beautiful,' she murmured, stretching out on top of him.

'I have made a new shade of blue, which gives

greater warmth, and I'm planning to improve my other colours.'

'Will you remake your old paintings?'

'I shall have to.'

'The beauty you have created makes this fortress almost pleasant.'

'Please let's not talk about work any more. I'd rather pay attention to the work of art I'm caressing.'

A wave of pleasure flowed through Windswept. Only Minos could make her forget her crimes.

The special reception hosted by the High Treasurer and his wife was an enormous success. Most of the Hyksos senior officers were present, and they thoroughly enjoyed their first experience of opium; they were sure to become loyal customers.

Windswept had set her cap at an official responsible for weapons. He had made a few acid remarks about the front at Qis, which sounded like criticism of the emperor's policy. If that were indeed so, she would draw out his confidences, and there would be a new candidate for the labyrinth.

Yima had made sure to congratulate Minos on the splendour of his sculptures, and Windswept was jealous to see that hussy getting too close to her lover. If she continued to do so, the emperor's sister would find a way to rid herself of her rival.

'Aren't you going to try our latest delicacy?' Khamudi asked Minos.

'Judging by the behaviour of those who have, it would make my hand shake.'

'Wouldn't it give you new ideas?'

'At the moment, I have plenty of those.'

'You'll come to the drug, I'm sure. How can an artist manage without it? You can rely upon me to obtain it for you at the best price.'

'Your concern touches me, High Treasurer.'

'What could be more natural, my young friend? I'm extremely fond of modern art.'

The reception was drawing to an end, and Minos managed to escape. Pretending to be returning to his own quarters, he walked away from the citadel, glancing round several times to see if he was being followed. As he headed towards the district where most of the senior officers lived, he almost walked straight into a patrol. His heart pounding, he slid into an alleyway, hoping that none of the men had noticed him.

He had to wait several minutes until he got his breath back; then he continued on his way. Ten times, the painter halted and looked around him. Reassured, he ran the last hundred paces that separated him from the house of the man he was to meet in such great secrecy.

As agreed, the house and its outbuildings were in darkness. Minos sneaked up to the entrance, and the door opened.

'Are you sure no one followed you?' asked a strained voice.

'Absolutely sure.'

'Come in, quickly.'

The two men sat down and spoke in hushed voices.

'Have you contacted any other dignitaries?' asked Minos.

'Only two, and I took the strictest precautions. But I cannot say that they are really reliable. In my opinion, it would be better to give up your plans. Conspiring against the emperor is much too dangerous. Everyone who has tried has died in agony.'

'If I can't get rid of Apophis, I'll never be able to return to Minoa – that would cause me agony, too. Overthrowing that tyrant is the only way.'

'The emperor has many networks of informants, not to mention Khamudi's agents. It's almost impossible to plan any kind of action against him.'

'"Almost" – there's hope in that word! We have two allies already. That's a start, isn't it?'

'Frankly, I'm afraid it won't be.'

'Aren't you determined to fight against Apophis, too?'

'I was, but he's grown so powerful that no one can oppose him. If you try, you'll end up in the labyrinth.'

'The emperor needs me,' Minos reminded him. 'Who else could decorate his citadel in the Minoan manner? He thinks I'm submissive and resigned, and I'm the last person he'd suspect. That's a big advantage, and we must exploit it.'

The other man wavered. 'There's some truth in that, but are you really aware of the danger?'

'I'm prepared to do anything at all to regain my freedom and return to my home. In the meantime, you must continue to make contact with future enemies of the emperor.'

Windswept would have liked to spend the night with Minos, but he had seemed in a hurry to leave the opium reception and go to bed. So she was thoroughly surprised to see him emerge from his quarters, taking a thousand precautions as he did.

Curious, she followed her lover, whose behaviour she found strange. When she saw him enter the house belonging to the weapons official suspected of plotting against the emperor, she felt a brutal pain in her heart.

Minos, the only man she had ever truly loved . . . Was he in league with a traitor?

CHAPTER 40

Each morning, Teti the Small summoned the officers responsible for security at the military base and in the town of Thebes. Lookout posts had been set up north and south of the city, to raise the alarm in the event of a Hyksos attack. Thanks to hard work by Heray, agriculture was flourishing again. Farmers were celebrating the birth of many, many calves, lambs and piglets; it was as if the herds and flocks felt reassured by the establishment of a lasting peace, and had returned to their normal fertility.

In addition, Neshi was proving an excellent Overseer of the Treasury. Having put an end to the black market, he was now applying the ancient rules, which stipulated that powerful people must not live at the expense of the weak. He reported to Teti about the size and nature of commercial exchanges, which were principally regulated by the temple at Karnak.

Although her days were busy, the old lady took time to oversee the upbringing of Prince Ahmose, who had become not only an excellent archer and a good swordsman, but also a scholar able to write in hieroglyphs or the language of government. Teti made him read stories and the teachings of sages like Ptah-hotep. The little boy's seriousness surprised his military instructors: obedient, determined, never balking at additional work, he pushed himself to the limits of his strength. He was gifted with a remarkable memory and a lively intelligence, and had a real thirst for knowledge of all kinds.

Ordinarily, Ahmose rose with the sun and breakfasted with his grandmother. When he did not appear, Teti asked her maid to wake him.

The servant soon came hurrying back. 'Majesty, the prince has a bad fever. His forehead is burning, and he's shaking all over.'

Teti went to him immediately. She felt responsible for him, and there might be a great destiny in store for him. There could be no doubt that his premature death would be a fatal blow to the queen.

Ahhotep had suffered from similar illnesses at that age, so Teti decided to use similar remedies to relieve the heart by unblocking the channels that led to and from it. This would enable the boy's life-energies to circulate properly again. Ignoring the fever, which was merely a symptom, she concentrated on three vital organs, the liver, the spleen and the lungs. She administered a potion whose ingredients – bull's meat, terebinth resin, sweet-clover, juniper leaves, sweet beer and fresh bread – had been carefully measured out.

The little boy held his grandmother's hand tightly. 'Do you think I'm going to die?'

'Certainly not. You still have too much to learn.'

'There are boats coming, Majesty,' announced Emheb.

'From which direction?' asked Kamose.

'The south.'

'Make the agreed signals.'

If it was Ahhotep, she would reply by hoisting a sail on which was painted a boat containing the moon's disc. If it was not, battle must be joined on the river.

The sail ran up slowly; too slowly. Because of the intense midday sun, it was impossible to see if the sign was there. The Thebans' nerves stretched gradually to breaking-point.

'The moon! I can see it!' exclaimed Emheb. 'It is indeed the queen's flotilla.'

The symbol of Ahhotep and the rebel movement shone from the top of her ship's mast. The drums began to beat a joyful rhythm, celebrating the unification of all the Egyptian forces.

While the young king kissed his mother, the soldiers congratulated each other.

Ahhotep said, in some surprise, 'I am bringing you only meagre reinforcements, my son, but you seem to have recruited many more.'

Kamose could not hide his pride. 'They're boatmen, merchants, former mercenaries serving the Hyksos. They had to be persuaded that they had chosen the wrong side. It wasn't always easy, but in the end they realized where their interests lay. Our victory will ensure that their lives are far more pleasant than under the Hyksos.'

Ahhotep smiled joyfully. 'You are becoming a true pharaoh, Kamose.'

The queen's presence had had a consequence no one had dared hope for: it had united the disparate elements of the Egyptian army. In addition, the men's minds were no longer haunted by fear, but were now nourished by the wildest of dreams: defeating the empire of darkness.

A heavy silence lay over the front at Qis. Everyone was waiting for the council of war's decision. Many had wagered that it would be the sensible one of making Qis Thebes's new northern frontier by erecting fortifications there.

'I've sworn to break through the obstacle posed by Khmun,' Kamose told the council. 'The Hyksos control-post must be dismantled.'

'The Jar of Predictions is said to be hidden in the temple,' added Ahhotep. 'We need it if we are to decide our strategy and save many lives.'

'Let us attack Khmun,' proposed Kamose.

Calm and steady as ever, Emheb felt it necessary to bring the young monarch back to reality. 'Majesty, Khmun is out of reach.'

'Why?'

'While we've been holding the front at Qis, we've had time to study the Hyksos positions. At great risk to their lives, two scouts got through the enemy front line and discovered their rear base. It is Nefrusy, capital of the sixteenth province of Upper Egypt, which is governed by a collaborator, Tita, son of Pepi.'

'Is there a fortress like the one at Per-Hathor?' asked Ahhotep.

'No, but Nefrusy is defended by very strong ramparts indeed, and I don't think our army can take it.'

'Has this Tita sold his soul to the emperor?' asked Kamose.

'Unfortunately, yes, Majesty. He was nothing but a simple boatman who made his fortune by transporting the invaders. He denounced the rebels and Apophis gave him the town as a reward. The only thing that matters to him is the empire, which ensures his wealth and power.'

'The perfect example of a coward and a traitor!' roared Kamose.

'Most of the present governors of the Northern provinces are like him,' lamented Emheb. 'They're convinced that the emperor is invincible and that our army will never get beyond Qis. You won't persuade any of them to change sides.'

'Then they shall die!'

'No one wants such vermin exterminated more than I do. But the Hyksos protect them and make them prosper.'

'Then what do you think would be the best strategy?'

'To make the frontier at Qis impregnable,' said Emheb, 'by building fortifications and blocking the Nile with cargo-boats lashed together.'

'What? And give up our goal of reunifying the Two Lands?' asked Ahhotep anxiously.

'By no means, Majesty. We shall merely be adapting to a given situation. At Edfu, at Thebes and at Qis, we analysed the situation correctly, and success smiled upon us. We must not spoil our progress by acting hastily.'

Neshi had always been opposed to caution. But this time he thought Emheb's analysis was sensible. Besides, no one could accuse the governor of lacking courage: without him, the front at Qis could not have held out for long.

Six days of high fever. Six days, during which little Ahmose was often delirious, imploring his dead father and his absent mother not to abandon him to the hungry mouths of the demons of night.

The palace doctor was pessimistic. He had not added anything to the remedies prescribed by Teti, who spent all her time at Ahmose's bedside and left Qaris to deal with pressing matters of government.

During his moments of lucidity, the sick child regretted being so puny and being unable to continue his weapons training. His grandmother reassured him and read him the teachings of sage Imhotep, the genius who had created the first stone pyramid at Saqqara, near the town of

Memphis, which was now occupied by the Hyksos.

Twice, Teti thought she had lost her grandson, whose breathing grew fainter and fainter. But the brightness in his eyes refused to yield to the dark, and he drew his last strength from her unshakeable confidence. Not for a moment did he ever sense doubt in her; she kept him firmly anchored to life.

It was this attitude, as much as the remedies, which brought about the prince's recovery. On the seventh day he rose and ate a hearty breakfast on the palace terrace, in the company of a joyful and very relieved grandmother.

CHAPTER 41

To people who, like the Syrians, had seen a bear, Tita, son of Pepi, looked just like a monstrous one, with his enormous head, bushy eyebrows and snout-shaped nose. He terrorized his underlings and never forgave even the smallest fault. An excellent pupil of the Hyksos, he based his power on violence and cruelty. In the emperor's image, each month Tita executed one of his fellow citizens, chosen at random. The people of Nefrusy were forced to attend the ceremony, which ended with a ritual song praising Apophis's greatness.

The bear was very pleased with his province and his capital, and wanted nothing but to rule there as absolute master. To thank him for his fidelity, the emperor had given him permission to build ramparts, which made Nefrusy look most impressive.

His wife, Anat, was equally notable. A blue-eyed Syrian with a fiery temperament, she constantly infuriated him by criticizing all his decisions, which she considered were as stupid as they were unjust. Fortunately for her, this particular contest was the only one that Tita enjoyed. Besides, the tussles always ended up in the vast sycamore-wood bed, his palace's finest ornament.

Tita expected to enjoy the day, because he was going to cut the throat of a youth guilty of rebellion against the emperor. Next, young girls would process past, singing a warlike poem composed by the bear himself. Anat had called it ridiculous doggerel, but it praised the emperor's genius.

'Aren't you ready yet?' asked Anat in surprise.

'I want to look particularly handsome, my darling,' said Tita. 'My public appearances must delight the common folk.'

'Is it really necessary to kill an innocent boy to cement your appalling reputation?'

'Of course. At the slightest sign of leniency, rebels would spring up like weeds.'

'I doubt if there are any left.'

'Mistrust, suspicion . . . you're wonderful. How does this new tunic look?'

'Too showy.'

'You really are unbearable, my darling.'

Shortly after dawn, Queen Ahhotep convened the Supreme Council, which had pronounced on the future of Egypt. Its members were hoping for firm orders and for the armed forces to be divided between Thebes and Qis.

'Tonight,' revealed the queen, 'Amon appeared to me, his sword in his hand. He was incarnate in the person of Pharaoh Kamose, and his eyes were as intensely bright as the noonday sun. "Did I not order you to destroy the Hyksos, and to carry out this mission whatever the obstacles?" he asked me. It is true that you are sensible and thoughtful men. It is true that the Hyksos are militarily superior to us. The front holds fast, Nefrusy is impregnable, and Khmun even more so. It is true that we have already achieved the impossible, and we have exhausted our reserves of *heka*, the only force capable of altering the cruel fate that has befallen our country. I know the reality. But it is my duty to reject it, not submit to it, because such is the will of Amon.

'The hour has come to go beyond Qis, to cross that frontier and to strike north. That is the only strategy that will make possible the reunification of the Two Lands. If we are defeated, Thebes will be destroyed and there will be no further resistance to barbarism. If we bend, the result will be the same. No doubt you consider my determination senseless and would prefer to take refuge in a false sense of security. That is why I shall take only volunteers with me when I leave for the front.'

Kamose raised his hands, palms turned upwards to the heavens, in a sign of worship. 'The pharaoh appointed by Amon has heard the voice of the Wife of God. His army will follow her. Any council members who disagree with our decision may return to Thebes immediately.'

No one moved.

⋆   ⋆   ⋆

'What an incredible woman,' murmured the Afghan for the hundredth time, as he watched Ahhotep speak to each soldier, instilling the courage they would all need.

'It's worth dying for her and for Egypt,' said Moustache. 'At least when we appear before the court of the otherworld, we shan't have to hang our heads in shame.'

When Kamose appeared at the prow of the flagship, wearing the White Crown, the soldiers raised their weapons to the skies and the drums began to beat a frenzied rhythm.

To break through the Hyksos defensive line, the pharaoh decided to launch a three-pronged attack using the river and both banks, thus involving all his forces. He had two pieces of luck: it was the time when the guards were relieved; and the general in charge of the Qis front was bedridden, suffering from intense pain in his kidneys.

Surprised by the scale of the offensive, the Hyksos lost precious minutes organizing themselves as best they could. Several of their boats were already burning when their camp was attacked from both east and west. As soon as Ahmes, son of Abana, had killed the senior officers, who thought they were safe on the mound from which they were observing the battle, the chain of command was broken and the defenders panicked.

Like an all-consuming flame, the Theban army poured into the many breaches in the Hyksos line, their battle-fever controlled and directed by Kamose's precise, efficient orders. Not until the last Hyksos was dead, burnt along with his camp, did the Thebans' passion die down.

Emheb was amazed. How could this motley assortment of raw troops have beaten the Hyksos, who greatly outnumbered them and were much better armed? The attackers' enthusiasm had been the decisive factor, it was true, but young King Kamose's exceptional leadership had also been vital. Trusting to nothing but his own instinct, he had struck in the right places at the right times. Ahhotep's magic must have been guiding him.

'What were our losses?' asked the queen.

'They were light, Majesty.'

'Send the seriously wounded by boat to Thebes. Are there any prisoners?'

'No, none.'

Kamose emerged from the smoke, his sword dripping blood; he looked so gruesome that even his own soldiers were nervous of him. All trace of youth was gone from his face, which for the rest of his life would bear the marks of all the brutal deaths he had inflicted.

'You exposed yourself to too much danger,' Ahhotep chided him.

'If I don't show an example, who will dare defy the darkness?' Wearily, the king sat down on a modest throne of sycamore-wood; Laughter licked his hands, as if trying to wipe away all traces of the terrible battle. 'You were right, Mother: we were indeed capable of breaking through the Hyksos front. This victory has strengthened our *heka*, and we have shown qualities we did not know we had. It was like a birth . . . We have given birth to formidable forces which Set himself would not deny. Is this really the path we must follow?'

'Answering violence with gentleness, cruelty with diplomacy and forgiveness – is that what you would like, my son? That policy would lead to the triumph of barbarism. We are facing not simple adversaries, with whom we could negotiate, but the Hyksos, invaders who want to destroy our bodies and our souls. It is because only Set can confront the dragon of darkness that he holds the prow of the sun's ship.'

Kamose closed his eyes. 'I had prepared myself to fight, but not for this war.'

'This is only the beginning,' said Ahhotep. 'Today you were reunited with the courage of your father, and you felt what he felt as he died for freedom.'

Kamose got to his feet. 'Like him, I shall fight to the end. A few days' rest, and then we shall take Nefrusy.'

Ahhotep sighed. 'I cannot let you have those few days. We must take advantage of this victory to force our advantage and swoop down like a falcon on our enemy.'

The Afghan and Moustache gulped down a frugal meal, collected their belongings together and climbed back on to their boat. Despite their status and decorations, they still behaved like simple rebel fighters.

'It would have been good to get our breath back,' grumbled a footsoldier.

'Do you really want to die?' asked the Afghan.

'Of course not.'

'Then be glad about your orders. The sooner we reach our next objective, the better chance we shall have of victory – and therefore of survival.'

'Are we going to fight again?'

'That's what you're here for, isn't it?'

The question plunged the soldier into confusion. 'There is some truth in that, Commander.'

'Come on, my lad. We haven't killed all the Hyksos yet.'

'Now that thought I like!' The soldier made his way happily up the gangplank.

Showing exemplary discipline, the soldiers of Theban army embarked in record time. Then it was the oarsmen's turn to show what they could do.

CHAPTER 42

The ceremony was at its height. Dozens of children were loudly singing Tita's song in praise of Apophis.

Suddenly, shouts shattered the apparent peace. Enraged, Tita signalled to his soldiers to arrest the troublemakers and have them executed immediately. But the shouts grew louder, and soon it was clear that they came from outside the town.

'It's the peasants, my lord,' said a soldier. 'They're begging us to open the great gate.'

Terminating the celebration, Tita climbed up on to the ramparts and looked down. It was an appalling sight: dozens of farm-workers had left their fields and were trying to take refuge in the city. Across the rich fields of the vast plain, the Theban army was advancing. At its head was Pharaoh Kamose.

'We must give the peasants shelter quickly,' urged the commander of the archers.

'No, we can't risk it. Kill them.'

'Kill them? You mean . . . kill our peasants, our own peasants?'

'Opening the gate is out of the question. Obey

my orders, then fire on the enemy, so that they cannot get near our walls.'

Watched in horror by the Egyptians, the unarmed peasants were slaughtered by Tita's archers. A young Theban captain and a few foot-soldiers were so appalled that they rushed to the peasants' aid, but they, too, were all shot down.

'No one is to try anything similar,' ordered Kamose. 'You can see what the results would be.'

'We must recover back the bodies of our men,' said Emheb.

'Not by sacrificing other lives. First, we must encircle the town.'

The Egyptian forces were deployed out of range of the Hyksos archers. Tents were pitched, and Neshi ensured that the men were fed. On Ahhotep's orders, the elite regiments commanded by the Afghan and Moustache were posted to the north of the town to prevent any reinforcements from breaking the siege.

As soon as the sun went down, Ahmes and ten volunteers climbed up to the place where their comrades had fallen. They succeeded in bringing back the bodies and also three seriously wounded men, whom She-Cat treated before they were sent back to Thebes by boat.

'The walls look very solid,' observed Emheb. 'An effective siege will take a long time.'

'I am going to my cabin,' said Kamose.

★   ★   ★

277

Despite the threat posed by the Theban army, Tita had decided to go ahead with the banquet organized in his honour, and was presiding over it with his wife.

'At least pretend to be enjoying yourself, Anat.'

'Have you forgotten that we're under siege?'

The bear sank his teeth into a leg of goose. 'That band of rebels won't threaten us for long.'

'Are you sure about that?'

'Hyksos reinforcements will destroy them first thing tomorrow morning – they'll take those fools by surprise. I'll send any survivors to Avaris, where they will be tortured to entertain the emperor. In return, Apophis will grant me new privileges. In fact, the arrival of these madmen is a stroke of luck: I shall benefit richly from it.'

A troupe of flute- and oboe-players was apathetically playing a droning melody which irritated him. 'Get out, you idiots,' he bellowed.

The musicians fled.

'Have you taken all the necessary measures?' asked Anat anxiously.

'My archers are patrolling the battlements, and no one can get near. Don't worry, my sweet. We aren't in any danger.'

'Are you really sure that the Hyksos are invincible?'

'They are. You can be sure of that.'

Kamose was pacing up and down in his cabin like a caged animal. Unsure which plan to adopt, he repeatedly weighed the lives of his soldiers against the need to conquer Nefrusy. Eventually, still unable to decide, he went out on deck, where Ahhotep was enjoying the last rays of the setting sun.

'Have you made up your mind?' she asked.

'I can't. A long siege would destroy our impetus, and a badly planned attack would incur unacceptably heavy losses.'

'Your conclusions are the same as mine.'

'Then what do you suggest?'

'Tonight I shall consult the moon-god, the interpreter of the skies. He will send us a sign to guide us. Go and rest, my son.'

The Afghan and Moustache, with ten experienced soldiers, were travelling warily down the Nile aboard a light boat. They went very slowly, all their senses alert.

'There they are,' whispered Moustache. 'We were right.'

Two Hyksos war-ships lay moored to the bank. The sailors had pitched camp ashore, and the sentries looked very relaxed. Clearly, the reinforcements for Nefrusy believed that in conquered territory they had nothing to fear.

A member of the raiding-party went back to alert the two elite regiments posted not far away. Less than two hours later, they were ready to begin work.

'First we must seize the ships,' said the Afghan. 'Our best swimmers will approach from the stern and climb aboard. The sailors on guard will be killed quickly and silently. When that is done, one man only is to return to us. The others will prepare to cast off.'

If the operation failed, the Hyksos would immediately search the surrounding area. A pitched battle would be inevitable. The minutes seemed to last for ever.

Then a head emerged from the water, and the swimmer reported, 'The enemy sailors are all dead. The ships are ours.'

'We shall divide into three groups,' said Moustache. 'As soon as the Hyksos are asleep, we shall attack.'

Kamose could not sleep. Ever since his coronation, he had managed only one or two hours' sleep a night, though his energy had not been affected. He thought constantly of his father, and sometimes felt sharp pains in the parts of his body where Seqen had been wounded.

There was a knock at his cabin door.

'There are two Hyksos ships coming,' said Emheb.

Kamose rushed to the prow of the flagship, but it was almost too late to take action. How could he have foreseen that warships would risk travelling in the middle of the night?

Waking with a start, the Egyptian sailors ran to their posts.

'Look at the top of the leading mast!' shouted one of them. 'It's Moustache!'

The tension relaxed. The two ships glided gently to their moorings, and their crews gave shouts of victory.

'Majesty,' declared the Afghan, 'our fleet now has two more boats. As for the reinforcements Tita was expecting, they'll never reach him.'

'That's excellent work.'

'We surprised the Hyksos while they were asleep. On our side, there are three dead and fifteen wounded.'

'See that the wounded are cared for, and then go and rest.'

'If you are planning to attack at dawn, Majesty, we have just enough time for a quick bite to eat.'

The king did not reply.

As the first glimmers of light pierced the darkness, Queen Ahhotep came towards him. Despite a sleepless night, she was surprisingly fresh-faced.

'Mother, did the moon-god speak to you?'

A falcon with multicoloured plumage soared up from the east and flew across the sky. Its wings looked immense, as if they had taken possession of the entire space.

'He has just spoken,' said the pharaoh, 'and I have heard him.'

CHAPTER 43

Like a falcon, Pharaoh Kamose swooped down on Nefrusy at the head of his army. Hampered by the light of the rising sun in their eyes, the Hyksos archers fired wide; Ahmes and the Theban archers did not.

Abruptly awoken, Tita responded quickly to this unexpected attack. Arming himself with a sling-shot, he rushed up to the ramparts, from where he killed a Theban officer marching at the head of his troops.

'Fire! Defend yourselves!' he ordered.

The instinct for survival provoked a response from his men, who, despite their fear, unleashed a barrage of missiles to prevent the attackers approaching the walls.

'We need battering-rams,' said Moustache.

'The masts from the Hyksos ships will serve very well,' suggested Emheb.

'They're retreating,' exclaimed Tita. 'We've driven them back.'

Although he could hardly believe it, he had won. That is, he had gained the respite he needed in which to escape. The Egyptians would mount a siege and Nefrusy would eventually fall, but he would not be among its victims. He would take with him only a few servants, to carry his most precious possessions. As for his wife, she would be a useless burden – there was no shortage of women in Avaris.

The Thebans had attacked from the east, so Tita planned to leave by the western gate. But to his horror he found that the enemy had massed troops on the nearby low hills, as well as in the southern and northern plains. Nefrusy was surrounded.

'You weren't going to run away, were you?' asked Anat pointedly.

'No, of course not! I was working out how best to strengthen the defences.'

'Don't you think it would be wiser to surrender?'

'Surrender? That would be madness.'

'One way or another, you will be killed. If you order your men to lay down their arms, you would at least spare the people further suffering.'

'I've been their benefactor, haven't I? They must fight beside me and defend me.'

'You are cruel and cowardly. End your life with one generous deed: open the gates of the city and beg the pharaoh's forgiveness.'

Tita glared at his wife. 'You wouldn't be thinking of betraying me, would you, my beauty? Yes, that's it. You think I'm already beaten and you're switching to the Thebans' side.'

'Don't be ridiculous. Face reality.'

'Go to your bedchamber immediately. Two guards will be posted outside your door. When I've finished with the Thebans, I shall deal with you.'

'My lord, they are coming back.'

Standing high on the ramparts, Tita saw the Theban army attacking again, from all four directions. Protected both by archers and by big, thick shields held by auxiliaries, men carrying battering-rams charged at the gates of Nefrusy.

He spotted the White Crown as Kamose reached the eastern gate, and hurled a javelin with all his might, but it missed. The battering-ram stove in the great gate; the noise of wood breaking and splintering struck terror into Tita's troops. A few moments later, the three other gates gave way.

While the footsoldiers poured into the town, the rammers withdrew and then advanced again to attack the brick walls.

Tita ran to his palace. His men would not hold out for long, and he must hide somewhere to wait for the pharaoh and beg his mercy. After all, he, Tita, was a victim of the Hyksos, too, and the Theban army's arrival was a real miracle, which he had been hoping for with all his heart. From now on, he would be a loyal servant of Kamose. All that remained was for him to kill his evil genius, the traitor Anat, who was the cause of all Nefrusy's woes. As proof of his good faith, he had placed her under arrest.

Some thirty women, whose children Tita had had executed, barred his way to the palace.

'Stand aside!' he roared.

'You killed my son,' declared a tall redhead armed with a cauldron.

'You killed my daughter,' said another, who was clutching a pestle.

Each of the women solemnly stated her grievance.

'Let me pass, and go and fight alongside the troops.'

All at once, they threw themselves upon him and beat him to death with their kitchen utensils, while the rams battered down the walls of Nefrusy.

Kamose had single-handedly killed more than thirty of the enemy, including the head of Tita's bodyguard. The man had tried to stab him in the back, but the king, benefiting from his intensive training, seemed to have eyes in the back of his head.

Spurred on by their leader's almost superhuman bravery, his soldiers had fought valiantly, and the enemy, despite showing the courage born of despair, had inflicted only slight losses before succumbing to force of numbers.

Believing the lies put out day after day by Tita, and thinking Hyksos reinforcements would arrive at any moment, many citizens had fought along-side the emperor's men. So by the middle of the afternoon the streets of Nefrusy were strewn with bodies.

A group of mothers pointed out Tita's body, which was almost unrecognizable.

'Have it burnt, and then raze the whole town to the ground,' ordered Kamose.

In the face of such destruction, Ahhotep's heart was in her mouth. This was only Nefrusy, a small town compared with Khmun, which was itself insignificant compared with Avaris. How many dead would the monster of darkness devour before the words of the song to the Creator, 'Awake in peace', could be sung?

She-Cat, who had been appointed by Ahhotep to take charge of treating the troops, was remarkably efficient. With her Nubian remedies, she eased the men's pain, and she gave hope to even the most seriously wounded. Everyone envied Moustache for having such a mistress, who had become one of the heroines of the war.

After entrusting the White Crown to his mother, Kamose washed thoroughly and changed his clothes. It would take the washermen a long time to cleanse his blood-spattered breastplate.

The young king was neither exhilarated nor downcast. Solemnly contemplating the next battle already, he was simply fulfilling his mission.

Supervised by Emheb, the victors took away the survivors, livestock, jars of oil, milk and honey, weapons and anything else useful, before the flames consumed Nefrusy.

'The palace is still standing, Majesty,' said Emheb, 'Do you wish to be the first to enter it?'

Dressed in a white tunic, Kamose stepped through the doorway of a fine, pillared building. The rooms, although quite small, were filled with beautiful furniture. At the end of the private apartments was a door, held shut by a wooden bolt.

Kamose drew it back and opened the door. Sitting on a low chair with ebony arm-rests was a beautiful young woman with blue eyes.

'Has my husband sent you to kill me?' she asked.

'If you are the wife of Tita, son of Pepi, I must tell you that he will give no more orders to anyone.'

Anat stood up. 'So he is dead. Then justice does exist! Whoever you are, you have given me wonderful news. Now I can die in peace.'

'Why did you marry him?'

Her eyes filled with sadness. 'I made the mistake of thinking he loved me. But he thought so little of me that he had decided to kill me.'

'Nefrusy has been utterly destroyed, and those who fought against me have been punished. Do you also wish to fight me?'

Anat stared at him in astonishment. 'Do you mean . . . ? Are you the pharaoh, come from Thebes?'

'Either you become my loyal subject, or you will share the fate of my enemies.'

CHAPTER 44

Being a trade-control official at Khmun was a coveted privilege. Only Hyksos soldiers with excellent service records and good connections in Avaris could gain appointment to the largest control-post in occupied Egypt.

The Hyksos imposed a toll upon everything and everyone that passed through Khmun: men, women, children, animals, boats, goods . . . Only the emperor's soldiers were exempt and could move around freely. An official tariff decreed the maximum rate that could be levied from prostitutes who entertained the military, but trade-control officials were free to alter other people's conditions of passage according to their own whims, and could swindle travellers as much as they liked.

Always aggressive, they would take exception to even the most innocent remark. The offender was instantly stripped of his clothes and possessions, abused and sentenced. If he continued to protest his good faith or, even worse, his innocence, he was sent to prison where he would be forgotten for as long as the government pleased.

En-Ilusa, the Libyan who ruled the Khmun control-post, had a small moustache and sly eyes. Appointed by his friend Khamudi, to whom he paid a portion of his illicit earnings, he ruled his domain with a rod of iron. He never needed even to raise his voice. All he had to do was issue his orders, which no one dared question.

En-Ilusa behaved like a little emperor, and dreamt of one day leaving Khmun to take up a more important post in Avaris. He specialized in playing a double game, and ruthlessly betrayed anyone who made the mistake of confiding in him, as soon as they were no longer useful. Through Khamudi's good offices, he hoped to obtain promotion in the coming months. Then he would really show what he could do.

He was not worried about the Theban rebellion. The front would remain fixed at Qis until the moment when the emperor decided to kill Ahhotep.

As he did every morning, En-Ilusa inspected the main trade-control building. A pernickety man, he demanded that everything be in its proper place and that nothing ever changed. He was also strict about the cleanliness of uniforms, and anyone who fell short of his standards was fined several days' pay. Above all, En-Ilusa liked to stir up discord among the officers by encouraging informers and the spread of malicious gossip.

One thing was annoying him: in recent weeks business had fallen slightly, indicating that some of his underlings were being lax. As soon as he had identified them, the miscreants would be transferred to some miserable small town.

En-Ilusa was just beginning to read the previous day's reports when a grain inspector entered his office.

'Sir, we're going to have a great deal of work. Three cargo-boats are approaching from the south.'

En-Ilusa smiled avariciously. 'They're going to pay a high price.'

Ahhotep's plan had been enthusiastically received by Pharaoh Kamose and his council of war: the battle for Khmun would take place in three stages. First, three supply-boats would arrive at the control-post; they would be made to look like ordinary trading-vessels, and so would be allowed through the floating barricade of boats that protected Khmun. Next, a raiding-party would attack from the riverbank, taking the troops by surprise. Finally, the war-fleet would come as quickly as possible to join the fight. Co-ordination would be vital: any confusion would lead to a disaster from which the Thebans could never recover.

The three heavy cargo-boats advanced with prudent slowness towards the floating barricade. Many soldiers were hidden aboard, lying flat on the decks, ready to leap into action the moment the order was given.

When Emheb appeared at the prow of the leading ship, En-Ilusa took him for what he seemed to be: a good-hearted, round-bellied fellow with an open smile. Ideal prey.

As soon as the boats were moored, Emheb would send Rascal back to the war-fleet, which was commanded by Moon. Moon would know that the fight was beginning and that he must set off, urging the oarsmen to row with all possible speed.

The first wave of the Egyptian attack would necessarily entail heavy losses, and Emheb himself might be killed. But what about Queen Ahhotep, who was leading the raiding-party on land? No soldier would let himself show less courage than she did.

The boats nudged gently against the bank, watched covetously by En-Ilusa and his men, who were already mentally sharing out the booty they would obtain legally, by levying their myriad taxes. In accordance with instructions, they arranged themselves in a line along the quay.

En-Ilusa stepped forward and spoke the usual words: 'Have you anything to declare?'

'Not very much,' replied Emheb affably. 'You will soon be finished with my cargo.'

A greedy smile lit up En-Ilusa's cold face. 'That would surprise me. I am very scrupulous and I believe that these three boats are crammed full of both authorized and unauthorized goods.'

Emheb scratched his chin. 'To be frank, you are not entirely wrong.'

'So you admit it already? That's very sensible of you. It's always better to co-operate.'

The governor nodded.

'Continue to be sensible,' recommended En-Ilusa. 'What is your most illicit merchandise?'

'I will gladly tell you, but you won't profit from it.'

'Come on, tell me!'

'Be sure to listen carefully. You won't have much time to appreciate its song.'

Unsheathing his dagger, Emheb threw it with force and accuracy. It hissed viciously through the air, and plunged into En-Ilusa's chest. His eyes filled with astonishment, the man died without even understanding what was happening.

At Emheb's signal, all the Egyptian archers stood up and fired on the trade-control officials, who, lined up as they were, made excellent targets.

Although thrown into confusion by the un-expected attack and by their leader's death, the survivors attempted to fight back. But they were caught between the Egyptians firing on them from the decks of the three boats, and the footsoldiers charging at them along the riverbank, led by Pharaoh Kamose.

Emheb and his men exploited the situation expertly. Khmun's soldiers could have prevented the crushing defeat of the trade-control men, but they had to contain the assault by the raiding-party, which had taken them by surprise.

Moustache and the Afghan were particularly

skilled at this sort of fighting, and when they had Queen Ahhotep at their side nothing could stop them.

The Hyksos forces made the mistake of dividing, some rushing to the aid of the remaining trade-control officials, the others confronting the enemy footsoldiers. Before long, the survivors realized that the day was lost. They took refuge on some boats in the floating barricade, hoping to be able to cut them free and escape northwards. At that moment, they saw the Theban war-fleet appear. As soon the fleet closed with the barricade, Moon's sailors rushed to the attack. As in the previous battles, no prisoners were taken.

Kamose was greatly surprised by how easily his army had broken through at Khmun, which many had thought was indestructible. Ahhotep's plan had succeeded, as if the Wife of God could see beyond outward appearances.

On a sign from Emheb, the troops raised an enthusiastic cheer for the pharaoh and the queen. Yet Ahhotep seemed anxious.

'What is it, Mother?' asked Kamose. 'Nothing can halt our progress.'

'From Thebes to Khmun, Egypt has been liberated. But this reconquest may only be temporary.'

'What do you mean?'

'The troops we have defeated did not have the heavy weapons that enabled the Hyksos to conquer our country. The emperor must be sneering at our offensive. He is simply luring us deeper and deeper

293

into a trap, and eventually we shall have to face his real army.'

Once again, the queen's clear thinking convinced the young pharaoh. 'But we cannot be content just to establish a new front.'

'Before we go any further, I must decipher the message of Khmun, and find the Jar of Predictions.'

CHAPTER 45

At first, the people of Khmun refused to believe it. And then they saw that the news was true: there were no Hyksos guards on the streets, and everyone could express their hatred of the emperor without fear of reprisals. Eventually, even the most sceptical allowed themselves to show their joy when Pharaoh Kamose, wearing the White Crown, and Queen Ahhotep, crowned with a fine gold diadem, appeared before the great Temple of Thoth, which stood in the Valley of the Tamarisks.

'People of Khmun,' proclaimed the young king, 'you are free. The Hyksos have been wiped out, and the control-post destroyed. Pharaoh rules once again, as before and for ever. The darkness has been driven back; the righteousness and harmony of Ma'at are our only law. A great feast, to which you are all summoned, shall seal the return of happiness.'

Emheb, Moon, the Afghan and Moustache were borne aloft in triumph. The prettiest girls in the city had eyes only for the archers, particularly Ahmes. The only person who was not happy was

Neshi, who, instead of enjoying the feast, was responsible for organizing it and ensuring that it was a success.

While the city was preparing to celebrate its liberation, the queen went to the temple.

When she arrived there, a young man knelt before her. 'I beg you, Majesty, do not go any further.'

'Stand up, my boy, and explain yourself.'

He dared not look at this gloriously beautiful woman, whom everyone called the Queen of Freedom. Already, storytellers were spreading her legend from village to village. To find himself here, so close to her . . . He had never hoped for such an honour.

'Do not enter this temple, Majesty.'

'Is it filled with dangerous creatures?'

'The Hyksos killed the priests, stole the precious objects and turned the shrine into a storehouse. They took stones and filled up the well that led down to the primordial ocean. The gods have departed, and all that remains is the spirit of evil. Do not challenge it, Majesty. We need you too much.' Surprised by his own boldness, the young man prostrated himself again.

'What work did you do under the occupation?'

'I looked after the temple garden, Majesty. It was not easy alone, but I avoided the worst.'

'I appoint you head gardener of the Temple of Thoth. Employ assistants immediately, to return this place to its past splendour, and begin by clearing out the sacred well.'

Ahhotep turned towards the door of the shrine.

'Majesty, you . . . you aren't going to enter that den of curses, are you?'

Ahhotep knew Khmun was not yet truly free. The military victory had been won, but the emperor fought with other weapons, too. Once the well was emptied, the energy that came from the primordial ocean would again fill the temple. But she believed Apophis would not have been content with this simple measure. Inside there must be a device capable of preventing the Thebans from making further progress. He would probably have chosen the most famous place: the library where the writings of the god Thoth were kept, his divine words inspired by the Word of Light.

As she walked through the great open-air court-yard, the queen felt an ache in her heart. The Hyksos had stored swords, armour and sacks of wheat there. The first covered hall was an even more distressing sight: the soldiers of darkness had turned it into latrines, and the stench of excrement was unbearable.

Suddenly, she heard a low growl. She headed towards the sound and came to the door of the library. All around were engraved effigies of ibis-headed Thoth and of Seshat, Queen of the House of Books, crowned with a seven-pointed star.

The growling became threatening. On the temple roof stood a she-leopard, the incarnation of the goddess Mafdet. Her role was to tear apart anyone who tried to violate the secrets of Thoth. On the ground lay bones covered in bloody Hyksos uniforms. After trying in vain to kill the divine animal, which no weapon could harm, the invaders had withdrawn, abandoning Mafdet's victims where they lay. Surely the sacred books must be inaccessible for ever.

Moving forward would make the animal attack, but going back was out of the question. Ahhotep absolutely had to go into the library, where the Jar of Predictions was kept. She had only one chance of pacifying the leopardess: to give her the *menat*-necklace of Hathor, in the hope that its power would turn her ferocity into gentleness.

Keeping her eyes fixed on Mafdet, Ahhotep lifted the symbol of love towards her.

At first, the leopard roared with rage, as if her prey were escaping, then she gave a howl of doubt and frustration, and then an incongruous mewling sound. Her terrifying deep voice had been reduced to the shrill sound of an irritated cat.

Holding the magical necklace high, Ahhotep advanced to the threshold of the library. The leopard turned and walked calmly and elegantly away. The queen's way was clear.

She drew back the copper bolt and entered the ancient hall of archives, where rolls of papyrus were carefully arranged on shelves and in wooden chests. Thanks to Mafdet's leopard, the writings of Thoth had escaped the barbarians.

Calm now, the queen examined the treasures of the ancient library, but could not find any jars. She lingered over a text which evoked the creative powers of the universe: the invisible, darkness, infinite space and limitless waters, each of them possessing a masculine and feminine aspect. Contained within the primordial egg, these eight things were the principal secret of the priests of Thoth, through which it was possible to perceive the ultimate reality of life.

For several hours, the queen forgot the war and devoted herself to the study of these inexhaustibly rich texts. While initiating herself into their mysteries and imbuing herself with their words of light, Ahhotep was still fighting. Overcoming Apophis required more than warlike qualities; she must also be the bearer of a spirituality which was powerful enough to dispel the night of tyranny and injustice.

When she left the library, the town was celebrating, under the protection of the moon.

Ten gardeners were working, supervised by their young overseer.

'Majesty, you are alive!' he cried. 'Thoth has guided your feet.'

'Have you ever heard of the Jar of Predictions?'

'Before he died, one of the priests told me that the Hyksos had taken it away to hide it in a tomb at Beni Hasan, from which it would never be recovered. But rumour has it that it was destroyed in the first days of the invasion.'

'Don't you want to join in the rejoicing?'

'My life is here, Majesty, and I shan't rejoice until the temple is as beautiful as it used to be. It will take months to clean everything, but I already have good assistants and we shall work every hour of the day.'

'Can you read?'

'Yes, Majesty. A priest taught me. I can write a little, too.'

Ahhotep was thinking of another gardener, Seqen, who had become her husband and a great pharaoh, and who had died in the name of freedom.

'Appoint one of your assistants to replace you,' she ordered.

The young man trembled. 'Majesty, have I done something wrong?'

'Shut yourself away in the library for as long as you need, in order to assimilate the message of Thoth. Then you shall assume the office of High Priest at the temple of Khmun.'

CHAPTER 46

Houses of eternity had been excavated in the cliff-face for the dignitaries of Beni Hasan, not far to the north of Khmun. This grand and lofty site looked out over a vast plain filled with palm-groves and villages served by canals. The majestic Nile flowed through it, forming elegant curves.

Despite their fears, the Egyptian army had encountered no resistance. According to the local inhabitants, who were all overjoyed to welcome their liberators, the emperor's soldiers had retreated from their positions two days earlier.

This serenely beautiful place seemed peaceful, far removed from the war. The countryside's tranquil charms were conducive to meditation. Nevertheless, though much preoccupied, Pharaoh Kamose deployed his troops as if they were about to face an immediate counter-offensive, both on land and from the river. No one, from Moon down to the simplest soldier, relaxed their guard for even a moment.

'This is where the emperor has erected a barrier of curses,' said Ahhotep. 'No one must try to cross it.'

'How can we destroy it?' asked Kamose.

'I must examine each tomb and find the one in which the Jar of Predictions has been placed.'

'But supposing the Hyksos have destroyed it?'

'Then we shall be blind and deaf.'

'Let me come with you.'

Ahhotep shook her head. 'Stay here and lead your army. If the enemy attacks, you must be able to respond instantly.'

She began to climb, watched by the soldiers. Some said that she was preparing to challenge a desert demon; others that she would combat evil spirits controlled by the emperor. The best-informed said that the continuation of the war depended on the confrontation between the Queen of Freedom and a dark force which was capable of eating away at the Thebans' souls.

As soon as she reached the rocky platform along which the tombs lay, Ahhotep knew that she had found the place where Apophis's would-be barrier of curses had been erected. Her head felt as though it were caught in a vice, her legs were leaden and her breathing difficult. It was as if she had been plunged into hell, even though a gentle sun was making the green fields and the white limestone shine magnificently.

Holding the *menat*-necklace tightly, Ahhotep managed to breathe almost normally and approached the tombs.

But a stele barred her way. On it were written these terrifying words: '*A curse upon anyone who crosses the threshold of this dwelling. All-consuming fire upon the profaner, everlasting damnation!'*

These words would never normally have been found in a place of profound peace, linked to eternity. Without any doubt, they had been engraved on the orders of Apophis, in order to create an impenetrable barrier. The Emperor of Darkness had corrupted an *akh*, a 'radiant spirit', distorting it and turning it into an aggressive, fearsome ghost.

Ahhotep addressed it, making the offering of the necklace.

A strong wind began to blow. The queen thought she could hear cries of pain, as if a lost soul were in unbearable agony.

Ahhotep tore the bodice of her dress into four strips, which she laid side by side between the stele and the entrance to the tomb.

The wind grew fiercer, and the moaning became louder.

Ahhotep laid her serpent-shaped staff upon the ground. The cornelian quivered and came to life, and a royal cobra reared up. Writhing on the linen strips, it set them alight.

Picking up these torches, the queen used them to make a path of fire. 'May the goddesses hidden in the flames stand guard by day and ensure protection by night,' she prayed. 'May they drive away visible and invisible enemies. May they cause light to enter the darkness.'

The wind dropped, and little by little the fire

grew less intense. When Ahhotep looked around, the menacing stele had disappeared, as if it had sunk into the cliff-face.

Staff in hand, Ahhotep entered the house of eternity of a noble called Amenemhat. She crossed a forecourt, passed beneath a pillared portico and meditated on the floor of the huge shrine, whose door stood open.

Had the emperor laid other traps?

Trusting in her own instincts, Ahhotep spoke the name of 'Amenemhat, of Just Voice', asking him to welcome her into his earthly paradise.

The paintings were extraordinarily fresh, and the queen allowed herself to be soothed by the charming depictions of birds, symbols of the metamorphoses of the soul. Suddenly, she sensed danger. Her eyes fixed upon unexpected scenes, devoted to wrestlers who were engaged in unarmed combat. They were using a great number of different holds, each movement clearly broken down to serve as an example.

The wrestlers' faces turned towards the queen, their eyes filled with the will to attack her. Soon, the seemingly immobile figures would come to life, step down from the walls and assail the intruder.

'I am the Queen of Egypt and the Wife of God. You are soldiers in the service of Pharaoh. May the emperor's enchantments leave your bodies and may your fighting skills enter the service of Kamose.' Defiantly, she held up the serpent-shaped staff in her left hand and the *menat*-necklace in her right. 'Obey me, or your images will be deprived of life. May each movement you make favour the light, not the darkness.'

For a few moments, the wrestlers seemed to confer. Then they returned to their original positions. The sense of danger was gone.

Ahhotep made her way to the alcove containing the statues of the tomb's owner and his wife. At their feet lay a jar.

In the jar was a papyrus on which were written the good and bad days of the current year, in accordance with the myths revealed in the different temples of Egypt. Any important action must respect this sacred calendar.

'Try again,' Moustache ordered a strong, thickset man who was most unhappy at having twice bitten the dust.

On the third attempt, the stocky man feinted at Moustache's head but, at the last moment, tried to hit him in the stomach. Not realizing what was happening to him, the fellow lost his balance, was lifted off his feet sideways, and fell heavily on to his back.

'This hold is truly amazing!' exclaimed Moustache delightedly.

Several scribes had made exact copies of the paintings of the wrestlers in Amenemhat's tomb, and the pictures were being used to teach the old techniques to the Theban soldiers. Moustache and the Afghan had proved best at this game. And they made sure that the training was intensive, so as to increase their men's chances of survival. Although the Hyksos had not counter-attacked, the troops were still on permanent alert.

Kamose was pawing the ground with impatience, but the Jar of Predictions had delivered its verdict: the coming days were unsuitable for military action. Obliged to respect the words of the Invisible, he feared that time was against the Thebans.

'You look worried, Majesty,' said beautiful Anat, who had been placed under confinement in the royal tent.

'That would that please you, no doubt.'

'On the contrary, since you freed me from my chains I wish only for your success.'

'You are very seductive, and you know it.'

'Is that a crime which merits punishment?'

'I have more important concerns than a woman's beauty.'

'But surely the war doesn't prevent you from loving? If it does, you will lack a strength which will be essential to your victory. What violence destroys, only love can successfully rebuild.'

'Do you really want to be loved, Anat?'

'By you, yes, provided you are sincere.'

Kamose took the blue-eyed Syrian into his arms and kissed her passionately.

CHAPTER 47

Jannas had crushed the Anatolian rebellion, but at what a price! Half the Hyksos war-fleet had been wiped out, many of his best soldiers were dead, and an enormous number of wounded men would not be fit to rejoin the army for a long time, if ever. And hostilities would break out again some day, for the mountain-men of Anatolia would never accept Hyksos domination.

Despite these grim facts, when he returned to Avaris Jannas was celebrated as a hero by a huge crowd of officers and men, who had total confidence in the empire's most highly renowned warrior.

As a sign of honour, High Treasurer Khamudi himself greeted Jannas at the entrance to the citadel. 'The emperor has been awaiting your return with impatience, Commander.'

'I acted as fast as I could.'

'Of course, of course. No one doubts that. Are you satisfied with the results?'

'That information is for the emperor's ears alone.'

'Of course. I shall take you to the audience chamber.'

★ ★ ★

Apophis was in an indescribable rage. That morning, he had secretly tried to put on the Red Crown of Lower Egypt for an appearance before the Temple of Set. But he was immediately attacked by such severe pain that he had had to remove the accursed crown and return it to its hiding-place. No one must ever know that it had rejected him.

From his spy's reports and by consulting his blue flask with its map of Egypt, Apophis knew that the Thebans had reconquered Qis, Nefrusy and Khmun, and were drawn up north of Beni Hasan. So Queen Ahhotep had succeeded in shattering the magic barrier. She was undoubtedly a formidable enemy, who had escaped trap after trap.

This war would be decisive. The queen and her son had thrown all the rebel forces into the battle, and Egypt would be drained dry after their defeat. It was an ideal opportunity to destroy the ancient spirituality of the pharaohs for ever.

Jannas bowed before Apophis.

'You have arrived at the right time, Commander. You are no doubt tired after that long campaign, but unfortunately I cannot let you rest.'

'I am yours to command, Majesty.'

'Are we at last done with the Anatolians?'

Jannas hesitated.

'You may speak freely in front of Khamudi.'

The commander could not disobey an order

from the emperor. 'I have killed enough rebels to ensure that Anatolia will cause you no concern for several months. But it is impossible to wipe them out completely. In a year, or perhaps two, we shall have to strike at them again.'

Apophis did not seem angry. 'Our army is not made for sleep, Commander. The greatness of the empire will always demand this sort of action. For the moment, you are to deal with Egypt.'

'Egypt? Do you not think a simple frontal operation—'

'The situation has changed. It was necessary that Queen Ahhotep became bold and that her son Kamose, the puppet king, believed in victory. The further north they advance, the closer they come to the terrain which we know best and on which we shall use our heavy weapons. The rebels are over-confident, and will throw all their forces into a head-on clash which they think they can win. Also, I wanted to re-organize the trade-control post at Khmun and rid myself of the petty tyrant at Nefrusy. By killing a few useless individuals, Ahhotep has done me a service.'

'Is our information about the enemy's movements accurate?'

'It could not be more accurate. The spy who enabled me to kill Seqen continues to serve me efficiently.'

'Then I can attack the Thebans at once.'

Apophis gave one of his icy smiles. 'There is

something else more urgent, and we shall use another strategy, beginning with Lisht and Per-shaq.'

Jannas was a soldier and a Hyksos, so he would obey his emperor's orders to the letter. However, he considered them beneath his dignity as leader of the empire's forces. Khamudi and his men would have been quite good enough to carry out this task. But the commander forced himself to believe that Apophis saw further than he did, and that these orders were necessary.

As he made his way to his official residence, Jannas saw fifty old men, women and children pass by, laden with bundles and chained together. They were surrounded by a detachment of Hyksos guards, commanded by Aberia.

'My lady, where are you taking these people?' asked Jannas.

'That is a secret matter of state,' replied Aberia.

'It is your duty to tell me.'

'They are convicted criminals – nothing but dangerous criminals.'

'Dangerous, those miserable wretches? Do you take me for a fool?'

'I am merely obeying orders.'

The pitiful procession continued on its way, and Jannas went to Khamudi's house, where the High Treasurer was totting up his receipts from the last sales of drugs to the notables of Avaris.

'I would like to know,' said Jannas coldly, 'how many matters of state are kept secret from the commander of the Hyksos armies.'

Seeing the commander's anger, Khamudi realized that he must tread carefully if he was to avert an explosion of anger.

'How many? Why, none, Commander.'

'That is not the lady Aberia's view.'

'I'm sure it is only a misunderstanding.'

'In that case, tell me where she is taking old men, children and women whom she describes as dangerous.'

Khamudi looked rather uncomfortable. 'The lady Aberia is not entirely wrong. These people may look harmless, but in fact they are a real threat because they spread dangerous ideas. That is why it is necessary to expel them.'

'Only expel them?'

'We intern them in a place where they cannot cause any more trouble.'

'You mean a prison camp. Where is it?'

'At Sharuhen.'

'But Sharuhen's in Palestine. Why there?'

'It is far enough from Avaris, and the rebels receive just punishment there.'

'In that harsh land, many of them must die very quickly.'

'Surely you don't regret the deaths of the emperor's enemies?' said Khamudi. 'He approves both of the camp, which he considers essential, and also of the deportation of troublemakers. By expelling them, we rid Avaris of all undesirable elements. Isn't it a good idea?'

'Very good. Now, what else is there that I ought to know?'

'Nothing, I assure you.'

'I am glad to hear it, High Treasurer.'

Khamudi smiled. 'My wife and I are holding a reception this evening, with a few young girls who are to be deported tomorrow. It should be amusing, so won't you join us?'

'I have already told you I am not interested in amusements like that. Good night, High Treasurer.'

CHAPTER 48

Minos was as ardent as ever when he made love to Windswept, and she still found matchless happiness in her lover's arms. But she could not forget his secret meeting with an official suspected of conspiring against Apophis.

If Minos really was guilty of that crime, she ought to denounce him to the emperor, who would delight in sending a new victim to the bull or the labyrinth. But Windswept would not let herself believe in his treason, and kept her suspicions to herself.

She caressed the Minoan's chest with her long, slender hands. 'I have the feeling you're hiding something from me, my love.'

'Don't you think you know everything about me?'

'Sometimes I wonder.'

'You're right.'

At last, he was going to confess. 'You can tell me everything, Minos.'

'It's very intimate, very serious . . .'

'Trust me.'

The artist swallowed hard. 'I'm having doubts about my talent. My early paintings seem colourless to me now, but I can't help wondering if they aren't more accomplished than the new ones. I worry about it so much that I can't sleep. My hand should be my only guide, but I'm afraid it's losing its precision. Is this a new stage, which will improve my work, or is my inspiration running dry?'

Windswept kissed him passionately. 'As long as you love me, you'll have all the inspiration you could want.'

After the midday meal, when most people were asleep, Minos left the fortress, bidding good day to the guards. They regarded him with contempt: this dauber was no use to anyone – he couldn't even handle a weapon.

He walked along with no apparent goal in mind, and turned into a street lined with officers' houses. Several times, he halted and looked around. Then he suddenly dived into a blind alley where grainstores stood. Since they were not due to be filled for another week, there were no guards there.

In fact, there was no one at all there. And yet his accomplice had agreed to meet him here. His absence must mean that he had been arrested and that Minos would soon be caught, too.

'Come closer,' whispered an anxious voice.

Nervously, Minos did so.

The man was there, crouching between two grainstores.

'Have you made any more contacts?' asked Minos.

'Jannas's return made it impossible – there are guards everywhere.'

'At the palace, people are whispering that Jannas hates Khamudi. Some say that the commander would make a good emperor.'

'He has the army's trust, certainly, but he's absolutely loyal to Apophis and would never support a conspiracy against him.'

'Then is it impossible for us to do what we must?'

'For the moment, yes. But Jannas is leaving to fight the Theban rebels. When he returns, the enmity between him and Khamudi is bound to take a new turn. Perhaps we can profit from it. Until then, we must wait and stay calm.'

Disappointed, Minos set off back to the palace. The man seemed too afraid to do anything, even in favourable circumstances. It was up to Minos to act, together with the other Minoans who were forced to live in this sinister town. Only the emperor's death would give them back their freedom.

Taking ample precautions so that she would not be spotted, Windswept had almost lost Minos. Choosing the right direction, she had finally found him again and had hidden in the corner of the blind alley where, it was clear, the Minoan was making contact with someone.

By climbing on to the roof of a grain-store, she could have eavesdropped on their conversation, but the stores' convex shape would have made that too dangerous. She had had to be content with watching her lover leave, lost in thought and visibly dejected.

The man who mattered was the other one. When she saw that he was the weapons official who was already under suspicion, the terrible reality hit her full in the face.

Minos was indeed a conspirator. He had lied to her, and she must denounce him.

In Jannas's eyes, there could be no exceptions to the rule of obedience. But he had never to carry out a mission as strange as the one to Per-shaq, and he felt that it lay well outside the duties of a soldier with his experience. He had therefore not gone himself, delegating one of his subordinates to execute the emperor's orders.

When the officer returned, Jannas summoned him at once, and asked, 'Is it done?

'Yes, Commander.'

'Any problems?'

'No, sir.'

'What is the latest information on the enemy army?'

'According to our scouts, it's moving slowly towards Per-shaq. They say it's a real army, sir, and surprisingly well organized, and the fleet is big. But the Theban scouts are not unskilled, so ours could not observe at close quarters.'

'Ensure that our operation is thoroughly prepared. I will not tolerate any laxity.'

The site of Lisht,* abandoned since the Hyksos invasion, included pyramids built by illustrious pharaohs of ancient times and the tombs of their senior officials. A profound peace reigned there, as if the kings of that bygone age were still passing on their wisdom.

It was precisely that wisdom which Apophis wanted to see disappear.

'Find me the entrances to these monuments,' Jannas ordered his engineers, 'and unblock the ways to the treasure-chambers.'

The pyramid of Amenemhat I, the most northerly, was as tall as thirty men; that of Sesostris I, which was surrounded by ten small pyramids, was even taller. Despite the precautions taken by the builders, the Hyksos succeeded in breaking into them. The mummies were removed from their sarcophagi, their bandages ripped off, their protective amulets scattered. Precious papyri, covered with texts describing the never-ending metamorphoses of the royal soul in the universe, were burnt.

Apophis's will had been done. Deprived of the protection of their glorious ancestors, Ahhotep and Kamose would find their momentum destroyed.

*Lisht is about 50km south of Cairo. Its ruined pyramids date from the twentieth century BC.

Nevertheless, the desecration of the royal remains was carried out in heavy silence. Jannas's soldiers were unaccustomed to fighting dead men, and the mummies' serene faces disturbed more than one soldier.

'The operation has been completed, sir,' said Jannas's second-in-command.

'Perhaps . . .'

'Have we forgotten something, sir?'

'Look at those pyramids. You would swear they're alive and defying us, as if violating the tombs had served no use.'

'What do you suggest we do?'

'We ought to destroy them stone by stone, but we haven't the time. I have received new orders.'

CHAPTER 49

As the Theban army advanced towards Per-shaq, they knew that a head-on clash with Hyksos forces was inevitable. In the ranks, there was talk of monstrous animals which the emperor controlled with his mind, of long spears which could run through three men at once, and unknown weapons against which even Queen Ahhotep had no defence.

At the head of the war-fleet, Moon had taken up his helmsman's staff again to sound the Nile. As alert as a cat, he watched for the slightest sign of danger. At his side were Moustache and the Afghan, who knew the region well.

'We're very near Per-shaq,' said Moustache, who was getting increasingly edgy.

'Still nothing,' said Moon. 'But they may well have laid an ambush for us.'

'The best way of finding out,' suggested the Afghan, 'would be to send out scouts.'

Moon halted the boats. Ahhotep and the pharaoh agreed with the Afghan's reasoning, but refused to let him command the patrol himself.

'You're too senior,' Moustache pointed out, 'and you have too many decorations. I'll go instead.'

'No, you will not,' replied Ahhotep, 'because you hold the same rank and decorations as the Afghan.'

'Majesty, we cannot send a few inexperienced boys out. Without a skilled leader, not one of them will get back alive.'

'Do you consider me a skilled leader?' asked Kamose.

Moustache and the Afghan stared, open-mouthed.

The king bowed to his mother. 'Queen of Egypt, it is my responsibility, and mine alone, to lead my men into battle. Then they will know that I am not afraid, and that the commander of the army of freedom will face all the risks they do. My father and you yourself have always acted in this way.'

The man who stood in front of Ahhotep was neither a braggart nor irresponsible. He was a twenty-year-old pharaoh who was insistent upon carrying out his duties to the full. Although, as a mother, she felt her heart was breaking, the queen could not oppose his decision.

'If I fall,' whispered Kamose, 'I know you will pick me up again.'

The king had disembarked with a hundred men, less than an hour's march from Per-shaq. As soon as the enemy was spotted, he would release Rascal with a brief message outlining the situation.

'Still nothing,' fretted Moustache, pacing up and

down the deck of the flagship, 'and they've been gone for ages.'

'It may be a good sign,' said the Afghan.

'Supposing the king's been taken prisoner? Supposing Rascal's been killed? We must do something.'

But only Ahhotep could give the order, and she said nothing.

'There's something wrong,' declared Moustache. 'I can feel it.'

'I am beginning to agree with you,' said the Afghan. 'Let's go and see the queen.'

At that moment, Rascal appeared above them with a flutter of wings, and landed gently on the queen's forearm. His bright eyes shone with the joy of a job well done.

The message, written in the king's hand, was decidedly surprising.

'He says there's nothing to report,' said Ahhotep. 'He is waiting for us at the gates of the town.'

Per-shaq was deserted. There was not a living soul in its narrow streets, not even a stray dog. Profoundly suspicious, Emheb ordered some of his men to inspect all the houses. All had been abandoned. In the cellars food had been left, untouched.

'The Hyksos must be hiding,' said Emheb. 'They're waiting for a large body of our troops to enter the town, and then they'll encircle us.'

Kamose deployed his men. This time, Moustache

and the Afghan walked at the head of their regiments, ready to fight. But there was not a single Hyksos to be seen.

Outside the city, Moustache spotted significant tracks in the damp earth. There were footprints, hoofmarks – much larger than those of donkeys – and strange furrows.

'They have left and headed north,' he said after studying the tracks.

'The Hyksos have fled!' declared the pharaoh incredulously.

This bloodless victory unleashed joy in the whole army. So this was all the emperor's terrifying forces amounted to: a band of cowards who ran away at the enemy's approach and did not even try to hold their positions!

Ahhotep, however, did not join in the jubilation. True, the Hyksos had left Per-shaq, but where were its citizens?

Embheb came hurrying up to her. 'Majesty, come quickly!'

He led Ahhotep and Kamose to the area where the granaries stood. There was blood everywhere, and a terrible stench filled the air. Emheb's archers took up their positions, as if the enemy was at last about to emerge from the shadows.

'Open the doors of the granaries,' ordered Ahhotep.

Several young soldiers did so. Instantly, they bent over and vomited. One of them cried out, and beat his fist so hard against his forehead that an officer had to intervene to stop him injuring himself seriously.

The pharaoh and his mother went to the granary doors. What they saw brought them to the brink of fainting. Holloweyed, hearts pounding and breath coming in gasps, they could not believe such barbarity.

The bodies of the inhabitants of Per-shaq were heaped on top of each other, together with those of dogs, cats, geese and little monkeys. Not a single human being, not one animal or bird, had been spared. All had had their throats cut. All had been flung on to the piles like rubbish.

The pharaoh picked up the misshapen body of an old man, which lay across a fat man's back. Before murdering him, they had broken his legs.

Kamose could not weep. 'Remove these victims, human and animal, from this charnel-house with respect,' he ordered, 'and bury them in the earth. The Wife of God will conduct a funeral rite so that their souls may be reunited and at peace.'

A slow procession began, while the artificers started digging tombs.

Most of the soldiers were in tears, and even the Afghan, who had seemed to have no chinks in his armour, could not hold back his sobs as he carried the body of a young woman whose belly and breasts had been slashed to ribbons.

Twenty granaries at Per-shaq were emptied. The queen and the pharaoh looked upon each of the victims. Most had been appallingly tortured before being killed.

Ahhotep could sense her son faltering. But she could not hide from him a fact which she alone seemed to have noticed: 'Among these unfortunates, there is not a single child.'

'They must have been taken away to become slaves.'

'There are still three granaries left,' said the queen.

His head reeling, the king himself opened the door of one of them. He gave a sigh of profound relief. 'Jars – nothing but jars.'

For a moment, Ahhotep wanted to believe that the Hyksos had been merciful, but she had to check. She removed the coarse stopper of clay from an oil-jar. Inside lay the body of a three-year-old girl, her skull smashed.

Every single jar contained the body of a child; each child had been tortured before being killed. The Hyksos troops had carried out the emperor's orders to the letter.

CHAPTER 50

The burial ceremony was conducted with a fervour which united the living and the dead through their shared faith in the justice of Osiris. Afterwards, everyone felt as if they'd plunged into a kind of abyss, from which only the comradeship of battle could offer an escape. The soldiers gathered in groups to talk about their dear ones, and to prove to themselves that, despite the horrors of Per-shaq, a future still existed.

Alone in her cabin with Laughter, who was lying in front of the door, Ahhotep called upon Pharaoh Seqen's radiant soul to give her back the strength she had lost by offering all her love to the victims of the Hyksos. After the slaughter of those innocents, after the torture of women, children, men and animals, the face of this war had changed.

If there still was a war. The emperor's intentions were clear: if the Theban army continued to defy him, thousands of Egyptians would be slaughtered with unparalleled cruelty. Could the twenty-year-old king live with the responsibility for that happening? Deeply scarred already, he wanted only to return to Thebes.

The murderers of Per-shaq had not struck at random, and their appalling crime would prove as effective as even their most destructive weapons of war.

So Ahhotep must stand in the path of her own son, and show him that any backward step would lead to defeat.

'Your attitude is unworthy of a pharaoh,' declared Anat.

'If you had seen—'

'I did see. I also saw Tita cut the throats of innocent people to establish his reign of terror. Those are the methods the Hyksos use.'

'If we continue our offensive,' said Kamose, 'the emperor will order more massacres.'

'If you take refuge in the illusory safety of Thebes, first he will order more massacres, and then his army will charge south and destroy you. The more you hesitate, the more Apophis's fury will be unleashed upon innocent people. Once you attack the Emperor of Darkness, you can never go back. That is what Queen Ahhotep thinks, and it is what I think, too.'

'Has my mother confided in you?'

'No, Majesty, but all I needed to do was look into her eyes. Even if she had to continue the fight alone, or with just a handful of supporters, she would not hesitate. Apophis knows now that he will never subjugate the Egyptians, so he has decided to kill them all. Your army's retreat would not save a single life.'

'So our early victories were nothing but illusions,' said Kamose bitterly.

'Illusions? Breaking through the front at Qis, taking Nefrusy and Khmun? Of course they weren't.'

'When the Hyksos use their heavy weapons—'

'They may be too confident in those weapons' power. You must strive to be worthy of wearing the White Crown when the sons of the light confront those of the dark.'

Ahhotep gazed up at the full moon, the symbol of successful rebirth. Once again, the sun of night had vanquished the forces of chaos, to light up the starry sky and become the interpreter of the hidden light. But from this day onward, the Jar of Predictions had no more to say.

Kamose came up to her. 'Mother, I have made my decision. In the voice of Anat, the woman I love, I heard your voice. And you have set out the only possible way.'

'Destiny is asking a great deal of one so young – perhaps too much. A whole lifetime of suffering and drama has been imposed upon you in a few weeks, and you have been given no chance to regroup. But you are the pharaoh, and your age is of no importance. The only thing that matters is your office, for it is the hope of an entire people.'

'At dawn, I shall inform the army that we intend to continue northwards.'

The small town of Sako, where the army next

halted, had suffered the same fate as Per-shaq. Their macabre discoveries once again horrified and sickened the soldiers, and it took all Pharaoh's authority to maintain order in the ranks. The Wife of God conducted the funerary rites, and her nobility calmed the men. Everyone realized that they were fighting not only to free Egypt but also to destroy a monster whose cruelty was limitless.

The king and queen were finishing a frugal evening meal when Moustache came in, pushing in front of him a small, frightened-looking man in a black breastplate.

'Look what I found,' said Moustache. 'He was hiding in a cellar. If Your Majesties permit, I shall hand him over to my men.'

The Hyksos fell to his knees, eyes lowered. 'Don't kill me,' he begged. 'I'm only a messenger. I haven't hurt anyone – I've never even carried a weapon.'

'Why did you not leave with the others?' demanded Kamose.

'I hid in a house so as not to see what they were doing, and I fell asleep.'

'Who is in command of these murderers?'

'Commander Jannas himself.'

'And where is he now?'

'I don't know, my lord, truly I don't know. I'm just a messenger and—'

'Deal with him, Moustache.'

'Wait a moment,' cut in Ahhotep. 'It's possible that he might be useful.'

★ ★ ★

'You wished to see me urgently, little sister?' The emperor was surprised. 'You look upset.'

Face to face with Apophis, who was colder than the north wind in winter, even Windswept felt uneasy. But it was too late to go back now.

'I . . . I have some information.'

'The name of a conspirator?'

'Exactly.'

'You're wonderful, little sister, far more efficient than my spies. Tell me quickly, who dares devise dark plans against my august person?'

Windswept remembered Minos's body, his caresses, his fervour, the hours of pleasure which only he could give her. 'Someone important, someone we'd never have suspected.'

'Come on, don't keep me waiting. The traitor will enter the labyrinth this very evening and you shall sit beside me to watch him die.'

Windswept took a deep breath. 'He is one of the officials in charge of weapons,' she said.

The arrest warrant had scarcely been signed when a furious Khamudi came in and presented the emperor with a papyrus. 'Majesty, it's a letter from Pharaoh Kamose.'

'How did it reach us?'

'It was brought by a messenger the Thebans captured but then released. I tortured the imbecile, of course, but he died without saying anything interesting.'

'Well, read me the message.'

'Majesty, I don't think—'

'Read it.'

Khamudi did so, in an indignant voice.

> I, Pharaoh Kamose, regard Apophis as nothing
> but a petty warlord who has been driven back,
> together with his armies. Your speech is miser-
> able. It calls to mind the headsman's block on
> which you will perish. Terrible rumours are
> circulating in your city, where your defeat is
> already being announced. You desire nothing
> but evil, and by evil you shall fall. The women
> of Avaris will no longer be able to conceive,
> for their hearts will no longer open in their
> bodies when they hear the war-cries of my
> soldiers. Look behind you as you flee, for the
> army of Pharaoh Kamose and Queen Ahhotep
> is advancing towards you.

Khamudi was quivering with rage. 'Majesty,
should Jannas not immediately crush this vermin
who dares insult you?'

The emperor was unperturbed. 'This contemptible letter is intended to provoke me and draw
me into a trap. The Egyptians would like us to fight
at Sako, on their terrain. But we shall not make that
mistake, and Jannas shall continue his cleansing. We
shall destroy the rebels at the right place and time,
just as we have planned.'

CHAPTER 51

'Nothing to report, Majesty,' said the commander of the scouts; he was as disappointed as the pharaoh and Queen Ahhotep.

Although his vanity must certainly have been wounded, Apophis had not reacted as they had hoped, so all the measures they had taken around Sako had been for nothing.

'Nevertheless, we have learnt something important,' said Ahhotep. 'Apophis has a specific plan, and nothing will divert him from it, not even insufferable insults to his power.'

'Massacring innocent people and pretending to retreat,' said Kamose furiously, 'that's all his vile plan is.'

'There may be more to it than that,' warned the queen.

Her words worried the king. 'What do you suspect?'

'We must not underestimate Apophis, even for a second. Although we are advancing, he is still in control of the situation. There are three vital questions. First, how far back will he withdraw,

331

and where will he finally join battle? Second, do these tactics mask preparations for a surprise attack? Third, we have still not caught the Hyksos spy: what is he plotting?'

'He must have gone back to Avaris, or else be dead. Otherwise he would have done us serious harm.'

Kamose's argument seemed convincing, but the queen was still doubtful.

'This is what I advise,' she said. 'Soon we shall have to face Jannas, and we have no idea what form the confrontation will take. So I propose dividing our troops into two: one half will remain at Sako, while the other makes for Fayum. The carrier-pigeons will enable us to remain in constant contact, and if we need to join forces we shall be able to do so quickly.'

'Then I shall leave for Fayum.'

'No, Kamose, I shall go.'

'Mother, I don't—'

'It must be so.'

The governor of Fayum, Joseph, was a Hebrew. After suffering the jealousy and hatred of his brothers, who had tried to kill him, he had found happiness, wealth and respect in Egypt. As he was not suspected of collaborating with the enemies of the Hyksos, Apophis had appointed him to govern the little paradise the pharaohs of old had created by irrigating the area, which was about three days' march south-west of Memphis.

Criss-crossed by canals fed by a tributary of the Nile, Fayum was an immense garden and a haven for game and fish.

Joseph was an excellent administrator. He now lived in opulence, in a big house surrounded by gardens and palm-trees, but he had never forgotten the unhappy times, or what it was like to be hungry. He cared about every inhabitant of his province, and intervened personally to help anyone who was in difficulties. His people lived a pleasant life amid the greenery, far from the ferocity of the desert and the ferocity of war.

The governor was therefore very surprised when Jannas arrived at his house.

'Is everything quiet here?' asked Jannas. 'Has there been any trouble with rebels?'

'No, of course not. There's been no unrest in Fayum for a long time.'

'All good things come to an end. The Theban army is heading this way.'

'The Thebans? How can that be?'

'You do not ask questions, you obey the emperor's orders. I am leaving you two hundred soldiers, under the command of Captain Antreb.'

'That's a very small force to defend the whole of Fayum.'

Jannas looked out at the garden. 'Who said anything about defending it? Their mission is to burn all the villages and crops.'

Joseph thought he must be having a nightmare. 'That's impossible! Surely you aren't serious?'

'Those are the orders, and I demand your full co-operation.'

'But . . . what about the people?'

'They will be killed.'

'What have they done wrong?' asked Joseph rebelliously.

'The emperor's will must not be questioned.'

'Surely you aren't going to kill the children?'

'The emperor said everyone. When it's done, Captain Antreb will take you to Avaris, where Apophis will reward you.'

Captain Antreb was a short, stocky, round-faced man who looked rather like Khamudi. He was a particularly brutal man and loved killing, which was why Jannas had appointed him. He and his murderous troops would thoroughly enjoy their work, especially when the victims begged for their lives. As Antreb had a little time to spare, he was planning to extend the period of torture. In a region as pleasant as Fayum, his men would enjoy the extra entertainment.

Antreb was staying at Joseph's villa, and was revelling in the delicious food, fine wines and other benefits. Never had he been so assiduously massaged and shaved.

'Are you satisfied with my hospitality?' Joseph asked him.

'More than satisfied, overwhelmed. But there's work to be done.'

'This province did not grow rich in a day. Why

ruin so many years of work? You can see for yourself that the villagers of Fayum are peaceful people,
whose only interest is their gardens and fields. The
emperor has nothing to fear from them.'

'That's irrelevant. The only thing that matters
to me is my orders.'

'Think again, I beg of you! What good will
massacring all these innocent people do you?'

'With the villages and crops destroyed, the
Thebans will find no support along their way, only
corpses.'

'May I go to Avaris and plead Fayum's cause to
the emperor?'

'That's out of the question. My work will begin
tomorrow morning and will be finished by the
evening. Not a single village will be spared. Do
you hear me? Not one. And if you drag your feet,
you might just have an . . . accident. Do I make
myself clear?'

'Very clear.'

'We shall begin with the largest village. You will
tell all the people, including the children, to
assemble in the main square because you have
some good news to announce to them. Then I
shall take over.'

Moon had insisted on commanding the fleet on
its voyage to Fayum. Aboard were the regiments
led by Moustache and the Afghan, and the archers
commanded by Ahmes, son of Abana. Emheb had
remained in Sako with the pharaoh, as had Neshi.

335

Everyone was very tense. Ahhotep stood at the prow of the flagship, scanning the riverbanks.

'The Hyksos have destroyed everything in their path,' grieved Moon. 'There's probably not a single villager left alive.'

As they neared Fayum, the air grew fragrant. The province was like one huge oasis, where the very idea of war seemed out of place. Trees as far as the eye could see, gardens in the shade of palmgroves, herds of cattle browsing on juicy grass, and even the sound of a flute playing, as if there was still such a thing as a happy peasant.

'It is a trap!' exclaimed Moon. 'To your combat stations!'

While it was in the middle of the river, the fleet had nothing to fear. And, surprisingly, the lookout at the top of the highest mast did not give the signal that meant enemy vessels were near.

'The Hyksos must be hidden among the trees,' said the Afghan. 'As soon as we disembark, they will attack.'

'There's one,' said Moustache, pointing to the riverbank where a man had just appeared.

Arms raised above his head, the man ran towards the Egyptian ships.

'Do not fire,' ordered the queen. 'He is unarmed.'

The man waded thigh-deep into the river. 'I am Joseph, governor of Fayum,' he shouted, 'and I need your help.'

CHAPTER 52

'I'll deal with him,' declared Moustache, diving into the Nile.

The Egyptian archers aimed their bows. If this man Joseph was in fact a decoy, he would not live long.

'You must help me,' he repeated. 'The Hyksos want to slaughter all the people of Fayum! Their leader is at my house, and he's about to begin the killing.'

'How many Hyksos are there?' asked Moustache.

'Two hundred – two hundred torturers determined to destroy Fayum! You're the only ones who can stop them.'

Moustache scanned the area suspiciously. There were no Hyksos in sight, so Joseph might not be lying. He beckoned to the war-fleet.

As soon as the ships were moored, Ahhotep was first to descend the gangplank.

At the sight of her, Joseph was overcome. He knew instantly that she was the famous Queen of Freedom, whose legend grew greater every day. This sublimely beautiful woman radiated a light whose intensity made the heart swell. At that moment, he knew he had been right to hope she would come.

'We must act quickly, Majesty,' he said, prostrating himself. 'Please do not abandon my people.'

It was a pitiful Joseph who presented himself before Captain Antreb.

The Hyksos adjusted his black breastplate. 'Here you are at last. If I'd had to wait much longer, I'd have cut your servants' throats to relieve the boredom.'

'Your orders have been carried out, Captain. The villagers have gathered and are waiting for the good news I promised them.'

Antreb put on his black helmet. 'Excellent. Carry on like this, Joseph, and you'll save your skin.'

'Will you at least spare those closest to me?'

'That depends how tired we are when we've finished with the others.'

Antreb had some difficulty gathering his men together, as most of them were drunk. When they entered the main square of the village, which was fringed with palm-trees, they found all the men, women and children huddled together in terror. The soldiers knew they were going to enjoy some fine sport.

'I have two pieces of news, one good and one bad,' announced Antreb jauntily. 'The bad news is that you are all, including your governor, dangerous rebels.' He grabbed Joseph by the shoulder and hurled him into the huddle of villagers. 'I hate Hebrews, so I shan't spare you, after all.

'Now, here's the good news: the emperor has ordered me to prevent you from doing harm. We're going to torture you to make you confess what you are plotting against our sovereign. Those of you who tell us absolutely everything will be allowed to die quickly. For those who are stubborn, death will be very slow and very painful.'

The torturers held up thick clubs studded with metal. There was nothing more effective for interrogating victims.

A man emerged from the mass of villagers. 'You, Hyksos, are you aware that you are a murderer?'

Antreb was so astounded that for a moment he was speechless. Then he said, 'Who the devil are you? Some sort of priest?'

'No, just someone who will no longer tolerate the rule of tyranny and blind violence.'

Antreb turned to his men. 'You see? They really are rebels. As for you, little man, with your fine words, I have a special fate in store for you: you will be roasted alive over a slow fire.'

'That's unbelievable.'

Antreb was amazed again at this peasant's fearlessness. 'You're making a big mistake if you think I won't do it, my lad!'

'The unbelievable thing is that that's exactly what I intend to do to you.'

Antreb's third attack of astonishment proved fatal, for Moustache dived at his legs and, using one of the holds he had learnt from the wrestling scenes at Beni Hasan, hoisted him high before dropping him heavily on the back of his neck.

The Hyksos soldiers were cut down by the Egyptian archers' arrows. Ahhotep had ordered that they were to be shot in the back, so that they would die like the cowards they were. In just a few minutes, all the torturers were dead.

Antreb lay still, his eyes glassy.

'Good grief,' grumbled Moustache, 'even that vermin's neck was weak!'

'You took an unnecessary risk again,' scolded the Afghan.

'No I didn't – you were covering me. Besides, I really wanted to try out that hold.'

The villagers embraced their rescuers.

'Last week,' Joseph told Moustache, 'we received supplies from the North. With those and what we grow here, I can promise you and your men an unforgettable meal.'

The joints of meat cooked in milk were as delicious as anyone could wish. Fayum had been transformed into a gigantic open-air banqueting-hall, where its return to freedom would be joyously celebrated. Kamose was welcomed with shouts of joy, as if he had been sent from another world, where Ma'at still reigned.

Before the celebrations began, the Wife of God

had celebrated a ritual in honour of the ancestors and of Amon, lord of Thebes. As she did so, she sensed a presence close by, a gentle warmth, a loving caress, a south wind enveloping her whole body in tenderness. It was he, it was Seqen, intensely present at that moment when a new part of Egypt had been torn from the emperor's clutches. Never before had the late pharaoh manifested himself in such tangible form, as if the queen needed a new kind of energy, sent from the otherworld, before facing terrible ordeals.

'Aren't you hungry, Mother?' asked Kamose.

'We ought to be thinking about the future.'

'I cannot really share the people's happiness, either,' he admitted.

The queen and the pharaoh withdrew into the royal tent, to study Qaris's model of Egypt.

How far they had come since young Ahhotep's rebellion, since the time when only the Theban enclave knew any freedom at all. Many provinces and towns had been reconquered, but there had also been many atrocities and much suffering, and there were still innumerable obstacles between them and true victory.

Ahhotep leant over the model. 'That's where Jannas is waiting for us. That's where he plans to crush us.' She pointed to Memphis.

Memphis, 'the Balance of the Two Lands', had been Egypt's capital at the time of the pyramids, the heart of the country's system of trade, and it was made sacred by the Temple of Ptah. Memphis, gateway to the Delta for the South, and to the Nile valley for the North. Through his policy of destroying villages and crops, the emperor planned to lure in all the Theban forces, which would have no chance of defeating the main Hyksos army.

'Then the battle at Memphis will be decisive,' said Kamose. 'But Apophis must not find out that we know it and that we shan't throw ourselves head-first into his trap. He ought to have launched a surprise attack by now, before we can reach Memphis. He probably has absolute confidence in his own military power, so whatever tactics we adopt will seem ridiculous to him.'

Ahhotep said pensively, 'Do you remember the three questions I posed? We have the answer to the first, but there are still the other two. Memphis is so obvious that it may conceal another trap which is still hidden from us.'

'How can we detect it?'

'Let us pray to Amon, and ask him not to abandon us but to offer us a sign.'

CHAPTER 53

The Afghan and Moustache were always among the first to rise in the morning. They had acquired this habit in their early days as rebels, at a time when they had feared they might be caught at any moment. It gave them a chance to inspect the camp and see if anything was amiss.

This morning, despite a dreadful headache resulting from the previous night's excesses, the Afghan noticed something unusual.

'What's wrong?' asked Moustache.

'Have we set up enough guard-posts?'

'I saw to it myself. If there'd been even the slightest problem, we'd have been warned immediately.'

The Afghan sniffed the air like a lion on the prowl. Then he delivered his verdict: 'There's someone coming, from the south.'

A moment later, the ground shuddered under the weight of heavy, powerful feet. A colossal ram with spiralling horns emerged from a dense thicket of tamarisks. The majestic animal halted and stared at the humans. A supernatural light shone in its eyes.

'Go and fetch the queen and the pharaoh,' Moustache told the Afghan.

The sovereigns meditated before the incarnation of Amon. Then their eyes began to speak, and the ram moved off, heading due west.

'Judging by the shape of its horns, that was a Nubian ram,' observed the queen.

'Does that mean the Nubians are still a danger?' asked the pharaoh. 'Surely that's impossible – they're much too far from here.'

'I must follow the direction the beast of Amon showed us,' said Ahhotep.

'But, Mother, all you'll find will be the desert and then an oasis.'

'As soon as I have found another sign, I'll send Rascal to you.'

'You know how much the army will need you during the battle for Memphis.'

'We must not attack blindly. Gather together as many fighters as you can and, together with your council, draw up a battle-plan which does not involve any fighting on land. Our best weapon is our fleet. And we have one other ally: the Nile flood.'

Way-Finder guided Ahhotep and her troop of soldiers. For him, following the trail left by Amon's ram was easy, but he set such a fast pace that some of the soldiers had difficulty keeping up. The queen knew he had a good reason for hurrying, so stops were kept to a minimum and everyone remained on the alert at all times.

Suddenly, they saw a white antelope standing

on top of a rocky outcrop. Way-Finder halted, and nuzzled the queen's shoulder.

Ahhotep went slowly towards the antelope. It was the incarnation of Satis, wife of the ram-headed potter-god Khnum, and the new sign sent by Amon. And this sign, too, pointed to the Great South and Nubia. The animal licked the queen's hands, and its infinitely gentle eyes told her that it would guide her to her goal.

In the Bahariya oasis, which was ordinarily calm and far removed from the sounds of war that disturbed the Nile valley, the atmosphere had abruptly grown tense. Usually, the governor was content to collaborate limply with the Hyksos, who showed only a cursory interest in this obscure place, a mere staging-post for army messengers.

It was, in fact, by way of the oases of the Western Desert that messages passed between Avaris and Kerma, the capital of Nubia. True, it was a long and difficult route, but the Thebans did not know of it.

This time, the head messenger was accompanied by a hundred particularly savage Hyksos soldiers, and they had joined up with as many Nubians, who were just as menacing. The Bahariyans had to give them all free beer, wine and date alcohol.

'Do not cause any trouble here,' the governor told the messenger.

Backed by so many soldiers, the messenger was

openly scornful of the stocky, bearded man who dared admonish him. 'This oasis belongs to the emperor, like the rest of Egypt. Or have you forgotten that?'

'We pay him enormous taxes, and he takes almost everything we have. So let him at least allow us to live in peace. This place is of no strategic importance.'

'That's where you're wrong, my fine friend.'

The governor frowned. 'What does that mean?'

The messenger relished his moment of glory. 'You see, these Nubians are only a forward detachment, whose job it is to collect a very important letter to King Nedjeh. Before long, hundreds of Nubian warriors will be arriving here, and you are to serve them zealously.'

'I won't do it! I—'

'You cannot refuse to help the emperor and his allies – unless, of course, you're a rebel, a supporter of Queen Ahhotep.'

'No, I swear I'm not!' said the governor.

'Now I see what your game is. Still, it doesn't work out too badly for me. I've had enough of being a messenger. I shall enjoy being the new governor of Bahariya.'

The governor panicked and tried to escape. He ran towards the edge of the desert, pursued by two Nubians.

He was almost at his last gasp when all at once, there before him, he saw a magnificent white antelope, which bounded off into the desert. In its place stood a majestic woman, wearing a red band round her hair and a tunic of the same colour. She was so beautiful that he forgot his fear.

The two Nubians thought they could kill their quarry with one blow from their clubs, but they suddenly froze: they were facing a whole army. They heard arrows whistle through the air, and scarcely had time to register the fact that they were about to die.

The governor was shaking from head to foot. 'Majesty, you . . . ? Are you . . . ?'

'How many Nubians are there in the oasis?' asked Ahhotep.

'About a hundred, and the same number of Hyksos, but they're all trying to drink themselves into a stupor. Majesty, they want to turn Bahariya into a military base.'

The matter was quickly resolved. Dead drunk and caught by surprise, the enemy offered only feeble resistance.

The sole survivor was the head messenger, who had taken a little girl hostage.

'Don't touch me,' he yelped, 'or I'll break her neck. If you spare my life, I'll give you an important letter.'

'Give it to me,' ordered Ahhotep.

He handed her an official letter, marked with the emperor's seal.

The queen read it and learnt a great deal.

From Emperor Apophis to King Nedjeh:
Do you know what Egypt has undertaken against me?
Kamose is attacking me in my own domain. He is persecuting the Two Lands, yours and mine, and he is ravaging them. Come to Avaris without fear. I shall hold Kamose until you arrive, and no one can intercept you as you traverse Egypt, because all the enemy forces are in the North. We shall defeat them and share the country between us.

So that was the answer to Ahhotep's second question: the emperor was indeed planning to entrap the Egyptian army. While it was pinned down by the Hyksos, it would be attacked from the south by the Nubians.

'Will you spare my life?' whined the messenger.

'On two conditions: that you carry a letter to the emperor and that you release that child immediately.'

He obeyed. The little girl ran to hide in the queen's arms and Ahhotep comforted her for a long time.

While the man stood waiting, not daring to move, Ahhotep wrote a biting letter informing Apophis that the route through the oases was now under Egyptian control, that his message would never reach Kerma, and that the Nubians would not leave their province.

CHAPTER 54

The emperor had ordered Jannas to remain at Memphis and to mass troops there on the plain, to prevent the enemy from advancing. Soon, the Nubians would charge down on the Thebans, whose only option would be to retreat to the north, where Jannas was waiting to wipe them out.

Jannas did not approve of this plan. Never in all his brilliant career had he depended on the actions of third parties like the Nubians, whose lack of discipline worried him. There was something else, too: the annual Nile flood had begun, which made it impossible to leave chariot regiments on the plain. He had had to pull them back to the east of Memphis where, for the moment, they would be of no use whatsoever. Redeploying his forces would take several days.

In Kamose's place, he would have chosen this ideal moment to launch an offensive. But the young pharaoh was inexperienced in war, and his early victories had probably turned his head. As for Queen Ahhotep, she suffered from an incurable fault: being a woman, and therefore incapable of holding a command. In fright, she would persuade her son not to venture too far forward, for fear of losing what had been gained.

The river was rising fast.

'It will be a very fine flood,' predicted Moon.

'All the finer because it has already forced Jannas to withdraw his chariots,' said the Afghan, who had just received the reports from his scouts.

'We should attack immediately,' said Kamose.

'Give us one day, Majesty,' begged Moustache, 'one single day, so that we can try to revive our networks of supporters in Memphis. If we manage to make a large proportion of the population rebel, Jannas will have to face another and unexpected opponent.'

'That is very dangerous.'

'The Afghan and I can pass unnoticed.'

Kamose turned to Ahhotep, who nodded. 'Tomorrow at dawn,' he said, 'our fleet will enter the port of Memphis. Kill as many Hyksos as possible.'

Memphis was Moustache's favourite town. With its white walls, dating from the first dynasties, and its great temples, which had alas been burnt down by the Hyksos, the former capital retained its proud appearance despite the occupation. But this was no time for contemplation, and the two water-carriers were bent double under the weight of heavy jars as they arrived at one of the gates, which was guarded by Hyksos soldiers.

'Who are you?' one of them demanded.

'Conscripted peasants,' replied the Afghan. 'Because of the flood, the river water is no longer fit to drink. We've been told to bring reserves to the barracks.'

'You may enter.'

The town was in upheaval. It was clear that the chariots' forced retreat had obliged the high command to alter its plans. The Afghan and Moustache headed for the poor district around the ruined Temple of Ptah, where they hoped the last members of their rebel network might have gone to ground.

In a deserted alleyway, close to a safe-house, they heard characteristic barking: a rebel dog was sounding the alert, according to the agreed code.

The two men laid down their burdens and took off their tattered tunics to show that they were not carrying any hidden weapons.

'It really is us,' said the Afghan. 'Have we changed so much?'

The heavy silence that followed this question ought to have made them run for safety, but neither man moved.

'We're in rather a hurry, friends. If you want to kill some Hyksos, now is the time.'

The blade of a dagger pressed against the Afghan's back.

'A good move, little one, but a bad final position.'

Using one of the wrestling holds from Beni Hasan, the Afghan tripped the youth who was threatening him, disarmed him and twisted his arm behind his back. 'If you want to fight, my lad, you still have a lot to learn.'

Five rebels emerged from the house, among them a priest of Ptah who had escaped the mass arrests. 'I know them,' he said. 'They led our group. Everyone thought they were dead.'

The Afghan smiled. 'Well, we aren't. And – can you believe it? – we've even been decorated by Queen Ahhotep! Tomorrow at dawn, the Egyptian fleet will attack the town. Can an uprising be organized?'

'Too many people would get themselves killed.'

'You don't get anything for nothing,' Moustache reminded him. 'If the townspeople can put the city guards out of action and set fire to the docks, our army will take care of the rest.'

'The whole city is ready to rise up,' declared the youth. 'If we spread the message through every district straight away, we'll succeed.'

Jannas did not sleep well: he had a nightmare in which fire destroyed the Hyksos war-fleet. Thinking about the vital new precautions he must take, he did not fall asleep again until the small hours.

He was awakened by a smell of burning, which made him leap out of bed. From the window of the barracks, he saw that the docks were on fire.

His second-in-command rushed into the room.

'The Egyptians are attacking, sir! Several boats have breached our first line of defence.'

'The queen and her little king aren't as incompetent as I thought,' admitted Jannas. 'Every man to his post.'

'There are several fires, sir, and loud shouting can be heard in most districts – it's as if the whole of Memphis is rebelling.'

'It is. Let's hope the city guards can contain the rioters. I have other priorities.'

Very soon, Jannas realized that the enemy had carried out a masterly manoeuvre. Taking advantage of the flood, war-boats had sailed right up as far as some of the city ramparts, from where Pharaoh's archers were ideally placed to aim at the Hyksos defenders, who retaliated furiously. Kneeling on the roof of a cabin, along with the other elite archers, Ahmes, son of Abana, cut down several officers, causing consternation among the enemy ranks.

As soon as Emheb and his men succeeded in setting foot on the battlements of the citadel, the Hyksos weakened. Galvanized, Egyptian soldiers appeared from everywhere. And in the town, under the command of Moustache and the Afghan, the guards were killed with mattocks, stools, carpenters' mallets and anything else that would serve as a weapon. The Memphites gave full vent to their rage.

Before long, under the onslaught by over seven thousand soldiers, all as reckless as their pharaoh, the Hyksos army began to buckle.

'Is there still no news of the Nubians?' Jannas asked his second-in-command.

'No, sir.'

'That stupid plan has failed. It's impossible to defend Memphis any longer. We must get out of this hornets' nest as fast as possible.'

It was the first time that Jannas had ever been forced to beat a retreat. But circumstances were against him, and he found himself with no choice. To continue to fight in such bad conditions would have been madness. He therefore sacrificed a small part of his troops to ensure that the rest could pull back to the north-east. Soldiers, chariots and horses were loaded on to boats which headed rapidly away from Memphis.

Jannas had prevented the worst. True, he had barely scratched the enemy army and was abandoning a great city to them, but his forces were almost intact, and the fact that the Egyptian victory was spectacular did not mean it was decisive.

Kamose himself shattered the skull of the last Hyksos footsoldier, who had obeyed Jannas's orders by holding his position to the death.

In disbelief, the Egyptians realized that the battle was over. Memphis, capital of Egypt during the time of the pyramids, was free again. In the residential districts, where not a single Hyksos guard had been spared, people were singing and dancing. Old men were weeping, the prison gates had been thrown open, and children were already beginning to play in the streets again, while doctors and nurses, under She-Cat's vigorous direction, were taking care of the many wounded.

In the palace, Ahhotep and Kamose received the homage of the surviving town dignitaries, most of whom had suffered torture and interrogation. Standing in the front row, Anat marvelled at the pharaoh's bearing.

When, a little weary, the Afghan and Moustache went into the palace, they met Emheb, who had been wounded in the arm.

'So you two have survived again,' he commented.

'It would have been a pity to miss this,' replied Moustache. 'You should get that arm seen to.'

'Can you imagine how the queen must feel?' asked the Afghan.

At that moment, Ahhotep had only one thought in her head: the road to Avaris, the Emperor of Darkness's lair, lay wide open.

CHAPTER 55

Like all the soldiers of the Egyptian army, the Afghan and Moustache were shaved and perfumed, and their skin was rubbed with a pomade made from honey, red natron and sea-salt. This was vital to keep the skin healthy and protect it from insects, which were more numerous in the marshy areas of the Delta than in the Nile valley.

Ahhotep and Kamose had just made known their decision: the Egyptian fleet was to sail for Avaris, taking full advantage of the flood, which had turned the vast stretches of the Northern provinces into one immense lake.

'This time,' enthused Neshi at the final council of war before departure, 'we shall strike the emperor a death-blow!'

'It won't be that easy,' warned Emheb. 'The Hyksos army is almost intact and we don't know the system of defences around Avaris.'

'The emperor is not expecting an attack,' said Ahhotep. 'Logic dictates that we establish our main military base at Memphis and take the time necessary to prepare for a decisive attack.'

'Our boats are ready,' said Kamose. 'We shall leave tomorrow morning.'

A liaison officer asked permission to speak. 'Majesty, we've had a message from Sako. The town has been attacked, and the officer in charge of our detachment requests urgent assistance.'

'Do you know any more details?'

'Unfortunately not. And the carrier-pigeon arrived exhausted and wounded – we couldn't save it.'

'I shall go to Sako immediately,' decided the queen. 'If the Hyksos counter-attack isn't halted, Thebes will be in peril. Nevertheless, we must not delay our attack on Avaris.'

The pharaoh and his counsellors were worried. Without Ahhotep, the Egyptian army would be deprived of its soul.

'The White Crown and the steering-oar of the flagship, with its gold-covered prow, shall guide Pharaoh along the waterways of the Delta,' said Ahhotep. 'He will find the quickest route to Avaris and will swoop down like a falcon upon the tyrant's city.'

The young king rose. 'Commander Moon, prepare to embark.'

The golden ship made good speed, with the war-fleet in her wake. At the helm, Moon was having a strange experience: the steering-oar seemed to have a life of its own, and he was no more than a witness to its movements as it steered the boat in the right direction.

Almost all the soldiers were seeing the Delta for the first time, and it was very different from the Nile valley. Here, the land was flat as far as the eye could see, criss-crossed by canals and tributaries. Alongside the fields grew veritable forests of papyrus and reeds, partly submerged by the flood.

The fleet was not planning to stop anywhere. It had passed by the towns of Iunu, Taremu and Bubastis, all of which it could have attacked, so as not to lose a second on the way to Avaris.

Still elated by the conquest of Memphis, the young soldiers were joking about the Hyksos' cowardice.

'They're good lads,' mumbled Moustache, through a mouthful of dried fish. 'It's better that they don't know the truth.'

'Don't you think we'll succeed in taking Avaris?' asked the Afghan.

'We've had a lot of good luck since the beginning of the war, but this time the queen isn't here to lead us.'

'All the same, we'll have the benefit of surprise.'

'Can you imagine the fortress of Avaris? We shall break our teeth on it.'

The Afghan shook his head.

Emheb came over to them. 'Wouldn't you like something better to eat?'

'Not hungry,' replied Moustache.

'I know Avaris is getting closer,' said Emheb, 'but isn't it pleasanter to fight with a full stomach?

In the front line we'll have no chance of coming through alive, but we must make sure that Kamose does. Pass on the order.'

Moustache went to join She-Cat. He wanted to taste the pleasures of love one last time.

Fascinated by the beauty of Lower Egypt, the kingdom of the Red Crown, Kamose retired to his cabin shortly before Avaris came into view. Travelling across provinces which were still beneath the Hyksos yoke gave him an immeasurable desire for victory.

Gently he took Anat's face in his hands. Her blue eyes expressed an increasingly intense passion for the king, whose most intimate life she now shared.

'Do you think what I'm about to do is mad?' he asked.

'It has taken many mad acts to get so close to the monster, in the hope of plunging your sword into his back. By believing himself invincible, the emperor gives you a chance of victory.'

Kamose opened a phial which had been given to him by a perfume-maker in Memphis. Slowly he spread its contents over the young woman's neck and shoulders.

'I am a foreigner and the widow of a traitor,' she said. 'How can you love me?'

'Will you marry me, Anat?'

'That's impossible; you know it is. You are Pharaoh of Egypt, and I—'

'You are the woman I love, and you love me, too. There's no law forbidding our marriage.'

'Please, don't say any more. Not another word.'

Almost everyone was delighted by the flood. Born of Hapy, the vital energy of the Nile, it deposited silt which made the earth black and fertile. It also acted as an immense purifying wave which drowned a vast numbers of rodents, scorpions and even snakes. At the moment, it was disturbing a big herd of hippopotamus, who were accustomed to remaining submerged during the daytime and climbing out on to the banks at night to find food.

The hippopotamus's only enemy was the crocodile, which was apt to seize and carry off calves at the very moment of birth, unless it was fought off by one or more females. Although the hippopotamus looked placid, if disturbed or frightened it sometimes became enraged and very dangerous.

'I've never seen so many,' said Moustache. 'Fortunately, there's room to pass, otherwise they might capsize our boats.'

'It won't be easy,' warned Moon. 'I fear we may incur serious damage.'

'We could spear them,' suggested the Afghan.

'We'd never be able to kill enough of them,' objected Emheb.

'Then let us use them as a weapon,' said Kamose. 'Let us turn the strength of Set within them to our own advantage.'

'How, Majesty?'

'By using a good old method well known in Thebes: to anger a hippopotamus, all you have to do is tickle its nostrils with a reed. We shall gather reeds long enough to keep risks to a minimum, and try to drive the herd northwards. The hippos will be the perfect first attack-wave.'

Several good swimmers volunteered for the task. They were linked to the boats by ropes tied round their waists, but in spite of this precaution two young men died, crushed between the angry animals.

At first it was chaos, as if the creatures' fury were summed up in the deafening din. Amid the turbulent waters, every animal bellowed more loudly than its neighbour. Then, led by the dominant male, some semblance of order was brought to the confusion. At last, the animals began to move in the right direction.

At the prow of the golden ship, Kamose donned the White Crown, which was under the protection of Set. He would need all its power to attack the capital of the Emperor of Darkness.

CHAPTER 56

Jannas found it difficult to contain his anger. He paced up and down the audience chamber at Avaris, which, infuriatingly, was empty. He had been waiting for the emperor for more than an hour.

At last High Treasurer Khamudi appeared.

'When can I see His Majesty?' demanded Jannas.

'The emperor is ill,' explained Khamudi. 'His ankles have swollen and his kidneys are not working properly. For the moment he is sleeping, and no one may disturb him.'

'Are you serious?'

'Those are his orders, and we must all obey them.'

'You don't understand the gravity of the situation. The Egyptian army is about to attack Avaris.'

The High Treasurer smiled condescendingly. 'You seem perturbed, Commander.'

'That army is a real army, with a real commander and real soldiers! Our Nubian allies never arrived in Memphis, so I had to retreat to save the majority of my troops. Besides, the flood means I cannot use my chariots. In Kamose's position I would

362

immediately attack Avaris, whose defences are laughable.'

'Kamose is nothing but a petty princeling. He has installed himself in Memphis, which you will retake without difficulty as soon as the flood is over. For the moment, in accordance with our emperor's instructions, march your regiments to Sharuhen. The lady Aberia will accompany you with a large convoy of deportees. Make sure none of them escapes.'

'Don't make another mistake, Khamudi. I shall be needed here.'

The High Treasurer's voice hardened. 'Just obey your orders, Commander.'

The emperor had burnt Ahhotep's letter and put the head messenger to death in the labyrinth. Angered by his plan's failure, he had shut himself away in the citadel's strongroom, to gaze upon the Red Crown of Lower Egypt. He handled it lustfully, hoping to see himself crowned with this sacred emblem. The ancient texts considered it to be an eye, which made the pharaoh able to see the invisible.

No one knew what the crown was made of; it was as solid as granite but as light as fabric. Soon Apophis would enclose it within the White Crown of Upper Egypt, taken from Kamose's dead body, thus forming the Double Crown, the total vision that would give him absolute power.

As he was preparing to place the Red Crown

upon his head, a burning pain ripped through his side and stopped him. His blue flask was glowing red like molten metal. The emperor cut the string that tied it to his belt.

As the flask fell to the ground, it exploded into fragments. With it vanished the map of Egypt that Apophis had manipulated for so many years.

The herd of hippopotamus surged along the eastern canal, which passed in front of the citadel of Avaris. They caused panic among the fishermen and the river-guards patrolling the area around the city.

Puzzled by the uproar, Tany, the emperor's wife, climbed to the top of the ramparts with her serving-women. Suddenly, a brilliant light blinded them.

'It's coming from the river,' said a frightened serving-woman. 'A golden boat . . . It's coming nearer.'

The powerful voice of Pharaoh Kamose rose into the sky above Avaris.

'Fledglings cowering in your nest, see: I have come, for destiny looks favourably upon me. My cause is just. The liberation of Egypt is in my hands.'

Flattened against the wall like lizards, Tany and her servants could not move.

The Egyptian fleet had no time to be impressed by the gigantic citadel that loomed over Avaris. After sinking the guards' boats, Kamose's soldiers recovered the heavy stones they used as anchors, and turned them into projectiles which they then used against a Hyksos war-boat, sending it straight to the bottom.

Khamudi was aghast. Jannas had left the capital and nobody, not even the High Treasurer, was permitted to enter the strong-room where the emperor had shut himself away.

It was like a dream. The pharaoh with the White Crown was cutting through the enemy defences, thanks to the agility and speed of his warships.

Nevertheless, the ramparts of the citadel were lined with archers, whose accurate aim was bound to cause serious losses in the Egyptian ranks.

'We cannot tackle this monstrous citadel from the river,' said Moon. 'Not even a very high flood would enable us to reach the ramparts.'

'Then we shall go round the other side,' said Kamose, 'and take the western canal.'

Once out of range of the Hyksos arrows, the war-fleet headed along a broad waterway which led directly to the trading-port. There they found three hundred cedarwood boats had just arrived, laden with gold, silver, jars of wine and oil, and other supplies from the provinces. They were about to be unloaded, and the appearance of the Egyptians caused utter chaos.

The dock-workers tried to take refuge in the guards' offices, but the Hyksos killed several of them. In fury, their colleagues attacked the killers, and the quays became the scene of a fierce fight.

Moustache and the Afghan were the first to jump from the prow of the flagship to tread Apophis's domain underfoot. Using light axes and short-swords, they cut a path towards the main building, where the official responsible for checking goods had just been trampled to death by the dock-workers.

'The Egyptians have seized the trading-port,' an officer told the High Treasurer. 'We must send reinforcements immediately, both from inside and along the canal. If we don't, Kamose will invade Avaris.'

Khamudi was wholly unprepared for such incredible news, but he owed it to himself to ensure the safety of the governing authorities. 'The citadel and its surroundings must not be left undefended,' he snapped. 'It must remain impregnable.'

'There are not enough soldiers at the port, High Treasurer. They will be massacred!'

'Tell them to do their duty and resist for as long as possible. The main body of our forces will stay here, in order to preserve the centre of the empire.' But when, he wondered, would Apophis decide to make his appearance?

Another officer rushed in. 'High Treasurer, the enemy is approaching!'

Well shielded behind an arrow-slit, Khamudi saw the White Crown glitter, and heard Kamose's voice ring out again.

'Apophis, vile, fallen tyrant, weak of heart: you

still dare to claim, "I am the master; everything as far as Khmun and even Per-Hathor belongs to me." You are nothing but a liar. Know this: I have wiped out those towns, and not one Hyksos remains there. I have burnt your lands, I have transformed them into bloody mounds because of the evil they inflicted upon Egypt by serving you.'

He turned to face the citadel, and raised a goblet. 'See, I am drinking wine from your vineyard! Your peasants, who are now my prisoners, will press the grapes for me. I shall cut down your trees, I shall lay waste your fields, and I shall seize your dwelling-place.'

Already, the Egyptian sailors were steering the boats out of port, laden with riches.

As Khamudi and the soldiers gazed in fascination at the pharaoh, whose bearing was deeply impressive, he felt an icy chill run round the ramparts. Apophis was standing there. Wrapped in a brown cloak, his head hooded, the emperor gazed down upon the disaster from the heights of his citadel.

'Majesty,' stammered Khamudi, 'I thought I was doing the right thing by—'

'Order Jannas back immediately. Tell him to gather together the largest force he can muster.'

CHAPTER 57

Because there was little or no wind, Ahhotep's journey took longer than planned. At last she sighted Sako, and all the boats in the flotilla were put on the alert.

Was there anything left of the Egyptian garrison? If it had been wiped out, how many Hyksos would still be there and what traps had they laid?

The queen watched Laughter constantly and was surprised by his calmness. The huge dog was dozing in the shade of an awning, showing not the slightest sign of anxiety.

'There's someone down there!' shouted the lookout.

The archers drew their bows.

'Don't fire,' ordered the queen. 'It's a child.'

The little boy ran up, waving his arms to greet the ships that bore Ahhotep's colours. Soon he was joined by several of his friends and their mothers, who were visibly enthusiastic. On the quayside, a crowd of civilians and soldiers gathered, waving palm-fronds as a sign of welcome. The boats berthed to the accompaniment of joyful shouts and spontaneous songs, celebrating the queen's return.

Forcing his way through, the commander of the little garrison prostrated himself before her.

She looked at him, puzzled. 'But you were attacked by the Hyksos, were you not?'

'No, Majesty. Everything is quiet here.'

'But Sako sent a message asking for help.'

'I don't understand, Majesty. There really is nothing amiss here.'

It had been a false message, designed to separate Ahhotep and Kamose, in order to weaken the army of liberation. The queen had the answer to her third question: not only was Apophis's spy still alive, but he had chosen a crucial moment to try to strike a fatal blow against his enemy.

Now a new dilemma arose. Should she go to the North and rejoin Kamose or continue southwards to Thebes, which was probably the real target of the coming Hyksos counter-attack?

Ahhotep did not hesitate for long. Kamose had proved his worth. He would know how to weigh up the situation and conduct the siege of Avaris. The thought of Thebes being attacked by barbarians was unbearable. If the Hyksos had the intelligence to hide troops in Middle Egypt, so as to strike at the heart of the rebels and destroy their main base, all that the Thebans had accomplished so far would be wiped out.

'I would like to organize a festival to celebrate your arrival, Majesty,' said the garrison commander.

'It is much too soon to rejoice.'

'But, Majesty, have we not defeated the Hyksos?'

'Certainly not, Commander. Your women and children must leave Sako and take refuge, under close guard, in a neighbouring village. Increase the number of lookout posts. If the enemy attacks in numbers, do not try to resist. You must go to Thebes.'

The Afghan caressed a little piece of lapis-lazuli, which he had been allowed to take from the supply delivered to the Hyksos.

'It must remind you of your homeland,' commented Moustache.

'Only the mountains of Afghanistan produce such beautiful stones. One day the trade will begin again, and I shall be rich again.'

'I don't want to be a pessimist, but we're still a long way from that. Have you seen the size of Avaris's citadel? It makes even *my* stomach turn over. There isn't a ladder in the world long enough to reach the top of the ramparts, and the Hyksos archers seem as good as our own.'

'All the same, we've given them a good shaking, haven't we?'

'We haven't killed very many. There are a lot of them left behind those walls – and tough ones, at that.'

'You really are feeling a bit pessimistic, aren't you?' said the Afghan.

'To be frank, I don't like this place. Even when the sun's hot, I feel cold.'

'Come and drink some of Apophis's wine. That'll cheer you up.'

The cargo-boats were now travelling south; the pharaoh thought of the moment when they would arrive in Thebes and be offered to Amon. Above all, though, he was preoccupied by the strange silence that filled Avaris. Holding the trading-port meant that they could block exchanges between Avaris and the outside world, but had the emperor's power really been diminished?

With his usual energy, Neshi was running around, checking that the men were well fed. Emheb was worried that the troops sheltering in the town and the citadel might try a lightning raid, so he had posted small groups of archers in many different places to give the alert.

'How shall we organize the siege, Majesty?' he asked.

'We must explore the surrounding area and see if it is possible to isolate the city and starve out the emperor.'

'That will take a very, very long time. Meanwhile, do you not find this lack of reaction surprising? Apophis certainly has enough men available to try and break through our blockade.'

'Perhaps he thinks otherwise.'

Emheb shook his head. 'No, Majesty. I think he is waiting for reinforcements, in the belief that they will crush us. Seeing us pinned down, he believes, heralds victory for him.'

'In other words, you advise me to retreat when we are right at the gates of Avaris?'

'I do not wish it any more than you do, Majesty,

but I believe it necessary for us to regroup if we are to avert a disaster.'

'You say that because we do not have Queen Ahhotep's magic with us. As soon as she is back among us, our doubts will be swept away and we shall take the citadel.'

There were three of them, three Hyksos guards who, instead of fighting the dock-workers with their comrades, had taken refuge in a guard-post. An officer there had arrested them and handed them over to his superior.

Tied to a stake in the courtyard of the citadel, they had been beaten with clubs. Their ribs broken, they feared a long prison sentence at the end of which they would be condemned to carry out the lowest menial work.

'Why did you behave like cowards?' demanded the icy voice of the emperor, who was accompanied by Aberia.

'Majesty, we thought the battle was lost and we would be more useful alive than dead. The dock-workers were in a blind rage – it was no longer possible to contain them.'

'Those are indeed the words of a coward,' said Apophis, 'and cowards have no place among the Hyksos. Whatever the circumstances, my men must obey orders and remain at their posts. Lady Aberia, carry out my sentence.'

'Have mercy, Majesty, and—'

Aberia's enormous hands choked him into

silence. She strangled him slowly, with obvious pleasure, and inflicted the same torture and death on the other two.

The emperor's calmness reassured his troops, who were champing at the bit at the thought of taking their revenge on the Egyptians. But Tany was so distressed that she had taken to her bed. A long procession of serving-women came to bathe her forehead and give her drinks. She was feverish and caught in a delirium of flames, torrents of mud and falling stones.

Yima soothed Tany's anxiety with the drug her husband had procured for her own use. No, the Hyksos Empire was not on the point of crumbling, and Apophis's knife would rid it of the Egyptian cancer.

As for Khamudi, he was not a happy man. The emperor had reproached him for sending Jannas away at the wrong time. But those had been the orders of Apophis himself, who did not wish to see the commander gain too much power.

Only the trading-port was under Kamose's effective control. He dared not attack the outskirts of the town, where Hyksos soldiers were ready to contain an attack.

High on the walls of the citadel, the emperor gazed down on his domain, which had been violated by a spirited young man who believed himself invincible because he was wearing the White Crown.

That illusion would cost him his life.

CHAPTER 58

Water-bags made from tanned goatskin turned inside out were distributed to the soldiers of the Egyptian army. The supplies were vital, because the river water would not be drinkable for a day or two and the heat was increasing. Balanite fruit and sweet almonds had been dropped into the water to keep it pure.

Neshi handed Kamose his water-skin, which was to be carried by a young footsoldier, proud to serve his king.

'The fleet is ready, Majesty,' announced Emheb.

Kamose had decided to sail down the eastern canal, pass the citadel, where many skilful archers would certainly be posted, and see if it was possible to attack from the north. If not, the war-boats would establish a blockade and, as soon as Ahhotep returned, the king planned to seize Avaris, district by district.

He drank a little water. 'How is the troops' morale, Emheb?'

'They will follow you to the end, Majesty.'

'Unless we take the citadel, all our achievements will have been in vain.'

'Every soldier knows that.'

Emheb's solidity reassured the young king. Through all these hard years of struggle, the governor had never once complained, never once given in to despair.

Just as the pharaoh was climbing the gangplank of the flagship, a lookout's warning shout stopped him in his tracks. Many Hyksos boats were approaching from the north. They were entering both the eastern and the western canals, and would trap the Egyptian fleet in the trading-port.

At last Jannas had received coherent orders: to assemble the regiments stationed in several Delta towns, then reduce Kamose's army to nothing.

Khamudi's insult and the emperor's indifference were forgotten. Jannas was once more fulfilling his role as commander-in-chief of the armed forces, and he would show the young pharaoh what Hyksos military power really meant.

Aboard ship, Jannas had absolute command and would not be hindered by the stupid decisions of a civilian like Khamudi. He would conduct the battle for Avaris as he chose. He was well aware that it would be ferocious, because of the quality of the enemy boats, which were fast and easily manoeuvrable, and the zeal of the Egyptians, who had been hardened in several battles.

The emperor had underestimated the enemy, but Jannas would not make the same foolish mistake. By surprising Kamose's fleet from the east and west simultaneously, he would force it to divide, and there by weaken itself. If the pharaoh had not thought of evacuating the cargo-vessels as a matter of urgency, he would be trapped in the port.

'Trading-port in sight,' announced the soldier on watch. 'No cargo-vessels.'

'That little king is not a bad leader,' thought Jannas, 'and the fight may be yet more difficult than I thought.'

'They want to ram us,' said Emheb. 'They're much heavier than we are, so it will be a massacre.'

'There is only one solution,' decided Kamose. 'Our ships must head east. We shall concentrate all our forces in the same direction.'

The manoeuvre was carried out with such cohesion and promptness that it took the Hyksos aback, and they had no time to turn side-on so as to form a wall. The flagship with the golden prow slipped between two enemy vessels, and for a few moments Kamose thought he might open up a breach. But the Hyksos threw out grappling-hooks and slowed his ship enough to board her.

The first to set foot on the deck did not enjoy his triumph for long, for Moustache's axe sank into his neck. The two men who followed him were felled by the Afghan's dagger, while the arrows fired by Ahmes and his men soon sapped the attackers' zeal.

Several Egyptian vessels escaped from the

Hyksos, but three were boarded and fierce hand-to-hand combat ensued. The flagship could not free herself. The boat carrying archers from Emheb's town of Edfu rushed to her aid and, firing arrow after arrow, held off another Hyksos boat which was trying to join the attack.

In the western canal, Jannas was hindered by his own vessels, which had no room to turn and come back at the Egyptians, some of whom sacrificed themselves to protect the pharaoh.

Kamose fought with incredible courage, and Moon himself took charge of the steering-oar. Seeing him threatened by a gigantic Asiatic, Moustache flung himself between them, and the man's axe-blade slid along his left temple. Despite the pain, he sank his short-sword into the belly of the enemy, who staggered backwards, collided with the ship's rail and fell into the water.

'We've done it! We're free!' roared Moon, and his words gave renewed courage to his crew. The flagship had indeed freed herself at last.

With two precise slashes of her dagger, beautiful Anat hamstrung a veritable wild beast of a Hyksos, who was about to stab the Afghan in the back. As an Egyptian sailor finished him off, she looked up and saw a Hyksos aiming his spear at Kamose, who was standing at the prow.

Shouting would be futile – the pharaoh would not hear. Leaping forward with all her strength, Anat threw herself in front of the spear, which plunged into her chest.

At that moment Kamose turned, and he saw her sacrifice. Maddened with grief, he dashed across the deck, jumping over corpses. Bringing down his sword in fury, he sliced the murderer's skull almost in two.

It was the hardest battle Jannas had ever had to fight. True, the Egyptian losses were severe, but the Hyksos' were even worse, because of Kamose's tactics and the manoeuvrability of his boats.

'Are we going to follow them, sir?' asked his second-in-command.

'They are too fast, and Kamose may lave laid traps for us to the south of the city. But the flood will not last for ever and, however skilful the adversary may be, he will one day come up against our chariots. For the moment, let us concentrate on bandaging our wounds and taking effective measures to ensure the safety of our capital.'

Standing on the highest tower of the citadel, Khamudi had watched Jannas achieve victory, hailed by cheers from the Hyksos archers. Already very popular, the commander was now seen as the saviour of the Hyksos and the emperor's true right arm, in place of the High Treasurer, who from now on would have to treat him with the greatest respect.

Khamudi knew he had neglected the army in favour of the city and provincial guards. As soon as possible, he would make good that mistake.

His wife ran to meet him. 'We're saved, aren't we? We're saved!'

'Go and comfort the lady Tany. I must go and give the good news to the emperor.'

Apophis was sitting on his austere throne, in the half-light of the audience chamber.

'Majesty, Commander Jannas has put the Egyptians to flight.'

'Did you ever doubt that he would, my friend?'

'No, of course not! But we have lost a great many boats and sailors. That is no doubt why the commander chose not to pursue the defeated fleet but to ensure the defence of Avaris. Unfortunately, our victory is not complete, because Kamose is unscathed.'

'Are you quite sure of that?' asked the emperor's icy voice.

CHAPTER 59

She-Cat was horrified to find Moustache's body. She leant closer: he was still breathing. To her relief, most of the wounds were superficial, though his left ear had been almost completely sliced through.

'A remedy for pain, quickly!'

One of her assistants brought her a small round vase, containing a powerful pain-reliever based on opium. Opening Moustache's mouth a little way, she made him take enough to ensure that he would feel no pain for several hours.

With a linen net soaked in sycamore-sap, she cleaned the wound and removed the fragments of tissue that might become septic, then brought together the two parts of the ear. Using bronze needles and linen thread, she sewed it up.

'Do you think it will work?' asked the Afghan.

'When I do something,' retorted She-Cat in annoyance, 'I do it well. Do you want me to see to your shoulder? At first glance, it doesn't look too good.'

The Afghan's eyes rolled upward. More

seriously wounded than he wanted to admit, he fainted.

Kamose held Anat's hands for some time after she died. Then he tenderly wrapped a shroud round her body. He loved her, and she had given her life to save him, but there was no time now to grieve for her.

'About turn!' he ordered.

'The men are exhausted,' objected Emheb, who was himself at the end of his strength.

'We must show the Hyksos that we are capable of taking the offensive again.'

'Majesty . . .'

'Order to all vessels in the fleet: about turn and head for Avaris. Tell the soldiers to wash, change their clothes, and prepare for battle.'

Under Moon's direction, the boats carried out the manoeuvre.

She-Cat emerged from the cabin where the wounded were being treated. 'What is happening?' she asked Emheb, who was sitting on a coil of rope nearby.

'We are turning back to attack Avaris. The Hyksos believe we have been put to flight, and the king thinks the effect of surprise will be decisive because Jannas has not yet had time to organize the city's defence.'

'But our losses were heavy, and the enemy outnumbers us enormously.'

'That's true,' said Emheb.

'And Jannas is an experienced commander, who won't be thrown into confusion even by a surprise attack?'

'That's true, too.'

'So if we launch this attack, we shall all die?'

'And so is that.'

The heat, the sun, the sparkling waters of the Nile: the Hyksos lookout thought he was seeing a mirage. It could not possibly be an enemy boat coming back towards Avaris.

He signalled to his colleagues to alert them, and they relayed the message to Jannas, who with his officers was studying the capital's future system of defence.

'That little king is becoming a serious problem,' said Jannas. 'He wants to take us by the throat even though he has not one chance in a hundred of succeeding. In his place and at his age, I might perhaps have committed the same folly.'

'Are we in any real danger?' asked an officer anxiously.

'Kamose does not know the size of the reinforcements I have not yet committed – they're waiting to the north of the city. He is committing suicide.'

The pharaoh stood at the prow of the flagship, thinking of Ahhotep. If she had been here, she would have done exactly the same. The Hyksos could not possibly have guessed that the Egyptians would find the resources necessary to resume the fight.

The sombre expression of the sailors, including Moon, told Kamose that they thought his decision pure madness. But he knew that none of them would flinch from the challenge.

'A lookout has sighted us,' said Moon. 'Shall we continue at full speed, Majesty?'

Kamose could not reply. The river was becoming confused with the sky, the riverbanks were spinning. Large drops of sweat trickled down his face.

'Majesty, are you ill?'

The sensation of vertigo was so great that Kamose swayed.

Moon helped him sit down. 'Have you been wounded?'

'No. No, I don't think so.' But he could hardly breathe.

'She-Cat must examine you.'

The Nubian could find no wound. 'This is a sickness I don't know,' she confessed. 'The king must drink plenty of water, and rest in his cabin.'

'Am I to order the attack, Majesty?' asked Moon.

Kamose took several seconds to understand the question and to realize what it implied. His brain had slowed down, and he had to make an intense effort to compose his reply.

'No, Commander. We shall stay here for a few hours, then head back towards Thebes.'

'The Egyptian fleet is withdrawing, Commander,' said Jannas's second-in-command.

Jannas frowned.

'Are we to give chase, sir?'

'Absolutely not. Obviously, Kamose wants to lure us after him and into a trap. He has proved that he can attack Avaris again, and he hopes to provoke just that reaction from us. Further south, there are other troops commanded by Ahhotep. If we pursued Kamose, we'd be mauled by the claws of that she-panther.'

'Then what are your orders, sir?'

'Remove the wrecked ships from the trading-port, bury the dead, and strengthen Avaris's defences to the maximum. I am to be alerted as soon as an enemy boat makes a move.'

Jannas had many details to sort out, notably the reorganization of the army and the war-fleet. From now on he intended to be their true commander-in-chief, free from the influence of Khamudi and his henchmen. True, he would have to be careful not to put too much emphasis on Khamudi's incompetence, because the emperor trusted Khamudi completely as regards government and the economy; but Apophis must accept that the Egyptian army was not just a collection of bunglers, and that there was a real war to fight, a war between Lower and Upper Egypt, between the North and the South.

Because of their speed, the Egyptian warships quickly rejoined the cargo-vessels captured from the Hyksos. Throughout the journey to Thebes, liberated towns and villages greeted Kamose's fleet in triumph.

Wonderful news was spreading: the pharaoh had beaten the Hyksos, the White Crown was victorious! Everywhere, feasts and other celebrations were being organized. Everywhere, people were singing and dancing. In the summer sky the sun shone, driving away the darkness.

Despite his exhaustion, the pharaoh stood at the prow of the golden vessel at each principal stopping-place, notably Memphis, Khmun and Qis, the scenes of his great victories. Cheered by the people, Kamose had believed his strength would return. But the dizziness was wearing him out, his legs gave way under him, and he had to stay lying down, even though he could not sleep.

Moustache and the Afghan were leaning on the ship's rail. Moustache's ear was healing well, but the Afghan was still a bit weak from his wound.

'We're nearly at Thebes,' said Moustache. 'I don't understand why Queen Ahhotep withdrew instead of joining us at Avaris.'

'And I don't understand why our system of carrier-pigeons isn't working,' added the Afghan.

'Still, we reached Avaris and stood up to Jannas.'

'Yes, we did, and it was a great achievement. But the emperor and his citadel are untouched, and I doubt if Jannas's troops will stay on the defensive for ever.'

Moustache thought about the next battle, in

which Jannas was sure to use his heavy weapons. But he soon shook off the thought, for there ahead of them were the green banks of Thebes and a crowd mad with joy, awaiting the heroes to congratulate them and celebrate their triumph.

CHAPTER 60

Married soldiers fell into their wives' arms, while the others enjoyed the attentions of enthusiastic young Theban girls who wanted to touch the victors and show their undying admiration.

Already, the cargo-vessels' precious contents were being unloaded, while the people of Thebes watched in awe. Seeing this, they did not doubt for a moment that Kamose had defeated the Hyksos.

Supported by Moon and Emheb, the pharaoh was cheered for a long time. Officially, he was suffering from a leg wound which made it difficult for him to walk. But, as soon as she held him to her heart, Ahhotep realized that her elder son was dying.

Putting on the bravest face she could, so as not to spoil the Thebans' happiness, she saw him helped into his travelling-chair to be borne to the palace, and then climbed into her own.

Teti and Ahmose greeted them, Ahmose rapturously happy to have his elder brother home again.

'You've got very thin,' exclaimed the boy.

'The battles were very hard,' explained Kamose.

'Did you kill all the Hyksos?'

'No, I have left you a few.' He suddenly felt ill again, and had to be helped by Qaris.

'Kamose must rest,' said Ahhotep. 'I shall make the ritual offerings in his place.'

The riches from Avaris were offered to Amon, in his temple at Karnak, before being distributed to the Thebans, with the exception of the gold and lapis-lazuli, which would be used to adorn the temple.

Concealing her anguish, the Wife of God spoke the ancient words that enabled the Invisible One to manifest himself upon earth. This caused the light that had appeared on the world's first morning to shine out, as it had done upon the mound that emerged from the primordial ocean, at the very spot where Karnak had been built.

As soon as the ceremony was at an end, Ahhotep returned to the palace and hurried towards Kamose's bedchamber.

In the passageway outside, she was met by Qaris, who, despite his anxiety about the king, was supervising preparations for the victory banquet. 'Majesty, do you think . . . ?'

'All this noise must stop at once.' The head palace doctor appeared in the doorway of the patient's bedchamber. 'Majesty, my diagnosis is definite: Pharaoh Kamose has been poisoned. It is impossible to cure him, for the heart of his being has been affected. The poison has spread through all his vessels, and the king's life-energy is almost spent.'

Ahhotep entered the room and closed the door behind her.

Kamose was sitting down, his head resting on a cushion, and was gazing at the Peak of the West. She took his hand gently.

'Avaris is intact and the emperor is still alive,' he whispered, 'but we inflicted severe losses on him, and I have shown him that we can strike at any moment. Jannas knows that our army can fight. We must strengthen our positions, then seize Avaris and finally liberate the Delta. But the course of my life is run. It falls to you, my mother, to continue the struggle that you yourself began. Forgive me for leaving you this superhuman task, but my breath is leaving me; I can no longer hold it within me.'

Scalding tears flowed down Ahhotep's cheeks, but her voice was steady. 'It was the Hyksos spy who took me away from you, and it was he who poisoned you, in order to make the attack on Avaris fail.'

Kamose managed a small smile. 'So he believed that I would win victory. A victory which you will achieve in my name and in my father's, won't you?'

'I give you my oath upon it.'

'I have tried to be worthy of him and you. I hope my brother will fight at your side, and I ask one last favour.'

'You are Pharaoh. Speak, and I shall obey you.'

'Will you have stelae engraved, telling of my fight for freedom?'

'Nothing that you have accomplished will be forgotten, my son. These monuments will sing of your exploits and your bravery, and they will be displayed in the temple at Karnak, where your glory will be preserved among the gods.'*

'It is not easy to die so young. But you are beside me, and I have the good fortune to gaze upon the western bank where the soul's peace reigns. For several years I have been unable to sleep. Now I am going to rest.'

Kamose raised his eyes to the heavens and his hand gripped his mother's very tightly.

'The mummy is cold, Majesty,' a priest told the queen. 'That is an excellent sign: it signifies that the deceased has expelled his bad heat, which is made up of passions and resentments, and that his soul has been purified. Henceforth, Pharaoh Kamose possesses the serenity of Osiris.'

A widow, now in mourning for a twenty-year-old son, Ahhotep yet again refused to succumb to the blows of fate. Since Kamose had no son or successor, it was she who must lead the funeral rites. Just as she had done after the death of her husband, she took on the office of regent queen and governed Egypt.

Kamose's sarcophagus was decorated with feathers evoking the travels of the soul-bird in the heavens. Inside, she laid a gold and ebony fan to ensure him eternal breath, axes, and a gold boat,

*Two stelae were indeed found at Karnak. Their texts have provided much valuable information.

in which his spirit would sail for ever across the universe.

With surprising gravity and composure for a child of ten, Ahmose had followed every stage of the mourning, from the mummification of his elder brother to the interment in the burial-ground on the western bank of Thebes. But, after all, the sages of Egypt considered ten to be the age at which one became fully responsible for one's own actions.

Ahhotep had a threefold mission: to continue the war of liberation, to prepare Ahmose to become pharaoh, and to discover the identity of the Hyksos spy, that person who was so close to her and who had already inflicted so much suffering upon her.

As the funeral procession went towards the river-bank, Emheb approached the queen.

'Majesty, I can no longer keep my thoughts to myself.'

'What is it, Emheb?'

'I saw the citadel of Avaris at close quarters, and it is impregnable. Everyone knows that you have achieved many miracles and that the gods have filled your heart with magical power. But the emperor has built himself an indestructible lair. We can certainly attack it and attack it again, but each time we will lose many men. I believe that is exactly what Apophis is hoping for, and that when we have been weakened enough he in turn will attack us.'

'For the time being, in accordance with the wishes of Pharaoh Kamose, you are to go to Memphis, strengthen its defences and consolidate our positions in the liberated provinces.'

Sorely tired, Teti the Small had not been present at the final stages of the funeral ceremonies. She could not accept that death had spared her, only to strike down a young king of twenty summers. And she knew that little Ahmose would never laugh as he had done before, and that from now on he could no longer enjoy the carefree existence of childhood.

Kamose's death had put a premature end to rejoicing and reality had imposed itself again, with all its cruelty: the war was far from over, Hyksos military power remained almost intact, and even the survival of Thebes was uncertain.

Ahhotep helped her mother to her feet.

'I am so tired,' said Teti. 'Leave me to sleep.'

'Qaris has prepared us an excellent dinner, and you need to regain your strength. Don't forget that Ahmose's education is not complete and that he still needs you.'

'I admire you so much, my daughter. Where do you get so much courage from?'

'From the will to be free.'

To show herself worthy of her rank, Teti joined her family for the meal. And when Ahmose asked her to tell him about the Age of Gold, she realized that she could not slacken her efforts. She had to educate a future pharaoh; that must be the joy of her old age.

Accompanied by Laughter, Ahhotep was walking in the palace garden. Suddenly, the dog stopped. Neshi was coming to meet them.

The queen stroked the dog, whose eyes remained fixed on the official.

'Forgive me for disturbing you, Majesty, but I have something important to tell you.'

Was Ahhotep at last about to find out the appalling truth?

'I served Pharaoh Kamose faithfully,' said Neshi, 'and I approved of all his decisions. But now he is dead, and so am I, in a way. For that reason, I wish to resign from my offices, while beseeching you to save this country, which needs you so much.'

'Neither our country nor any other needs a saviour, Neshi. What it does need is righteousness. When Ma'at once again governs the Two Lands, misfortune will disappear. Put aside your devotion to one man, and serve only that righteousness. Then, and then alone, will you deserve to be called a true servant of Egypt.'

Ahhotep walked away, followed by her dog. She needed to be alone with her husband and her elder son, two pharaohs who had given their lives fighting the Emperor of Darkness. And the Queen of Freedom gazed up at the waxing moon, her protector, praying that it would grant her the faith necessary to re-establish the reign of Light.